THE
BUTCHER
OF
ABERDEEN

THE BUTCHER OF ABERDEEN

A Story of Sex, Madness, and Murder

ROJÉ AUGUSTIN

A POST HILL PRESS BOOK
ISBN: 979-8-8-9565-159-9
ISBN (eBook): 979-8-89565-160-5

Post Hill Press
New York • Nashville
posthillpress.com

Published in the United States of America
1 2 3 4 5 6 7 8 9 10

AUTHOR'S NOTE

January 3, 2026. Sydney, New South Wales, Australia.

This book is a dramatized account of a true story. It is based on extensive research grounded in court documents, sentencing reports, transcripts, legal judgments, and media coverage. Although the book contains numerous quotes made by witnesses and authorities, I did not personally interview these individuals; their comments were drawn from public records. Furthermore, all major events depicted in these pages are real and supported by these documents.

There are, however, gaps in the record—gaps that represent the private moments, the unspoken thoughts, the conversations no one but Katherine and her victims would have been privy to. To tell the story in a way that conveyed the lived reality of the people involved, I have taken dramatic license to reconstruct scenes, emotional beats, and dialogue to underline the facts in the case. As such, these scenes are not strictly inventions; they are grounded in documented patterns of behavior and psychiatric analysis. Where characters argue, reflect, or reveal themselves on the page, those moments arise from what is known about their relationships, histories, behaviors, and desires.

A small number of names have been changed for narrative clarity or privacy. Dialogue throughout the book blends direct quotations from court transcripts with speculative exchanges meant to plausibly represent what likely would have or could have happened and what might have been said. Chapters involving the forensic psychiatric interviews are dramatized reconstructions inspired by documented sessions Katherine Knight had with three forensic psychiatrists, all of whom handed down a diagnosis of borderline personality disorder in their reports to the court. The three psychiatrists have been woven into the composite character of Dr. Robert Martin.

This book is not a work of fantasy, nor is it a factual transcript of events. It is what I would call narrative nonfiction—a work that sits on the border between fact and imagination. Everything that happened, happened; what I have added here are the connective tissues of human experience.

My aim was not to sensationalize the violence, but to explore what led to it: the jealousy, the coercion, the assaults, the red flags no one acted on; to interpret and to guide the reader closer to the shifting contradictions of Katherine Knight's inner and outer life. I focused on the pivotal moments, and her time working at the abattoir. Slicing, boning, and bleeding out carcasses gave me a natural way to echo the kind of violence she later inflicted on John Price.

The Katherine Knight case matters for reasons that go beyond the brutality of her crime. It offers insight into the causes of extreme violence, and it highlights a topic that's still largely overlooked: domestic violence against men. In John Price's case, warning signs were ignored until it was too late, perhaps because people struggled to believe a man could be trapped by a woman. His story forces us to confront that cultural blind spot.

I also wanted to tell this story because, as much as I'm drawn to true crime and its causes, I'm even more drawn to the psychology behind it, namely the question of nature versus nurture.

And Katherine Knight was different. She was unlike the archetypes we expect, an abused woman turned vengeful. She was something rarer: a female psychopath who also suffered from borderline personality disorder. The more I learned about her, the more I wanted to understand her, to understand what happens when fear, sex, and violence fuse into something monstrous and human all at once. It seemed to me that understanding her required stepping into the uneasy space between what we know for sure and what we can only infer.

Katherine Knight was sent to Mulawa Women's Correctional Centre, known today as Silverwater Women's Correction Center, after her sentencing. She remains there to this day. I reached out to her requesting an interview, hoping to hear her own voice amid the many others who have told her story. But she declined to be interviewed. I later learned that since her incarceration, she has refused all interview requests. It has been reported that she has found a measure of peace and stability within the walls of Silverwater. The routine, the structure, the constant presence of others—these seem to have offered her a kind of order and safety, a stark contrast to the chaos and violence of her past. She has also reportedly never admitted the crime or apologized to John Price's family. I imagine the absence of an explanation or an apology likely leaves a heavy burden on their lives, a burden as heavy as the crime itself.

PART ONE

1

THE BUTCHER'S HANDIWORK

March 1, 2000. 84 St Andrews Street, Aberdeen, New South Wales, Australia.

After the slaughter, you dress the carcass. Start at the hocks. You're gonna draw a ring around the trotters, slice in clean, shallow strokes down the hock. The goal is to keep the hide intact, not tear or gouge the fat. You gotta respect what you're cutting. A good butcher doesn't hack. A good butcher doesn't force. You let the blade do the work. Now, ring the trotters proper all the way round with your knife, grab the skin, then start pulling down, open the legs right down the inside. Keep the blade shallow. The thin yellow membrane just beneath, see how it clings to the white fat? You have to know how deep to go. Not too shallow, or it won't lift. Not too deep, or you tear the tissue underneath. Use the back of the blade here. Not the edge. The heel of the knife, too. The connective tissue stretches and snaps like gauze. The knife barely moves, see? Just a steady tug, a flick of the wrist. Up over the ribs now. Keep your angle. You're not gutting—you're peeling. You come to the chest, slow it down. It's thick through there. Use the fingers. Loosen it by hand. The right pressure. You'll get resistance at the shoulders. Slice through the tendons under the scapula, and it'll drop for you. Once the shoulders let go, the whole front half rolls off like a rug. You wanna get the head off now. Two cuts. Don't pull…follow the joint. Remember that. Twist it when you're done. Feel the joint go. The head's heavy, especially if the blood's still in it. The tongue comes out last through the jaw once the head is gone. Run the blade clean under it. With the head detached, you can remove the skin in one pelt, nice and tidy. Save the face for last if you want it. That's where people can struggle. The skin is tighter there, stitched close around the jaw and cheekbones. The lips clinging. The ears are hard to free, too. Use the point of the blade to ring the eyes. One clean circle. Then under the jaw. Take your time. Beneath the chin, through the sinew and tendon. The nose'll come last. Don't tug. Slice above the cartilage. Go under the chin, just where it folds. Draw the knife up toward the ear. Then pivot. Turn it around. On the back, you'll see the neck bones give when you're in the right spot. You want to shallow-cut first. Open the outer layers with the tip. Then it comes free—the whole hide, pulled down like a shirt peeled from a sweating back. Lay it out flat. Hair side down. Now see what's left.…

2

THE CRIME SCENE

7:44 AM. March 1, 2000. Aberdeen, New South Wales.

The first officers to arrive at 84 St Andrews Street were Sergeant Furlonger, Senior Constable Maude, and Senior Constable Matthews—a "welfare check," as categorized at the time of dispatch.

The officers were met by Jon Collison, a neighbor who had alerted the police. Collison had explained to the detectives that John Price had not shown up for work that morning. Very unlike him, Collison had said. John was always one of the first to arrive at the mines, he'd said. Six AM sharp. For the last twenty years. No matter how much he'd drunk the night before. That was John.

Furthermore, Collison continued, a comment John had made at work only the day before had left his boss and colleagues uneasy. So, when John didn't show up for work, and when the boss couldn't reach him by phone, he called around to John's neighbors.

"Is it just John in the house?" Furlonger asked.

"Nah," Collison replied. "Katherine, his girlfriend, and her two little ones stay with him most nights." Collison told the detective that he and two other concerned neighbors had gone over to 84 St Andrews and had knocked on John's door; they had circled the house calling out his name, but to no avail. The men weren't sure what to do. They walked across the lawn toward the road. John's truck was still parked by the side of the house. Odd, they had all agreed. After years of friendship, they knew their mate's routine well.

"I think we should call the police," Collison had said as they peered through the windows of John's truck, hoping to find some sign of life.

At 8:10 AM Sergeant Furlonger pounded on the front door, three imposing bangs. "Mr. Price! Aberdeen Police, are you in there?!" Senior Constable Matthews walked over to the kitchen window and peered in against the glass through cupped hands. His eyes moved across the vestiges of the previous night: an open beer bottle on the kitchen counter, a work bag on the dining table flanked by keys and a wallet, a few prescription blister packs. There was one thing out of the ordinary he noted: a crumpled old curtain hanging from the kitchen archway.

The detectives all went around to the back of the house, leaving the neighbors on the front lawn and away from what had officially become a crime scene. As they walked, SC Matthews noticed a portion of meat thrown onto the lawn. But there was no sign of a dog. They managed to access the house through the laundry room door.

Sergeant Furlonger entered first, his firearm drawn and held out in front of him. He could immediately smell the sour, metallic trace of blood. The other two officers stood by the door, awaiting orders.

The house was silent, except for the faint hum of an air conditioner. Furlonger took a few cautious steps inside, then stopped abruptly in the hallway, staring straight ahead. "Jesus Christ," he muttered under his breath, then he raised his voice. "You'd better come in here!" The other officers stepped in behind Furlonger and also stopped dead in their tracks when they saw it. SC Matthews let out an audible gasp. SC Maude instinctively stepped back, his mouth forming a small "O." There was blood everywhere. The walls were smeared with the evidence of a violent and rapid demise. The officers followed the trail into the kitchen, slow and cautious, guns still drawn. Matthews led the grim procession, brushing aside the ratty curtain he'd first seen through the window. He immediately felt a cold wetness on his skin and looked down at his hand. Blood. He looked at the curtain and realized with horror that it was not a crumpled old curtain after all. It was human skin. The full pelt, including the hair, the ears, the genitals, the fingers and toes, all of it. Even what appeared to be knife gashes. The pelt hung from the architrave on a stainless-steel hook like a lurid Halloween costume.

"Oh God, she skinned him," Furlonger murmured in shocked disbelief.

He and Matthews suddenly turned their attention to the entrance hall, which was defiled by a large and deep pool of blood, roughly three feet by six feet in size, still wet, but darkly congealed at the edges. Adjacent to the entrance hall was the living room where, lying on the floor just beyond the archway, was John Price. At least they assumed it was John, because the corpse had no head. His entire body had been flayed with gruesome precision. His trunk and limbs were nothing but raw flesh, muscle, tendons, and fat. The legs were crossed casually at the ankles, the left ankle over the right. The genitals had been removed. One arm had been positioned over an empty plastic drink bottle. A butcher's knife lay near the body, as well as a butcher's steel. On the coffee table were a broken, framed picture of John Price and his children, and a note. As the detectives padded slowly about the horrific scene, Furlonger read the note—bloodstained and spattered with tiny speckles of flesh:

> "Time got you back Johathon for rapping my douter. You to Beck for Ross – for Little John. Now play with little Johns dick John Price."

His first thought was, where was John's girlfriend? And where were the children? Furlonger suddenly became aware again of the air conditioner, humming in one of the back rooms. He rejoined the search. Moving past the kitchen toward the bedrooms, Furlonger realized that something had been cooking on the stove. An aroma lingered faintly in the air. And he saw two plates of uneaten food on the dining table. Had they been about to sit down to dinner? He wondered.

They continued down the hall, walls smeared with blood, and arrived at the bathroom. A cursory inspection revealed specks of gray fleshy matter littering the drain holes of the bathtub and a black nightie stained with blood draped over the side of the tub.

Opposite the bathroom was a bedroom, which contained two empty single beds. To the left was a second bedroom, containing a wardrobe, a sofa, and a single bed—still no children and no Katherine. Adjacent to that was the master bedroom. As they approached, they heard snoring. Furlonger turned to the others with a finger pressed against his lips. They raised their firearms and quietly entered. There on the bed lay a fully clothed woman with red hair, face down. There were smears of blood on the sheets. Spatters of blood dripped down the wall above the bed. Congealed blood stained a wardrobe. A scatter of pills lay on the mattress beside the woman, who oddly had not a drop of blood on her. Furlonger raised his gun and stood above her. He shook her. "Katherine? Wake up. Katherine, it's the police. I need you to wake up." She started coming to. Furlonger motioned to Matthews to help, and together they hoisted Katherine upright with some effort. She was six feet tall and solidly built.

"Katherine, can you tell us what happened here?" Furlonger asked, practically yelling. Katherine didn't answer; she wobbled slightly on the bed, like a drunk person.

"Where are the children? Are they in the house?" Still, she did not answer, just rubbed her face and looked down at the floor. The children were nowhere to be found, and this worried the officers. SC Matthews cuffed her as soon as she was on her feet.

By the time she was led out of the house, in a plain black dress, it was 8:28 in the morning. St Andrews Street was already crowded with onlookers, drawn by the flashing blue and red lights of the police vehicles. A cluster of detectives had gathered outside John Price's redbrick, single-story home. Furlonger asked Collison to follow them down to the front lawn to get a statement.

From across the road, residents watched as they ushered Katherine to the patrol wagon. They looked to Collison, who was talking with Furlonger, for some sign of what had happened. After a moment, Collison looked back at them grimly and gave a subtle thumbs-down, and they knew.

Katherine sat on the pavement next to the patrol wagon. She looked clean, as if she'd recently had a shower. Her red hair clung damply to her forehead. Her face was puffy. She blinked against the sunlight. Her movements were slow and detached, an unbothered, slurry nonchalance that Furlonger and the others found unsettling. She sat compliantly enough—the only protest a searching, steady blinking of her eyes. Processing. Calculating. Disassociating. Looking not so much like a confused or guilty suspect, but like a woman who had already begun to write the story of her victimhood. Senior Constable Maude radioed the station for an ambulance and backup, his voice trembling despite his best efforts.

It was shaping up to be another brutally hot day, the kind that made the townsfolk of Aberdeen retreat indoors by midmorning. But today no one was going inside. Neighbors in this tight-knit community of fewer than two thousand residents stood on their front lawns in uneasy clusters, whispering and speculating amongst themselves. Some were still in their dressing gowns, arms folded tightly against their chests, as if to ward off the unnaturalness of it all.

The forensics team arrived around 8:35 AM, their vehicles peeling up the crowded street. The house was now a beehive of probing activity. Men walking to and fro, processing the scene, wearing blue disposable overalls with the word Forensics printed on the back in big yellow letters.

At 8:45 AM an ambulance came blaring up the street. Two paramedics jumped out, a tall man in his forties and a woman in her twenties, her brunette hair pulled into a loose ponytail. They approached the lawn, ducking under the checkered police tape that fluttered slightly in the breeze. Senior Constable Maude brought them up to speed.

"She's over there," he said, pointing to Katherine on the pavement, surrounded by police guards. "She's a bit groggy. We think she might have taken something," Maude continued. "There are pills on the kitchen counter, not empty, but not full either. And she was out cold when we found her, some pills on the bed."

The young paramedic said to the tall one, "You wanna grab the pills from the kitchen and the bed?" As the paramedic started toward the house, Maude reached out and caught him by the arm. "Brace yourself, mate."

Senior Detective Bob Wells arrived at the scene at 9:10 AM. He was a broad-shouldered handsome man in his mid-forties, with sharp blue eyes and short dark hair. He turned off the ignition and leaned back in his seat for a moment. He closed his eyes and took a few deep breaths. He had a habit of doing this—pausing before he entered a scene. It was a bid to draw some kind of emotional boundary between himself and whatever awaited him. After a moment, he stepped out of the sedan and started for the lawn, ducking beneath the police tape. He joined Furlonger, who was briefing one of the forensic photographers.

"Sergeant," Wells said as the photographer moved off.

"Detective," said Furlonger. Wells pulled out a small notepad and pen from his jacket pocket. "Let's hear it."

"John Price. Local guy in his forties. Worked at Bowditch Mines. He didn't show up for work this morning. His boss sent someone to check on him. There was no answer, so they rang us. We forced entry." Wells scanned the street. Neighbors continued to linger and speculate, their curiosity deepening.

"And?" Wells asked.

"And he's been murdered. Brutally. Seriously brutal. I don't want to get ahead of forensics, but…butchered would be the word for it."

Wells exhaled slowly. "Weapon?"

"Likely knives. We've got some in evidence already."

"Who else was in the house?"

"Katherine Knight, our only suspect so far." Sergeant Furlonger motioned in her direction. "We found her asleep in the back room with some pills; we're thinking it may have been a suicide attempt," he continued. "Taken into custody without incident. She's not saying much, except muttering about being tired. Still under sedation, or something. Paramedics are sorting that out."

"Katherine Knight," Wells repeated as he took notes.

"We also learned that she has two young children; we haven't located them yet. They usually stay with her at the victim's home. Sometimes they're with their father. We're not sure where they are right now."

Wells nodded. "Send a unit to her house. Quietly. Let's find those kids." He went into the house and took in the scene. He had seen death before, many times and many kinds. But it always surprised him how ordinary the surroundings were. Dishes in the sink. A toy truck on the couch. Boots by the doorway, like they'd just been taken off moments before. There was the faint smell of cooking.

"Who's working forensics?" Wells asked SC Maude, who was guarding the door.

"Muscio's team."

"Good. They're thorough. Any word on what happened before all this? Any arguments? Fights? Threats?"

"We're still interviewing neighbors and contacting family members. Most are saying they fought all the time. Screaming, throwing things. You know how it goes."

Wells sighed. "Unfortunately, yes."

Back on the lawn with Furlonger, Wells put on his sunglasses to shield from the sun. "Let's find out if someone knows where those kids might be. And get me whatever timeline you can of the last seventy-two hours. Pull everything you can on the victim and suspect." Furlonger was already scribbling notes.

"And keep the media away, please," Wells added. "They'll be circling soon enough."

While Detective Wells was getting the lay of the land, the young paramedic was slipping a blood pressure cuff around Katherine's arm. She had been sitting on the pavement for half an hour by then, with three officers standing guard. The paramedic checked her pupils with a small penlight. "Vitals seem okay. Is there anything in your system we need to know about?"

Katherine shook her head, "No, nothink." Like most of the locals, Katherine pronounced her "g" like a "k." *Nothink. Anythink. Everythink.* The tall paramedic returned with the blister pack in a gloved hand. "Promethazine and fluvoxamine. Looks like six tablets missing."

"All right. Katherine, are you sure you didn't take anything?" the young paramedic asked, as if talking to a child. "You wanna tell me?"

"I don't know. I don't remember anythink."

"Okay, we're going to get some blood off you," she said, slipping off the blood pressure cuff. She stood up and signaled for the stretcher. "Let's get her inside." At 9:15 AM they strapped Katherine onto the gurney, adjusting the webbing across her chest and thighs. She didn't move or protest. To a casual observer she would almost seem to be enjoying all the fuss. The two paramedics wheeled her into the ambulance and closed the doors with a finality that sounded louder than it should have. Senior Constable Matthews got in the ambulance with Katherine while the paramedics continued their triage. The sirens and lights flicked on, and soon the ambulance drove away from 84 St Andrews Street. It would be the last time Katherine Knight would ever set foot in that house again.

Inside the ambulance, the paramedics continued their triage. Katherine lay back and stared at the ceiling. The world outside seemed to flatten to her senses. She barely noticed the siren wailing, or the growl of the engine, or the occasional exchanges between the paramedics. Not even the steady, mechanical beeping of the monitor tracking her pulse could draw her from her dissociative haze.

SC Matthews sat to her left, arms folded and doing his best not to stare. He couldn't reconcile what he had seen that morning with this tall, middle-aged mother of four lying before him. She could have been the librarian at Aberdeen public, or the neighbor you chatted to at bingo, or ran into at the supermarket and stopped to share some gossip.

As if sensing this, Katherine turned to Matthews and squinted. "Did I look like I was sleeping when you found me?"

Matthews pulled a face. "What do you mean?"

"When you found me, did I look peaceful?"

"I don't know," was all Matthews could think to say. Now he stared at her. *What an odd thing to ask*, he thought to himself. But Katherine had already lost interest. She looked past him through the small windows at the back of the ambulance. She could see two vans with satellite dishes mounted on their roofs kicking up dust as they approached John's house. The media. The news had spread like a bushfire. They were coming for the story. And they were coming for her. They would call her a monster. The word flashed in her mind as a familiar tide began to rise in her. *Monster.* Her pulse drummed in her ears, and it registered on the machines with a quickening of *beep beep beeps*.

"I'm going to give you some oxygen to help you relax, okay?" said the young paramedic. Katherine went back to staring at the ceiling as an oxygen mask was placed over her face. She calmed down a little, but the tide flowed just beneath the surface. They would soon arrive at the hospital, Katherine realized, and the questions would begin.

Just before 10 AM, officers Mike Prentice, John Alderson, and Robert MacDonald knocked on the door of Katherine's small cottage on MacQueen Street, where she lived with her two children when not at John's. There was no answer, so the officers forced entry.

The cottage was no more than four cluttered and stale little rooms. The air carried a rusty, metallic odor, mixed with the smoke of a thousand cigarettes. What struck them most, however, was the decor. If you could call it that. Every surface—from the floors to the ceiling, from the shelves to the doors, even above the door frames—was decorated with instruments of violence and/or death. Animal hides. Skulls. Rusted saw blades. Traps. Coiled whips. Leather belts. Metal chains. Knives were mounted on the walls. Old axes rested in dark corners. Pitchforks, rakes, and shovels were fixed to the ceiling.

"*Jesus Christ*," Prentice muttered, his eyes bulging at the ceiling where a large snakeskin was tacked to a beam. In the lounge area, a shelving unit sagged under the weight of VHS tapes and DVDs. *Resurrection, The Texas Chainsaw Massacre, Cannibal Holocaust, Faces of Death. The Silence of the Lambs, Friday the 13th, Natural Born Killers, Cape Fear, Nightbreed, Misery….* All of it spoke emphatically of violence.

Prentice moved first, stepping through the room with careful footing. "Check the bedrooms," he said. Alderson took the hallway. He found two small bedrooms: one with a double bed, the other with singles, all of which were empty. He came back shaking his head. "No one."

Outside they searched the backyard before knocking on a neighbor's door. A man in a robe answered.

"Have you seen the kids that live next door?" Alderson asked.

"Eric and Sarah?" The man frowned. "Not for a few days. I think the boy stays with his dad sometimes, the sister sometimes stays with her older sibling, Natasha."

That was enough of a lead. They made a call to the station, tracked down an address, and soon enough, Natasha confirmed both kids were with her—safe, and unharmed. Prentice radioed Wells with the update.

Back at St Andrews Street, John Price's teenage son, Johnathon, sat on the front lawn, too stunned to speak. Two of his father's colleagues from work sat with him, trying to console the young man, painfully aware that this was probably the worst day of his life.

3

THE QUESTIONS

Saturday, March 4, 2000. Maitland Hospital.

Bob Wells arrived at Maitland hospital just after 10 AM. The chief psychiatrist had rung him earlier that morning with news that Katherine was now lucid and stable. Fit, at least in a clinical sense, to be interviewed.

By now, she had been in custody for three days, during which time Wells had interviewed Katherine's family, friends, and neighbors, building up a brief on the case. This would be his first and only interview with Katherine. The task of getting to the "why" of it all would fall to Dr. Robert Martin, the forensic psychiatrist for the prosecution. But today Wells would start the excavation. He hoped to extract some useful information out of her, if not a full confession.

He was allocated a small, windowless room at the end of the main corridor, clinical in its austerity, with pale blue walls and a standard table and chairs. He set up a tripod camera and a recording device on the table. He placed a notepad and pen next to the recorder. He sat and scanned through a slim folder of case notes he'd brought with him. It contained police reports from her arrest, details from Katherine's relatives and friends, relevant fragments of her life now flattened into statements. He checked his watch. 10:25 AM.

A few minutes later, Katherine entered with her solicitor, a male nurse, and four uniformed officers. She wore a blue-and-white print dress. Her hair was messy, her face pale and freckly beneath her glasses. After initial preliminaries, Wells began the interview.

"As I've told you, Kathy, I'm investigating the death of John Price. I have reason to believe that you may be the person responsible. Is there anything you can tell me about the matter?"

"I don't know anythink on it," Katherine replied bluntly.

"Can you recall the last thing that you do remember?"

"The last think I remember was going out for tea with me daughter and the kids coming home."

"Can you tell me anything about that?"

"No, then I don't know anythink about the next day then."

"Right. Can you tell me the last thing you remember about the previous day, Tuesday, when you went to dinner with your children?"

"Yeah, I had to go to Muswellbrook for the test, to show the doctor the bruises on me breast, and I asked me daughter would she like to go to tea, 'cause she was upset…. So, we went out for tea and we, I was watching a video, and it was too late to take the kids home to bed, so they spent the night at Tasha's, and I just went home to Pricey's."

"Do you know how you got to Pricey's?"

"Yeah, I drove me car."

"Do you recall going into Pricey's at all?"

"I really don't know nothink." She said it once, then again, and again. "I don't know nothink," a refrain she'd settled on with a firm grip. But Wells knew the value of silence, of drawing someone out until they grew uncomfortable. He sensed this was going to be a delicate matter. Her silence and denials and claims of amnesia opened the detectives up to the risk of leading questions, which her defense could use to their advantage in court.

"Can you tell me about your relationship with John Price?" Detective Wells asked, switching gears.

Katherine shifted in her chair. "Yeah, he was me fiancé, we were engaged. He bought me a ring and everythink." Wells watched her, letting the silence pool between them. "He could be real nasty sometimes," she continued, glancing around the room. "Nasty to me. Nasty to the kids."

"Mmmm. Can you tell me what you mean by that?"

"Yeah, he hit me," she said, waving a hand in the air like a slap. "Hit me when he was drunk. Yelled at the little ones."

"Did you ever report it?"

"Of course I did." Wells made a note of this. "You and John had an argument the Sunday before his death. Is that right?" She shifted again in her seat.

"What was the fight about?"

Katherine hesitated for a moment. "Uh…he told me to leave, leave the house, he wanted me out and I wasn't gonna leave. I didn't want to."

"And after that?"

"I took out a restraining order, 'cuz he was hittin' me." Wells nodded, making another note on his pad. He was aware of the AVO. He had learned that police had served the same on Price's behalf, as well as Katherine's, after Price had gone to the station bruised and furious, saying he feared for his life.

"Can you just take me to the last thing that you actually recall on that evening, which is the Tuesday, the twenty-ninth of February?" Wells asked.

"The last time I recall was, I don't know about your dates, but I went inside and watched a bit of TV."

"Right. Was Pricey there?"

"Mmm."

"Do you—can you tell me where he was?"

"Not particularly."

"Okay." Wells paused for a moment, thinking. "Do you remember going to bed?"

"Mmmm."

"Okay. Was Pricey in bed with you when you went to bed?"

"Mmmm…. He had to have been."

"Do you recall that he was there, or not?"

"I don't even remember myself, so, I just remember watching a bit of Star Trek."

"So, you recall going to bed and going to sleep?"

"I don't remember anythink, so, I would have had to have gone to sleep."

"Can you tell me the next thing that you remember after that?"

"Them telling me that I'm in the Mater Hospital." Katherine went on to tell the detective that Price's son, Johnathon, hated her because of what she had done in the Howick Mines incident. And, surprisingly, she admitted that she had stabbed John before the night of the murder.

"To go back to the Tuesday just past, when you tell me that the last thing you remember is going to bed after Star Trek on television. That still the case?"

"Yeah, I only watched a little bit and I went to bed." By now Wells had begun to develop the beginnings of a profile in his mind. Most striking was that Katherine had been with John Price for more than six years. And yet there was no apparent grief, no remorse, no tears. He decided he would not press her on the events that led to the murder. That would be for Dr. Martin to unravel. And judging by what he saw at the crime scene, he didn't want to know the details of that night.

At 11:50 AM Katherine was taken back to her room and Wells left the building. He drove with the windows up and the air conditioning on high. The videotaped interview lay in a padded envelope on the passenger seat. About fifteen minutes into the drive, the tension caught up with him. He felt a pounding in his chest, pressure in his ears. He pulled over, switching the car into park, and let his hands rest on the steering wheel while he calmed himself. It was the crash after days of adrenaline and too little sleep—his body finally demanding a moment to reset. But mostly it was also the sheer brutality of the crime, images of which kept flashing through his mind. He sat there until his breathing eased, then he started up the car again. The senior prosecutor was expecting him. Wells would show him the tape, and the blunt, remorseless way Katherine had evaded his questions. He thought of the stories he'd heard over the last three days during his interviews. Everyone had something to say about Katherine. Some said that she could be kind and generous, the sort of person who'd give you a lift to the doctor without being asked. Others said she loved to dance and to laugh when the mood caught her. Some said she'd once confided in them that she'd been abused as a child. Others were clear that you did not cross Katherine Knight, because her temper was explosive. They all said that she and John loved each other, but that they fought often and had been an on-again,-off-again couple for the last two or so years. *Loved each other.* Wells scoffed. A statement like that almost made him angry. How could there be love there? How could you butcher someone that you loved?

Sizing up the situation, it was clear that Katherine had murdered John Price. He would never say this officially at such an early stage of the investigation. But he knew. They all did. What he wanted—what he *needed*—was an answer to the question that would now eclipse the entire investigation. Why?

4

THREE YEARS EARLIER

Late August, 1997. MacQueen Street, Aberdeen, New South Wales.

It was a Friday night in spring. The air was humid with a developing storm. Katherine and John, dating now for a little over two years, were in the lounge room of Katherine's MacQueen Street cottage. John had come over straight after work to pick her up for a night of drinking at the Top Pub.

He leaned against the bookshelf in the lounge, his hands in his pockets, while he waited for her to adjust her Annie Get Your Gun cowgirl outfit, which she was wearing to the pub. John was casually watching the children, Eric and Sarah, while they played on the floor, surrounded by all of Katherine's morbid relics.

"You should just come and stay," he said. "Johnathon's moving out in a week to live with some mates in Muzzie. The house'll be empty. Bring the kids."

The words stopped Katherine in her tracks. They were words she had been waiting two years to hear. Her two eldest daughters, Melissa, nineteen, and Natasha, sixteen, had gone to live with their fathers. It was just her and the two youngest ones in the draughty weatherboard cottage.

As if reading her mind, John shrugged. "They could each have a bedroom if you want." *Yes*, Katherine thought. Bedrooms for each child. A bigger yard. A separate laundry. Air conditioning in summer, heating in winter. John's steady income. This was progress. A step toward financial security and a proper family. A step, even, toward marriage. Her dream, taking shape. She thought about how John was good to her kids. She saw the way Eric followed him around the yard, how Sarah would lean against his side during movies, eyes fixed on the screen, one hand curled into the hem of his shirt. It was a no-brainer. Of course she would move in.

"Next you'll be asking me to marry you," Katherine half-teased, intending to plant the seed. She laughed heartily after she said this.

Pricey shrugged his shoulders again. "What, and make an honest woman of ya? Mission impossible." They both laughed this time. Then John stepped closer and wrapped his arm around Katherine, his hands squeezing her bottom, then her breasts. And then he kissed her.

A week later, she was in. Not fully, but she had a key and could come and go as she pleased. She kept her cottage, of course. It was the only thing of any value that she owned. She brought with her only what she needed for the time being. John made space for her things in the wardrobe, and he bought new themed sheets for the children—Pocahontas for Sarah, and Toy Story for Eric.

About a month later, when he was at work, and the kids were at her sister's for the night with their cousins, Katherine had the house to herself. She made a builder's tea and stepped out onto the back patio and lit a cigarette. The late afternoon air was cool and dry. Magpies twilled in the distance. She sat on one of the lawn chairs and looked through the window into the dining room, warmly lit and spotless thanks to her tidying. She could see her knitting on the dining table, awaiting the return of her nimble fingers.

She took a sip of the sweet milky tea, then dragged contentedly on her cigarette, letting the smoke drift through her nose. A small sound, almost like a laugh, caught in her throat. It was her dream. It was the house. It was her kids, each with their own rooms. It was the smell of a roast in the oven. And the feeling, at last, of being rooted. She took another drag. Then another sip of her tea, while staring peacefully at nothing in particular. Such a simple moment, but one she would cherish.

It wasn't long before she heard John's truck rumble up the driveway. Him coming through the front door, his footsteps into the kitchen, him placing his work bag, keys, and wallet onto the kitchen table. She heard the fridge door open and close. And the soft clink of a beer bottle being opened. She looked through the window and saw him walking toward the patio. The sky had darkened slightly, clouds forming a lush veil across a half-moon. She stubbed out her cigarette and got to her feet, brushing the ash from her dress.

5

THE FORENSIC PSYCHIATRIST[1]

June 21, 2000. Mulawa Women's Correctional Centre. Mum Shirl Psychiatric Wing. Day 1.

Katherine sat in a small, windowless room. The walls were a scuffed white and in need of a fresh coat of paint. The lighting was flat in a way that dulled everything. A clock ticked audibly in the background. Katherine crossed her arms tightly against her chest as she waited for Dr. Martin to continue. It was 10 AM.

Dr. Martin was a tall man in his late forties, with a graying beard and a thin silvery curtain of hair around his head grown down to his ears. His hands were long and fine. When he spoke, it was often with his index fingers steepled beneath his chin, his elbows planted on the table, looking like a man in prayer. A legal pad lay on the table in front of him, scribbled with shorthand notations. It was day one of his interview. They had been in session for about an hour.

"It sounds like that was a good time for you and John," Dr. Martin said. "Would you say that?"

---

[1] *Speculative reconstruction inspired by documented psychiatric interviews.*

"Yeah, it was good."

The doctor leaned back a little in his chair. The light caught the lenses of his glasses while he let a few seconds pass. "I'm interested to know what changed, and when."

Katherine pretended to fuss over her dress without looking at him. Dr. Martin sat forward now, resting his elbows on the table, his fingers forming a steeple beneath his chin. He watched her for a moment. And then he said, "Katherine, we're going to be speaking for a number of hours over the next two days. I'm not here to snare you. I'm not here to make any judgments either. I'm here to understand what happened so that we can determine your…" He searched his mind for the right word. "Role," said finally. "Your role in all of this. Not just details of the night itself, but also your state of mind, your thoughts, your feelings. We need to discuss everything that led directly to that night, as well as the night itself. And our time is limited. So, back to my question. When did things in your relationship start to change?"

6

THE WILL

Late August, 1998. St Andrews Street, Aberdeen, New South Wales.

One year after John had given her the keys to his house, Katherine bought steaks to celebrate the occasion. She also bought a case of Tooheys, John's favorite beer, and a pack of smokes. That afternoon, she prepared everything for their celebratory dinner. Then she moved about the house tidying up as she went, so that everything would be perfect when John came home from work.

In the bedroom, while putting the laundry away, she accidentally knocked a shoebox off the shelf on John's side of the wardrobe. It fell to the floor, spilling not shoes but a small pile of folded papers. Among them was a document with bold lettering that caught Katherine's eye. Her spelling wasn't great, but she knew instantly what it was. *Last Will and Testament of John Price.* Katherine began to read what she could. As her eyes scanned the lines, her face tightened with alarm. It seemed that all of John's things, including the house she had come to see as their shared home, were to be left to his estranged wife, Colleen, and their children. Not a single mention of Katherine Knight anywhere.

What's more, the will was dated February 28, 1998, only six months ago.

The sense of betrayal was visceral. For more than three years, she had devoted herself to John, believing she was building a future with him. She had tended to his home, done his laundry, cooked his meals, made his lunch in the mornings, which she packed neatly into paper bags, and she never turned him down for sex. In fact, she had more often been the initiator. So how could he, after several good years together, leave her out in the wind like this? She sat there for a while, stewing and brooding and clenching her teeth, the offending document held in her fist. She thought of tearing it up, but then she heard John's truck pull up. She rose to her feet and marched out to confront him.

She found him in the kitchen, setting his things on the table. She wasted no time. "What's this bloody fucking thing, Pricey?" She held out the will in front of his face. John's gaze fell to the document and for a moment he was dumbfounded. "You going through my things?"

"Are you leaving the house to Col?"

John rubbed the back of his neck, searching for the right words. "It's an old will, Kath. I just haven't gotten round to updating it."

"It's from this year," she countered angrily. "February. I may not read so good, but I'm not stupid!" She shook the document in his face. "That's six feckin' months ago. We been together much longer than *that*."

"It's not that simple, for fuck's sake, Kath. My kids…. Me and Col got kids together." He sighed and scratched his head. "Look, don't fuckin' start. I'm tired. I had a shit fucking day at work. And I'm hungry as all get out." He moved to the fridge and grabbed a beer, opened it, and took a long gulp.

"Why haven't you fuckin' divorced that cunt yet? You said you were gonna divorce, but you haven't. Why haven't ya?"

John looked Katherine square in the face, his jaw clenching with suppressed rage. "First of all, don't fuckin' call her that. Second, this isn't about Colleen. It's about making sure my kids are sorted if something happens to me."

Katherine took a step closer, her voice dropping to a dangerous tone. "What about me? I stood by you, looked after your sorry ass, made this place a fuckin' home for you. What do I get?"

"Whaddaya mean, what do you get?" John pulled a face and stepped back. "You get me!" He held his hands out to his sides to show off the goods. He was attempting to de-escalate a situation he did not want to deal with.

Katherine glared at him like he was some kind of joke. "That's it? That's what I get? A puny, part-time man?"

"C'mon Kath—"

"I'm not gonna be tossed aside, Pricey. I'm telling you that right now! I want you to divorce Col, and lets you and me get hitched." There was a beat while John chose his words carefully—a silence in which the whole house seemed to hold its breath. "Listen," he said finally, "I'll talk to her, okay? I'll get the divorce sorted. Now, can we eat, please? I'm fuckin' starving." Still glaring, she waited.

"What?"

"Marry me, Pricey."

He sighed again. "Fuck, Kath, I'm not gettin' married again. That's not happening."

There was another pause during which Katherine's eyes darkened. And then suddenly, she exploded, startling John nearly off his feet. *Why fucking not!?*

"Babe, I've done it already. I don't need a piece of paper to prove my love for you."

"That's easy for you to say when everythink's fuckin' yours. Or *hers*!"

"I said I'll divorce her, all right? Let's just go with that and talk about the other stuff later. Now, please can we eat?"

But Katherine wouldn't let it go. Something inside her had cracked open, and it made her lunge at him. It made her slap the beer from his hand. It hit the floor and foamed out across the tiles. "How do I know you're really gonna do it?"

"Jesus Christ, Kath!"

"You think you can just keep me here, like your maid, like a whore who doesn't even get paid!?"

He backed away now with his hands raised. "Kath, that's bullshit, c'mon, what are you on about?"

"I give you everything!" she shouted, poking her finger hard into his chest. John winced. At five foot nine, he was several inches shorter than Katherine. He was beer-gut stocky, but she was tall and surprisingly strong. "And you'd still rather leave it all to that cow than put my name in your fuckin' will!? You haven't been with her for what, twelve years you said?"

John finally grabbed hold of her wrists—not hard, but enough to stop her flailing.

"Kath, stop it! Stop!" She yanked free and started scanning the kitchen counter—for a weapon, John sensed. He stepped back, his senses heightened with adrenaline.

"You keep pushing me, I swear to *Christ* I'll have you outta this house, you hear me? I'm not putting up with your jealous bullshit. I'll throw you and your kids out!"

Katherine froze momentarily, caught off guard by the icy finality of John's words, and his voice. This, she thought, was something new.

"Now you're listening, ain't ya? Yeah, I'll pack your shit up right now if you don't leave me in peace!" His face went red. There was nothing remotely playful in it. He marched past her and swung the fridge door open to grab another beer, catching his breath as he opened the bottle and hungrily gulped. "Clean that shit up," he said, pointing at the mess on the floor. Her eyes fell to the spilled beer and suddenly she picked up the bottle. Before John could stop her, she launched it at him, narrowly missing his head as he ducked out of the way.

Later, she shut the bedroom door behind her and sat on the bed. The silence on the other side of the wall was worse than any fighting. Kick her out, he'd said. Her and the kids. How could he say that about the kids? She thought again of the will, and of her own absence in the legal language, not that she could have read much of it. But she knew her own name.

For a moment she stared unblinking at the carpet, boiling in the ache of what felt to her like a blunt rejection. She thought of her own mother and father, how they had often fought, and how all she had ever wanted was for them to be happy and for the house to feel safe. She wanted, no, *needed*, to feel safe. She would have to fix this. She would have to go out there, crawl back into his good graces, and offer up the part of herself she knew he could never resist.

7

THE FORENSIC PSYCHIATRIST[2]

June 21, 2000. Mulawa Women's Correctional Centre. Mum Shirl Psychiatric Wing. Day 1.

"He got in the shower after the fight," Katherine explained to Dr. Martin. "When he was done, I said for him to come into the bedroom and we patched things up."

"How did you patch things up?"

"We got into it. Sex, I mean."

Dr. Martin nodded. "Okay, and then what happened?"

Katherine's mouth tightened. "That's when he said her name, when we were having sex."

---

2   *Speculative reconstruction inspired by documented psychiatric interviews.*

8

LIKE A SLAP IN THE FACE

Late August, 1998. 84 St Andrews Street, Aberdeen, New South Wales.

She hated the way it crept in, this feeling that maybe she had gone too far again. She had seen it in his face. That dull, masculine resignation she recognized in men just before they decided it was time to end things. But she wouldn't let him go. Not after everything. Not after all she had given him, not after all her efforts to be what he wanted, and frankly, needed. At forty-four, she was getting too old and too tired to start again.

She stood up from the bed with renewed purpose and crossed to the mirror. Her eyes were puffy, her makeup half-smeared, her hair frizzy and damp from exertion. She dabbed at her eyes with a tissue, reapplied a bit of lipstick, ran a comb through her hair. Then she changed her top for one that dipped low and clung to all the right places. She took a breath and exhaled slowly. This wasn't over. When words failed, when threats didn't land, there was always her body. Her softness. Her ability to make a man feel he was the only thing that mattered. Her ability to make him forget. This was the thing she knew well. The thing she understood at her core. Every man she had ever been with crumbled under the weight of her sexual inhibitions. She knew just where to touch, when to stop and start again, how to hold back and to submit.

She waited in the hall, leaning against the wall until she heard the shower turn off. John emerged a few moments later with a towel slung low around his hips, his eyes tired and distant.

"You going to bed?" she asked, her voice soft and low. He nodded cautiously. She stepped toward him and touched his arm. "Let's not fight anymore, love."

He lay sprawled on the bed, the wiry hairs on his chest damp from the shower, one hand gripping Katherine's head. She knelt between his legs on the mattress, her hair loose around her shoulders, moving with the sensuous focus of a woman who had learned that sex could be currency and control.

She wanted to make him forget about Colleen. She wanted to be married again. So, she worked him over with a raw, uninhibited intensity. No pretense of romance, no staged performance. Just brute sexuality. She felt his body tighten as he neared climax. Then, she slowed down to edge him out a bit longer. When he could no longer contain himself, he let out a grizzly moan as he exploded into her mouth.

"Oh, fuck! Oh fuck, Col!"

The words landed like a slap. Katherine, for all of her seductive manipulations, froze like a doe caught in headlights. For a half second, she stayed there as still as a held breath while the name—*Col*—hung in the air, unmistakably not hers. John, already sinking back into the pillow and catching his breath, didn't seem to notice at first, caught up in whatever fantasy had overtaken him.

"What the fuck did you just say?"

He blinked, a little disoriented. "What?"

"What did you just call me?"

John lifted his head up, confused. "I didn't call you anything. What are you on about?" Katherine sat up, her hands pressed against his chest. "You said her name, Col. You said, 'Oh fuck, Col!'"

"No, I didn't," he muttered. "I said, 'Oh fuck, doll.'" But Katherine was sure she'd heard Col. Not just the name, but the tone—tender and familiar, like a muscle memory that hadn't faded in the twelve years they'd been separated. Katherine's eyes darted across his body, fast and furious, working up a rage. She dug her nails into his chest, hard. His eyes bulged from the pain.

"What the fuck, Kath!" John's voice went high with a kind of indignant terror. He tried to sit up, but Katherine shoved him back down, pounding her fists against his chest, screaming incoherent accusations. He yelled for her to stop, and raised his arms against her jabs, trying to grab her wrists.

"You piece of shit!" Her voice came out strangled and snarled. "You stupid fuckin' cunt!" She struck him again and again, fists against his face, his shoulders, his chest. He shoved at her frantically, but she kept at it, finding the soft flesh of his cheeks.

He twisted beneath her. "Get off of me, Kath!"

"You pathetic little cunt and your cunty Col can fuck off!"

John bucked, finally managing to shove her off. She tumbled sideways, hitting the nightstand, and sent a half-full bottle of Tooheys onto the carpet.

"Jesus Christ, it wasn't what you're thinking!" he panted, pressing a hand against the scratches on his face. "I said, doll, doll! You're bloody fuckin' insane!"

Katherine scrambled back up, her eyes narrowed and steely. "You say that again, go on, say it." But John was already moving, grabbing his jeans from the floor, yanking them on. His face was flushed and bleeding, his breath coming in ragged bursts.

"Why are you calling her name, Pricey!?"

"I told you, I said *doll*. Christ! You just heard Col, 'cuz we were talking about her today, with the will and…you just had it in your head is all." He left the room in a huff, and the sound of the door slamming, the truck firing up outside and then speeding off, gave way to the most awful silence.

Katherine curled up on the bed, sweat beading on her forehead, her thoughts racing. She glanced around the room, hearing the blood pound in her ears. Her mind flicking from thought to thought. He thought he could just use her? Take her for granted? Make her look like a fool? Like she was nothing but his entertainment? Like she didn't exist without him? He did say her name.

Oh fuck, Col. Oh fuck, Col. Oh fuck, Col. She was sure of it.

But she didn't mention it the next morning. Instead, she acted like nothing had happened. He, too, appeared to put it behind him, but there was caution hidden somewhere beneath the ruse. She made him bacon and eggs and black coffee. She kissed him goodbye at the door. Watched from the window as his best mate, Laurie, picked him up for the drive to work, and waved goodbye like she wasn't still hearing those cutting words in her head on a loop.

9

THE FORENSIC PSYCHIATRIST[3]

June 21, 2000. Mulawa Women's Correctional Centre. Mum Shirl Psychiatric Wing. Day 1.

"He wouldn't commit, see? He wouldn't commit to me. I know he loved me. His mate Laurie told me so. He said, 'He loves you, Kath, but he won't marry you 'cuz he wants his kids to get all his possessions.'"

"You said earlier that you were engaged to him; is that correct?" Dr. Martin asked.

"Yeah, that's why I was so…that's why we fought, about him divorcing Col. It made no sense."

"Why do you think he wouldn't marry you if you were engaged? Or why would he get engaged in the first place if he didn't intend to ever marry again?"

"I don't know. You think I'm lying? We were engaged. He bought me a ring, like I said."

"I believe you. I just want to understand how you reconciled these two things," Dr. Martin said.

---

[3]   *Speculative reconstruction inspired by documented psychiatric interviews.*

"I don't know about reconciling, but he says another woman's name while he's inside me. What woman wouldn't get mad?"

"And what did you do after he said her name?"

"I got off him, and I went to the bathroom. I sat on the toilet with my knickers around me ankles and started crying."

"You didn't confront him?"

"Yeah, I confronted him."

Dr. Martin watched her face. Noted the pause in her speech and the way her eyes blinked. "Did you hit him?" he asked.

"No. He hit me, he yelled at me, then he hit me."

"But you did hit him before?"

She shrugged. "Only in self-defense."

Dr. Martin leaned back, steepling his fingers again to his chin. He let the silence return while he watched her.

10

THE WAY SHE KNEW IT WOULD

September, 1998. 84 St Andrews Street, Aberdeen, New South Wales.

A week or so after the sex incident, Katherine found an old photo of John and Colleen. It had been tucked away in a drawer in one of John's old wallets. The picture showed them at a backyard barbecue, arm in arm, beers in hand, smiling brightly, friends happily gathered around them. Katherine took the photograph back to her cottage that afternoon and kept it on her lap while she watched *The Texas Chainsaw Massacre*, periodically looking down at it with a wistful disgust.

She didn't sleep the night. Instead, she searched the house for an old video camera her twin sister, Joy, had given her. By dawn, she had torn the photo in half and had burned it in the sink, after which she made herself a cup of builder's tea and sat at the table in her nightgown, watching the daybreak through the curtains. Her posture was one of defiant resolve. It seemed to say, *Fine, let him think he won. For now.*

The following day, she and the children went back to John's. As always, she woke with John at 5:30 AM to begin the day.

John would go into the bathroom to get ready, and she, clad in a robe and slippers, would wander into the kitchen to make coffee. She moved efficiently, a woman used to routine and busywork. She started breakfast—bacon, two fried eggs—John's usual. One yolk accidentally burst when she flipped it, which agitated her. While she waited for the toast, she took two more slices of bread out and made John a Vegemite and butter sandwich, which she wrapped in grease-proof paper and tucked into a lunch bag. She added a packet of crisps, Smith's Original, and an apple.

She heard him pad down the hallway from the bathroom into the bedroom. She plated his breakfast and set it on the table. When he passed through the kitchen a few minutes later in his work clothes, his wet hair flopping in loose curls, she handed him his coffee.

"Hot," she said, softly.

He took it with a nod. "Ta, love." He sat down and ate his breakfast. By 6:30, he was shoving his feet into his boots and grabbing his things for work. He stood by the open door with Katherine.

"You right?" he asked, rubbing the back of his neck.

"'Course I'm right, you?"

"Yeah, good," he replied.

She kissed him gently, almost maternally. She spotted Laurie's truck coming up the road. "Laurie's here. Tell him not to drive like a maniac or I'll kill him."

"Yeah," John said wearily. She followed him out onto the veranda. Laurie's window was already down, one elbow out.

"Morning, Kath!" he called out cheerfully as John made his way to the truck.

Katherine gave a wave. "Morning, Laurie." John climbed into the passenger seat, and they both waved goodbye as they drove off.

Katherine stayed on the porch and watched them go. Then, she went inside, and cleared the dishes and wiped down the counter, then rolled a cigarette while she waited for the kettle to boil. Anyone watching would have seen a calm and serene housewife doing housewifery things. But underneath, a vengeful satisfaction was quietly brewing. She took her tea out to the back patio, where she sat by the window and smoked. All that was left now was to wait for the morning to unfold the way she knew it would.

11

THE HOWICK MINES INCIDENT

September, 1998. Howick Mines, Howick, New South Wales.

As soon as John and Laurie arrived at work, John was summoned to the boss's office. No reason had been given. He felt uneasy as he headed over, replaying the past few days in his mind for anything that might explain why his boss, who was less than a year on the job, would want to see him. But nothing came to mind; he hadn't done anything wrong that he knew of.

"Morning, John," the boss said when he entered. "Take a seat." He gestured to the chairs in front of his desk.

"What's going on?" John asked as he sat down.

"I got a video this morning, which apparently was delivered yesterday afternoon. You need to see it." He turned to the small TV behind his desk and hit play on a VHS machine. John immediately recognized his living room. The camera was shaky as it weaved through his house. Katherine's voice came over the audio, clear and matter-of-fact.

"That's your place, correct?" asked the boss.

John nodded, his pulse picking up. "Yeah, that's my place."

"And that's the missus talking?"

"Well, that's Kath. She's—we're not married. Just seeing each other." He watched the video with mounting dread. The camera moved through his house, with Katherine's commentary running in a harsh, accusatory tone. "And he brought these two vacuum cleaners home one day…and these two drums." Her hand came briefly into frame as she pointed them out. "Some kitchen items, this can of Mortein, some oil." The camera moved outside to John's Land Rover, which was parked by the side of the house. "These headlights in the Rover—they come from the mine supplies." She then walked to a shelving unit in a storage shed and zoomed in on a dusty first aid kit. "And this first aid kit, he brought this home just last week. Took it from the storeroom, he told me." It was then that she turned the camera on herself. "He's a thief. You sirs got a right thief on your hands." And the image froze on her face.

With a slow, heavy breath, John rose to his feet, his face beet red with shock and fury. "What the hell is that!? That, that's… that's not…. Those things were throwaways. They were getting binned!"

"Look, never mind the other stuff. It's the first aid kit that's the problem, John. Health and safety regulations—anything medical taken from the site without authorization is a problem. You know this."

John shook his head, trying to keep his voice steady. "Mate, the storeman, he was tossing it because it was expired. There were ointments out of date. I told him I'd take it off his hands…you know, for the, for the Band-Aids and the gauze and such. He was about to toss it, he told me so, I *swear* to ya. There were witnesses."

The boss sighed and rubbed his forehead. "It doesn't matter. The moment it leaves the premises without authority, it becomes a liability. If someone got hurt and there were no medical supplies, it would cost us. We're a mine, for God's sake; people get hurt here all the time." He paused for a moment while he looked down at his desk. "And we don't need this kind of drama here, Price, with your missus and all. It's too risky. I'm sorry, mate."

"What are you saying?"

"I have to let you go. We have to take this matter seriously."

"Are you kidding me!? I've given twenty years of my life to this place!" John felt his heart pounding as the realization sank in. He was being fired. His reputation would be ruined. His six-figure income would vanish overnight.

His boss gave a sympathetic nod. "I know you've been here a long time. Not a fella here has anything but good things to say about you. But it doesn't change what I have to do. And don't worry, we'll sort you out with a generous severance." He paused again, waiting for John to say something, but all John could do was stare and blink with his mouth slightly agape, trying to process it all. "It's best you head home now. And just so you know, you can't take the company car. But I can get one of the boys to give you a ride."

He sat back down at his desk and picked up the phone. It was clear to John that his boss was ready to exit the conversation. John hadn't had much to do with him in the months since he'd replaced the last boss, who had been a decent bloke. John could have explained things to that one; they had gotten on well. That boss would have listened to John. He would have understood. And John would not now be out of a job. He wasn't sure if this new boss believed him. Judging by the outcome, probably not.

Laurie gave John's shoulder a long, thoughtful squeeze when he heard the news.

"Mate, that's fucked," he offered in support.

He had become familiar with Katherine's mercurial nature, and he didn't like her for it. But he had never said anything to John, who seemed happy enough, at least on the surface. But in the last year or so, Laurie had begun to notice the cracks. He recalled how Katherine had once punched John so hard in the chest that it left a large, angry bruise that took more than two weeks to fade.

"I'm giving you a lift home," Laurie said.

"Nah, you can't leave work. I'll walk."

"Don't be stupid. It's a bloody long walk back to Aberdeen, and it's already heatin' up. You're not gonna make it far in those boots."

They drove in silence at first, with the windows down, the warm wind whipping through the cab. Laurie kept his hands gripped tensely on the wheel. Finally, he said, "That bloody woman."

John didn't answer, just stared at the passing scenes of suburbia, his mind going over the video and what Katherine had said. And then suddenly, it came to him. *The Rover.*

"That fuckin' bitch," he spat in a low voice. "She's been planning this for months."

Laurie shot him a glance. "How do you mean?"

"The headlights in the Rover. I sold that car right after I put in those lights. That was three months ago. Which means she took that video before I sold it. And she's been waitin' for the right moment to fuck me."

Laurie took a breath, the gears turning in his mind. "So, she's been buildin' this thing against you for three months. Just waitin' to spring it. Why now?"

"Hell if I know. She seemed fine. You saw her this morning. Sweet as pie. That lying…."

Laurie kept his eyes on the road. "Control. That's all it is, mate. She gets off on it."

John rubbed his face, the anger and anxiety building in a sheen of perspiration on his forehead. "And she'll be at the house, actin' like she's done nothin' wrong. Smilin' and cookin' up a fucking storm as usual." He was livid now. Years of loyalty wiped out with one vindictive act. "I won't get my pension now. Six months I'd be eligible, and now I'll get nothing." John could barely process how little time it took for him to lose so much. "Nearly twenty years I gave that place. Now it's all bloody gone."

The thought of now confronting her, of going back to the house and facing whatever twisted satisfaction awaited him, made his chest tighten with a foreboding dread. He'd not been this fearful of her before. Frustrated, fed up, angry, yes, all of these. But this feeling of dread was new—a dark entity on his heart.

Laurie pulled the truck over to the side of the road and turned to John. "Listen, mate. You need to get rid of her. Whatever it takes."

"I know that, Laurie!" John snapped. "But how? How do I get rid of her for good without her fucking me again? Look what she's already done."

Laurie shook his head. "You've gotta get the cops involved, make a statement. Take out an AVO. You got injuries to show. You can back it up. I'll back you up." Laurie gave John's shoulder another firm squeeze. "Don't let her win. Don't give her the satisfaction, mate. You've got your kids to think about."

John nodded and breathed a little easier, though still distant and thoughtful. He knew Laurie was right. But knowing it didn't lift the dread from his chest. Didn't make him feel any less trapped. How far would she go, he wondered. What else would she do?

He couldn't shake the thought of Katherine recording that video in a petty bid to destroy him. He couldn't shake the image of her through the camera, that cold, satisfied voice rolling off the tape. *He's a thief. You sirs got a right thief on your hands.* And he couldn't stand the arrogance he saw on her face when she spoke those words, like she'd finally found something with which to shatter him completely. But for what? His mind spun with questions. It must have been the will, he realized, and saying Col's name. What else had she done while he wasn't looking? What other footage did she have? What other lies would she spread?

He squeezed his eyes shut, trying to force down the panic. He'd never felt so cornered. Never imagined that loving a woman could unravel his life in this way. He thought of his kids, their easy smiles and hopeful plans for the future, and felt sick to his stomach. He thought of Colleen and how much he missed her.

Regret flooded him in that moment. If only he'd been a better husband to Colleen, paid more attention to her, spent more time with her like she'd wanted, instead of with his mates at the pub, he would not be in this mess. Maybe he deserved this. Maybe this was his punishment for taking their marriage for granted.

John and Laurie sat there a while longer, thinking things through as the sun crept higher in the sky. Laurie eventually started the engine again and pulled back onto the road, his jaw set with quiet determination. John lit a cigarette, fighting back emotions he didn't have names for. One gnawing question kept circling back: Could he get her out of his life without more damage?

As if reading his mind, Laurie said, "You need to get legal advice. Make it official. Tell the cops everything. Get her out before it's too late."

Again, John nodded. Again, he knew Laurie was right, but Katherine was tricky. Every time he had tried to cool things down, she had lashed out. Up until now, it was always with her hands. He could handle that. But now she had cost him his livelihood, which impacted his children. What would she do if he pushed her out for good?

They arrived at John's house. "You sure you don't want me to come in? I think I should come in," Laurie cautioned.

"Nah, I'll be right. You should head back before they sack you too. I'll call ya later. Thanks, mate."

"Okay, just be careful. And please go see a lawyer."

John watched Laurie reverse out of the driveway and disappear. Then he marched up the steps of the veranda and yanked open the screen door. He found Katherine in the lounge, barefoot and humming softly while she knitted.

"What's got into you?" she asked casually.

"You know perfectly well what's gotten into me! How could you do that?" he said, the words coming out rough, half-choked. "How could you?"

"John," she said, looking shocked. "What are you on about?"

"Don't fucking play games with me!" he shot back. "You know bloody well! You got me sacked! You sent that fucking tape in like the vulture that you are."

Katherine straightened up and narrowed her eyes. "If you hadn't called out her name, I wouldn't of done nothink. You think I like living with someone who treats me like shit?"

He scoffed as he paced the room. "You're unbelievable. Fuckin' unbelievable. You just ruined my life, and you're sittin' there actin' like it's all my fault? You cost me my job. That was the only thing keepin' us afloat, and you torched it, like a bloody idiot!"

She set her knitting down with a deliberate calm. "You drove me to it, Pricey. You pushed me and pushed me, calling out that cunt's name, giving her everythink, and now you're shocked that I'm defending meself. You have no one to blame but yourself."

John felt his hands curl into fists, fighting the urge to strike her, to make her see what she'd done. "You don't get it," he said, his voice choking with rage. "You can't just go around getting people sacked for nothing! And then blame it on them!? Like your shit doesn't stink up the joint! Like you aren't some fuckin' batty cunt."

"Oh." She sneered as she stood up. "I'm the crazy one? Is that what you're telling me?"

John gritted his teeth, his pulse pounding in his ears. "I've put up with you for long enough. More than anyone in their right mind ever should, and you just keep finding new ways to twist the knife."

She was on him in a second, shoving his chest hard enough to knock him back a step. "Guess what, you don't get to make me the bad guy!" she hissed. "You think you're so high and mighty? You're weak, Pricey. You've always been weak."

He grabbed her wrists, which prompted her to start thrashing and kicking, and screaming like a feral animal. He pushed her back, harder than he meant to, and she stumbled, catching herself on the edge of the counter. A thin stream of blood appeared on her bottom lip where she had bitten it.

"Get out!" he shouted. "I don't want you here anymore, get out!" Next thing she knew, John was running between the bedroom and the front door, tossing armfuls of Katherine's things on the veranda.

The phone was already in her hand, dialing. "Barry," she sobbed into the receiver, her voice high and panicked. "You gotta come get me. He's going mad, he's hurting me!"

Katherine sat on the steps of the veranda, surrounded by her possessions—clothing, knitting, pots and pans, shoes—as her older brother, Barry, pulled up in his Holden. He leapt out of the car and up the steps urgently. John emerged from inside and dumped Katherine's toiletries onto the pile.

"What the hell's goin' on here?" Barry asked, squinting against the midday sun.

"She's leaving," John huffed, forcing himself to stay calm. Barry looked from Katherine to John and back again. "He lay a hand on you?"

"No," John chimed in preemptively. "But she's tryin' to make it look that way."

Barry put a hand on Katherine's shoulder, pulling her close. "He lay a hand on you?"

She nodded, sniffing. "He's a monster, shoving me and yelling in me face."

Barry looked back at John with a cold stare.

"It's bullshit, mate. You know your sister. She started it! She got me sacked today. Did you she tell you that? Yeah, why don't you ask her about it?"

"I don't give a shit. You touch her again, and I'll end you," Barry seethed.

John opened his mouth to say something in his defense but thought better of it. At this point, he just wanted them gone. "Fine, whatever, just get her the fuck out of my life and there won't be any regrets. Get the fuck off my property, *now*."

He stood on the porch and watched until they were gone, her things tossed haphazardly into the back of Barry's truck. He'd done it, he'd gotten her out. He should have felt relieved, but a chill settled over him nonetheless as he entered the house. It felt different without her—emptier, but not the kind of empty that brought comfort or peace. He didn't feel at all comfortable or peaceful; he felt instead that ominous dread, like he was drifting further out to sea.

12

THE FORENSIC PSYCHIATRIST[4]

June 21, 2000. Mulawa Women's Correctional Centre. Mum Shirl Psychiatric Wing. Day 1.

"So you let him go off that morning like everything was normal?"

Katherine shrugged and glanced at the clock on the wall. It was 11:55 AM. "I need something to eat. Can we break for lunch?"

Dr. Martin sat forward and capped his pen. "Okay, let's take fifteen," he said as he pressed the stop button on the recorder.

---

[4]   *Speculative reconstruction inspired by documented psychiatric interviews.*

INTERIM FORENSIC NOTE 1[5]

June 21, 2000. Mulawa Women's Correctional Centre. Mum Shirl Psychiatric Wing. Day 1.

When Katherine was escorted out of the room, Dr. Martin flipped back a few pages in his notes. He wrote deliberately, underlining a few items, then reached forward and pressed record on the device.

"This is Dr. Robert Martin, forensic psychiatrist for the prosecution. Subject is Katherine Mary Knight, forty-four years old. In custody for the probable murder of John Charles Thomas Price. We are at the Mum Shirl Psychiatric Wing, interview room 3B, Mulawa Centre, approximately three hours into day 1 session, now at 12:10 PM. Today is twenty-first June 2000. This is my interim note 1, recorded during a lunch recess. After preliminary questions, subject has so far been cooperative, verbally forthcoming for the most part about the events leading up to the murder. No overt signs of psychosis. Affect somewhat flattened, though she has responded with some positive memories when recalling certain domestic scenes. Particularly those concerning the early stages of her relationship with John Price. We have spoken this morning about the period between 1995 and 1998. Her relocation to his home on St Andrews

---

[5] *Dramatized scene inspired by documented psychiatric interviews and diagnosis.*

Street. She describes this time as calm, and stable. Uses language like "proper," "settled," "family." However, her recollections on the reasons for the breakdown of their relationship are questionable and inconsistent. She speaks as if she is the *victima provocata*, admitting there were fights and some violence, but refusing to take responsibility for her role in it, which we now know to be considerable. From what I've read in Katherine's file, the testimony from people who knew them as a couple was that she was more often the aggressor. The picture that has begun to form in my mind isn't simply jealousy that sent her into a rage. It is displacement and rejection. For Katherine, intimacy is not about vulnerability. It's about dominance. What the sex blunder revealed wasn't just a possible infidelity on John Price's part. It also revealed an inability to self-regulate at the most private, primal level, and her terror of abandonment. And that, I believe, is her core trigger.

"I pressed into the 1998 incident at the Howick Mines, well known and corroborated by witnesses. What stands out clinically, besides the act itself, is the manner in which she narrated the event. Coolly, almost as though she were describing the weather, this has been her demeanor for most of the session. She told me she watched John Price leave that morning with his lunch in hand and a smile on his face, knowing what she'd done.

"In attempting to assess the subject's culpability, my early impression is this: Katherine Knight has serious issues with control. In fact, she may possess too much of a need for it, often held in tension until something ruptures, and it doesn't take much for a rupture. I believe what we are seeing is a woman who has tried to administer a great deal of control over others. Katherine Knight presents in this Howick Mines business as a very pathological example of a paybacker. For a partner to do something like that, which is, to me, gross; to do something to that extent is extreme, very extreme. She may well have a personality disorder, but more analysis is needed. That's it for now. Subject is returning. End interim note 1. 12:33 PM."

PART TWO

13

THE KNOWN OVER
THE UNKNOWN

November 1998. The Top Pub, Aberdeen, New South Wales.

Two months after the Howick Mines incident, Katherine went on the hunt for John. She found him on a Friday night, sitting at the corner of the bar in the Top Pub with his mates Laurie and Frank, having a couple of beers and a laugh. It was around 8:30 PM. Being a man of ritual and routine, Katherine knew she would eventually find him there; there weren't many places to frequent in Aberdeen. The nighttime crowd at the pub was already loud, though it hadn't yet tipped into raucous. Billard balls cracked against each other from the back patio. AC/DC wailed from the sound system. A few fellas from the mines were scattered throughout the pub, all of them, it seemed to Katherine as she strolled in, glancing and gossiping about what she'd done. It was the talk of the town.

John saw her first. *"Oh shit, here it comes"* summed up the expression on his face. Katherine noticed him whisper something to his friends before getting up and leaving the bar. He headed toward the back of the pub, out past the billiard tables and toward the rear parking lot. Katherine wondered if it was an attempt to avoid her, or a sign that he would talk, but only in private. As she followed after him, his mates watched her uneasily. Katherine knew they didn't like her. She strode past them with a cool defiance. *Fuck them*, said her posture, *let them judge the edge of her knife.*

John was sitting in his truck in the parking lot smoking a cigarette and drinking his beer when Katherine approached. "Pricey," she called out.

"What do you want?" he groaned without looking at her.

"You know what I want." She walked around to the passenger side and hopped in.

"Not a chance in hell, Kath."

"I told you, I only did it 'cuz you said her name. It was a bad time for me when you did that. It caused me serious distress, Pricey, a lot of distress. You knew it would. Why would you want to hurt me like that when I do everything for you?"

He leaned back to look at her square. "Yeah, well, you knew I'd be sacked. What did you think was gonna happen?"

"You're leaving everything to that…to Colleen. You don't want to marry me. How do you think that makes me feel, huh? Like I'm nothing to you, when all I do is look after you. What person wouldn't be upset? You tell me what person wouldn't be upset?"

"Yeah, all right." He sighed. "But I don't know if I can forgive you," he said, his voice hoarse. "You hurt me. You hurt my family. I don't know how to come back from something like that." He took a sip of his beer, swaying a bit in his seat.

There was a moment of silence before Katherine leaned closer and put her hand on his knee.

"I forgive you, John. Let's forget this whole business." She started rubbing his leg. John looked at her. Katherine held his gaze and then she leaned in for it. The action was calculated, the motivation unmistakable. It wasn't just an olive branch; it was an attempt to claw her way back into his life, to make him see that she wasn't just a woman who had hurt him—she was a woman who could make him forget that she had.

"Oh fuck, what are you doing, Kath?"

"Don't leave me. It would be a mistake, Pricey." She put a hand on his crotch and squeezed. He swayed and half-heartedly pushed it away, but she kept at it until he could no longer resist. She unzipped him. Their eyes locked as she pulled it out and slid her mouth around him, taking control of him instantly. She got off on that, and on the public nature of the act, the gritty surrounds of the parking lot, even the contorted discomfort of her performance from the passenger seat. All of it was a turn-on. After she was done, John sighed heavily as he stared at the roof of the car.

"How was that, Pricey?"

"Yeah, it was good," he said, zipping himself up. Katherine leaned back in her seat and wiped her mouth and hands with some tissue that had been in the glove box. John got out of the car. "I'll call ya later," he said as he walked back into the pub.

"Yeah, call me later." She watched him go. Then she lit a cigarette and just sat in the car and smoked. In the moments that followed, a memory came to her from when she was fourteen, just before she'd started working at the slaughterhouse. She had gone to visit one of the local pig farms with her father, who had a mate who worked there. They were given a tour of the facility. The thing she remembered most was the farrowing crates, where rows and rows of crates were lined up, each containing a sow and her suckling piglets. She remembered the deafening noise. The nonstop clamor of metal and machinery, of sows grunting and piglets squealing. The crates were designed to prevent the sow from lying down too quickly and crushing her babies, which meant they were barely wide enough for the sows to even move. They were essentially trapped, forced to lie on their sides to allow the piglets to feed safely. The sows would lay like that, restricted for weeks at a time, often developing angry pressure wounds. And because they couldn't move, they would defecate and urinate and even give birth right where they lay. Many piglets died for one reason or another. Either they somehow got stuck under their mother and were crushed to death, or they were sickly and too weak to feed, in which case they would be picked off by one of the foremen and slammed against the concrete until they were dead. The corpse would be left there in the walkway, in full view of its mother.

Katherine remembered finding a runt piglet that had been stumped. It lay there, small and pink and vulnerable, flung onto the walkway near a side door that had been left open for ventilation. The piglet hadn't died. Its legs twitched as it regained consciousness, and it began to squeal plaintively as it lay there, shivering against the concrete.

After a few seconds, the piglet staggered to its feet and sniffed the air, turning toward the open door, clearly detecting a scent blown in on a breeze, and for a moment Katherine thought it might run out to freedom. But the piglet didn't run outside; it ambled back to the crowded maw of the farrowing pen, trying desperately to rejoin its mother and the others. It had chosen the clamor of the pen over a chance at freedom. Katherine picked it up by the tail and dropped it back into the farrowing crate with its mother and siblings, a jostling mound of pink flesh. Katherine pulled on her cigarette. There would be no more talk of it being over. John was back. Tomorrow would come, and things would return to normal.

Meanwhile, John had wandered back to the bar. Laurie spotted him first and stood up, not out of excitement, but exasperation. His eyes skimmed the doorway behind John, looking for her. "Jesus, mate," Laurie announced as John pulled up beside him. "What happened?" John was sheepish, his face pink and damp. He ordered another beer and leaned against the bar with both elbows. Laurie and Frank looked at each other as the barman slid a schooner across to John, who took it and started gulping it down.

"Well, you gonna tell us what happened?" Frank pressed. After a long swill, John said, "I been thinkin'…you know, maybe I brought all that business on meself."

Laurie laughed heartily with disbelief. "What are you talking about!? Brought what business on yourself? The sacking? That's funny, mate; that's a good one." He laughed again, shaking his head, then took a sip of his beer.

"I'm serious. I reckon I treated her rough. Didn't listen when I should've."

Laurie and Frank stared at each other, shocked, then back at John. "Mate, are you fucking serious?" Laurie asked, bewildered.

"Yeah," added Frank, "you feeling all right?"

Laurie said, "Anyone that's set you up like that, how could you have any time for them again?" John just shook his head as if it were already settled. "I brought it on meself," he insisted. "I'll get another job."

Laurie watched John like he didn't know him anymore. "But look what she's cost ya!" He held out his palms to illustrate the weight of it all, the epic betrayal.

"I said I'll get another job." His friends were speechless. John shrugged. "Look, fellas, I love her; what can I say. I love her. Yeah, she loses her mind sometimes, but who doesn't? I know youse two have in the past." Laurie and Frank shook their heads in violent disagreement.

"Not like that, mate. After what she done to you, you still love her. Have you gone mad? Are you thinking with the right head?"

But John was resolved. Laurie turned away from him then and finished his beer. "Well, I want nothing to do with that speckled hen. You bring her around and I'm gone."

John knew in that moment that Laurie and Frank had lost respect for him, and indeed the others would too, soon enough. Word would get around town. But what none of them could understand was the foreboding that had burrowed deep into him. Such that John now found himself back in the web Katherine had so vengefully spun. He knew now that she would never stop until she got what she wanted; refusing her was a dangerous option. When she had come to him, with her soft promises and desperate manipulation, he'd felt a subsidence in him, like the ground falling away beneath him. He had wanted to resist, had wanted to push her away, but he was weak when it came to women, and she knew this.

His friends would say he was mad. But he just couldn't explain to them how deep his dread went, how every time he'd tried to slow things down in the past, there had been consequences, and how those consequences escalated. As much as he hated the idea, he believed that staying in a relationship with Katherine, keeping the "enemy" close, as it were, was the best way to protect himself and his children. He didn't know what lengths she would go to if he ended it for good, so it would have to be the known over the unknown. For now.

14

THE FORENSIC PSYCHIATRIST[6]

June 21, 2000. Mulawa Women's Correctional Centre. Mum Shirl Psychiatric Wing. Day 1.

"He came running back to me," she said, her eyes narrowing behind her glasses. "Said he couldn't stand being away from me. That he missed me and thinks like that. He said he made a mistake—driving me to where I had no choice. He admitted it was his fault." Katherine glanced down at her fingernails. "Men like Pricey, they don't know what they want until it's gone. That's the think. He was always going back and forth. He couldn't leave me alone. Not for good."

Dr. Martin, as usual, let the quiet stretch out between them.

"He said I was the only one who really knew how to please him," Katherine continued. "Not even Colleen. He said she never understood what he wanted, what he liked, not like I did. He even cried. I remember that. He begged me to come back."

"And what did you say when he begged you?" Dr. Martin asked.

---

[6] *Speculative reconstruction inspired by documented psychiatric interviews.*

Katherine shrugged, looked off toward the corner of the room. "I said maybe." Dr. Martin made a note.

"I don't want to talk about that anymore. Can we talk about somethink else?"

"All right, let's talk about your time at work."

Katherine's expression softened a bit, not with warmth exactly, but with a kind of private satisfaction, like someone settling into pride, and for the first time since the session began, she smiled.

15

THE ABATTOIR

January, 1971. Aberdeen Meatworks.

The first time Katherine set foot in a kill room was the summer of 1971. She was just shy of sixteen and a recent dropout of Muswellbrook High. The school was a torturous forty-five minutes each way by bus. The last time she had ridden the bus home was the day she had decided enough was enough. She had been sitting by the window near the front of the bus, her long legs jammed up against the seat in front of her when one of the boys in a back row called out to her.

"Oi, freckle face," he said, his voice cracking halfway through the insult. He and his mates laughed, their voices full of bravado and stupidity. Their taunts had been a regular occurrence for months.

"You better shut your fucking mouth before I shut it for you," Katherine warned them. The boy's friends elbowed him on, and the insults kept rolling. By the time they had turned off the New England Highway past the Top Pub, Katherine's fists were already tight in her lap. The bus slowed near the railway station, brakes hissing to a stop. Katherine and her sister got off along with a few of the boys. Inside the bus, the remaining children pressed their faces against the glass to see what would unfold.

"Hold my glasses," Katherine said, slipping them off and handing them to her sister Joy, who stood by watching. As the bus pulled away, Katherine was on them with her fists swinging. One boy's nose bloodied, the other yelped like a kicked dog. It wasn't elegant, but it worked. The boys soon scattered, tripping over each other, calling her names as they ran. Katherine stood there watching them flee, her eyes squinting, freckles flushed across her cheeks like dots of fire, her chest heaving up and down triumphantly. She did not return to school after that. It just wasn't for her. The boys teased her relentlessly. Her teachers only saw the wild in her and did not bother with the rest. Her marks were dismal and she could barely read or write. There was no point in going back as far as she was concerned.

A week later she walked into the Aberdeen meatworks. "I'm here for a job. Ken Knight is me dad," she told the manager. It took her two attempts to land what she called her "dream job."

On her first day, she was given a tour of the facility, following the supervisor around as he walked her through the plant. "In a meatworks you have the slaughter men at the top of the ladder," he said, nearly shouting over the din of machinery as he raised a hand above his head to illustrate how "at the top" slaughter men were. "They work in the kill room, that's men-only work. It's the kind of place where your boots will stick to the floor if you pause for too long, if you know what I mean. They do the stunnin' and the slaughterin'. Once the animals are slaughtered, they're skinned and dressed. So your organs are all removed and collected in the offal bins.

"Then they're refrigerated for a couple of weeks to help the meat settle."

They were by the cooling rooms now.

"Makes it better for the next stage, which is the boning and slicing."

He led Katherine into a large, clamoring space with rows of workers in white aprons and hair nets. Some operated giant hook-like machinery that helped to detach large portions of flesh and sinew from bone. The supervisor gestured with his chin. "Carcasses come into the boning room through there," he yelled.

A pair of doors swung inward with the next chain-load: sheep hanging upside down from a line of conveyor hooks. They had no skin, heads, or hooves. Pink and sinewy, open rib cages showing a hollow cavity, all remarkably uniform in their appearance.

"Over there's the boning gang," he continued. "Boners and slicers must keep their knives razor sharp. Let a blade go dull and it'll turn your meat to mush.

"You have your boning gang deboning the prime cuts and cleaning 'em up. And over here you have the slicers." He gestured to the other side of the room, where rows of men and women worked at stainless steel benches loaded with cuts of meat.

"They cut the primes into sub-primes and make 'em presentable and ready for distribution. Both of these jobs, boning and slicing, require a good amount of skill with the knife. And some knowledge of anatomy, so you have to work up to that."

He led her down the line to where the finished cuts were bagged, weighed, and labeled.

"Rumps, rounds, chuck, brisket. Sorted by grade—fat cap, marbling, you'll learn to see it. Market cuts go that way. Rest goes to mince or export."

Now they were in a medium-sized tiled room. "This is the offal room, where all your organs get processed. Down there, the skins are processed. Then you have the pre-trim room upstairs, and your rendering, where all the waste gets collected and turned into your sausages and your pet foods. I'm gonna start you in the offal room as a general laborer. You'll clean up before, during, and after your shifts, and whatever else is needed." He clapped his hands and rubbed them together. "And that's all she wrote. Any questions?"

Katherine didn't have any questions. She knew most of this already. Her father had worked at Aberdeen Meatworks as a slaughter man. In fact, nearly all of Katherine's family had been employed there at some point over the years, which Katherine thought the supervisor should have known. Most people in Aberdeen worked at the abattoir. It had been the lifeblood of the town for nearly a hundred years. It's where Katherine's parents first met.

"No questions," she said.

"Right, let's go. I'll show you where to change."

She was given an apron and a pair of rubber boots and spent the rest of that morning cleaning up the blood, scraps, and off-cuts from the floor. It was one of the best days of her life.

She rose through the ranks quickly. Within a year, she was promoted to the boning room as a slicer, separating the bones from meat and sinew, carving prime cuts into sub-primes, trimming away the fat and silver skin, cleaning it all up so it looked pretty.

Standing at the stainless-steel table with her knife slicing into meat, Katherine would often hear her father's voice in her mind, cutting through the noise and guiding her work. When she was younger, he had kept cattle on their farm in Tenterfield. Every four months or so he would knock one off and distribute the meat amongst family and friends. Ken and Katherine's older brother, Charlie, would slaughter and dress the cow. Her mother and uncle would then quarter, bone, and slice the carcass. Katherine and Joy were too young to help, but they would always watch, and Ken would talk them through the process, teaching them for when they were old enough to do it themselves.

Once the animal is slaughtered, begin at the ankles to start the skinning, a slice across each tendon. Pull the skin down gently, guiding it with your knife, not too deep or you'll destroy the meat and not too shallow or you'll destroy the skin, then start on the butchering. You want clean cuts, not chewed meat, right, here's your beast, that's a hindquarter, heavy bugger, see the marbling? That's good fat, creamy and white, you want to watch for yellow fat, too much gristle, or anything green, don't cut what you wouldn't eat. Lay it flat, start with the primary cuts, long, smooth strokes, not sawing, it's a knife, not a bread cutter. Let the blade do the work, open it up and follow the seams, every muscle's got its path, follow the line between them, nature's already drawn the map. If it tears, you've gone too hard, if it drags, you're too blunt, keep your angle clean, once it's boned, tidy it up, gristle, sinew, thick fat, trim it down, clean muscle, nothing stringy. Expose your bones, start close and keep it tight, no hacking, use short, firm cuts, not deep ones, don't waste meat, it's a sin to leave it hanging on the bone! Pressure should be steady, not rushed, control is everything when it comes to your knife....

Katherine drew hers through the flesh smoothly, hand braced flat against the muscle. The tip of the blade sank in near a hip bone. *Start wide, open her up. You want to see the shape of it before you start separating anything. Long, clean strokes—remember, you're drawing, not stabbing.* The fat parted like cream under her blade. She cut it down and in, pulling the meat from the bone with short, sharp movements. The muscle yielded to her, loin first, then the flank. *Good. Now follow the seams. That's where the cut wants to be. They'll come apart like pages if you're patient.* Vertebrae glinted pale beneath a layer of sinew. She slid the blade under the bone, flicked her wrist. *See that? Expose the bone, then stay tight.* The meat would sometimes give with a soft sound like tearing cotton and something inside Katherine would tingle. It was as if she could feel what the knife felt: dominance, control, efficiency.

During her breaks, she would visit the kill room. She liked to watch the pigs come down the line on the conveyor, one directly behind the other, trapped so tightly it was a miracle their legs didn't break from the pressure. As a pig came to the end of the line, David Kellett, one of the shift slaughter men, twenty-one and not long out of jail, would position the stunning rods behind the pig's ears and deliver six hundred volts of electricity into its brain for three seconds. Katherine was always amazed by how quickly they seized and dropped unconscious, their legs out-stretched, like an upside-down table.

David would then hoist the pig's snout up and slice its throat clean across. The blood would come gushing out of the pig's main artery onto the bleed trough in a steady, pulsing river of red. The actual slaughter was always quick and clinical, like an assembly line series of actions that betrayed a degree of monotony and even boredom on David's part. *I've done this a thousand times,* his movements seemed to say.

But that's if the process went smoothly. Unlike cows or sheep, the pigs seemed to know what was coming. Katherine could see it in their eyes—the fear and desperation. They would squirm violently, squealing with ungodly terror. Occasionally, a pig would manage to dislodge itself from the conveyor and wriggle free of the stunning rods before stumbling onto the floor, slipping and sliding in pools of blood, with that ear-splitting squeal, as it frantically tried to flee. David would seize the terrified creature by the ear, twisting it hard and calling one of the boys over to help. They would then hoist the pig back up onto the bleed trough and wrestle it into submission. The other pigs, bound up and trapped as they were, would witness everything, their panic permeating the air like a vapor. Katherine often felt that watching them was almost like watching human beings. Something about their eyes.

16

THE FORENSIC PSYCHIATRIST[7]

June 21, 2000. Mulawa Women's Correctional Centre. Mum Shirl Psychiatric Wing. Day 1.

Dr. Martin watched Katherine from across the table. She sat with her arms crossed, one leg tucked over the other. The recorder ran. The fluorescent lights glared. The clock ticked.

"I liked watching it, yeah," Katherine said, her eyes steady but detached, like she was reliving the moments in her mind. "And David was good at it."

"How old were you then?"

"Sixteen, seventeen."

Dr. Martin nodded slightly. His pen hovered but didn't touch the paper. "And the abattoir was your first job?"

"First proper one. I worked at a clothing store for a couple of months, when I didn't get the job the first time at the meatworks."

Dr. Martin let the silence breathe for a second.

"They had me cleaning up at first," she continued. "Scraps, fat, the off-cuts. Blood and thinks like that." She paused. "I'd

---

[7] *Speculative reconstruction inspired by documented psychiatric interviews.*

watch the slicers. Watch how they used the knife, where they held it. How quick they could strip the bone."

"You wanted to be doing what they were doing?" asked Dr. Martin.

"Yeah, it seemed right to me."

"And how did the men treat you when you started in the boning room, at such a young age?"

"Yeah, same as blokes always did, I guess."

17

PUT UP WITH IT AND STOP COMPLAINING

March 1973. Aberdeen Meatworks, New South Wales.

The men. They noticed Katherine. They noticed that she was a teenager. They noticed that she was tall and had fiery red hair. They noticed that she often murmured to herself while she worked, a running commentary whispered under her breath to some invisible presence. They noticed that her knife moved fast. Each cut landing clean and deliberate. And they noticed that she never asked questions. Never asked for help. Never chatted with the other girls, except for her sister, Joy. She just watched and worked. Some of the older blokes would glance at her as she broke down another forequarter.

"Reckon she's faster than Bretty," one muttered.

"Cleaner, too," said another.

"Yeah, but she's weird with it. She cuts like it's personal."

It wasn't long before a small tension began to take shape between Katherine and some of the other men. One morning, Vince, a wiry young slicer in his twenties, kept glancing her way. Sensing his gaze, Katherine shot him a look.

"What's your fuckin' problem?"

"Think you're the big dog now, eh?" Vince said as he walked around her. He flicked something at her—a strip of fat, or tendon. It slapped the side of Katherine's face and fell to the floor. In that moment, as she sized Vince up, a memory suddenly flooded her mind. From when she was thirteen. She had been walking along MacQueen Street with Joy and two friends one summer afternoon when they heard whistling and calling out from across the road. A group of three older boys was hanging out in front of the RSL Club.

"Why don't youse come over here and give us a kiss," one of them taunted.

It was Paul, a seventeen-year-old boy whom Katherine had had sex with only weeks ago. Some of the other girls in class had fellas or boys who liked them. But none of the boys ever paid much attention to Katherine except to tease and bully her. When Paul had shown interest in her, Katherine lapped it up. She wanted a boyfriend. He had pressured her to do things to him in the bathroom, and behind the school building. But she'd felt uncomfortable at the time because he touched her in a way that called up her childhood.

She had told her mum about it, hoping for some guidance. But all Barbara would say was, "Put up with it and stop complaining." That was her advice. And that's what Katherine did. She met Paul in the bathroom one afternoon, and he made her do things. Then he turned her around and penetrated her. Katherine was left in terrible pain by the end, wanting only his care and acknowledgment, even a gentle pat on the back would have done the trick. But he zipped himself back up and strolled out of the bathroom with a flippant "See you around, slut" as his parting words. His mates had been waiting outside for him, clearly aware of what was going on. When Katherine emerged, humiliated and furious, they had given her grief.

Paul disappeared from school after that and had not spoken another word to Katherine until now—calling out to her like he didn't already know her.

"Fuck off!" she'd shouted, giving them the finger. One of the boys kicked a football across the road at her. That's when Katherine pulled a long-bladed knife from somewhere on her person and advanced across the road toward them. The girls were stunned when they saw it. So were the boys.

"Come on then," Katherine goaded. "If you want to have a go, come on."

Attempting to save face, the boys called her bluff and held their ground. Katherine moved toward Paul without hesitation, the knife held out in front of her. But the boys finally ran off scared before she could reach them. Katherine never forgot the look on Paul's face, or how rousing it felt to be the victor.

Now, in the boning room, everything around her sharpened— the hum of the line, the rattle of hooks, the hiss of a floor hose some- where down the hall. She turned to Vince, the knife in her hand held out in front of her just like it had been that summer afternoon. Vince started to smirk, maybe say something, but Katherine was already in his face. Her chainmail-gloved hand closed around his throat and drove him back against the metal bench. He was shorter than Katherine and slight in frame, so it was no effort to restrain him. She brought up the knife and hovered it near the corner of his eye. Not a sound came from the others, just complete shock.

"If you ever fuck with me again, I will rip this through you."

Vince's terrified eyes locked with Katherine's.

"Think I'm kidding?" she hissed. "Try me." The foreman shouted across the room, "Katherine! That's enough!" Boots pounded on concrete. A tray hit the floor somewhere. Someone yelled for the line to stop....

18

THE FORENSIC PSYCHIATRIST[8]

June 21, 2000. Mulawa Women's Correctional Centre. Mum Shirl Psychiatric Wing. Day 1.

Dr. Martin steepled his fingers beneath his chin. "Vince embarrassed you. Provoked you. Like Paul did."

Katherine shrugged. "Yeah."

"And you liked him once, Vince?"

"Yeah, until I realized what a cunt he was."

Dr. Martin watched her. "When you feel humiliated, when someone rejects you, or offends you, your response is often violent; are you aware of that?"

Katherine's expression didn't change, but her knee started bouncing beneath the table.

"People don't get to laugh at me." She folded her arms. "I don't like being used. Or dismissed. Who would?"

"Well, no one, but most people don't retaliate with violence. Do you understand the difference?"

Katherine shrugged and looked off, feigning boredom.

---

[8] *Speculative reconstruction inspired by documented psychiatric interviews.*

Dr. Martin glanced at his notes, then back to her. "Okay, let's talk about the others. The ones who came after Paul and Vince." He paused. "What happened with them?"

Katherine bit her nails as she stared at the floor. Dr. Martin waited.

She shrugged again. "Why do you want to know?"

"Well, it seems to me," said Dr. Martin, "that for you, sex has become a kind of tool, if you will. A way to gain the upper hand. Would that be fair to say?"

19

DAVID KELLET

1973. Aberdeen, New South Wales.

They hadn't known each other long by the time David's back hit the tin wall behind the garbage shed, Katherine pressing into him, her hands on his shoulders, her mouth smashed into his. She slid her fingers beneath his shirt, grazing the skin just above his belt. They were on their shift break and had snuck out behind one of the outbuildings of the abattoir, beside a scrabbly thicket of weeds and trash.

A few weeks earlier, Katherine's brother Charlie had been sharing a cigarette with David, who was new in town and recently hired.

"My sister's in the boning room," Charlie told him. "Tall. Redhead. You can't miss her."

David had seen her. Bent over a carcass, slicing away with fast efficiency. She had looked up, met his eyes without blinking. "What the fuck you starin' at?" she'd said. "Nothing, just your brother Charlie told me I'd find you here." They chatted a lot after that. Katherine thought he was cute, and she would visit him in the kill room when he was rostered for slaughtering. She liked to watch him stun the pigs.

Her breath was hot in his ear. "You gotta girlfriend?"

"Yeah, Maxine," he replied breathlessly.

"Not anymore," Katherine said coyly. All hands and heat, she rubbed herself against his erection, pulling him closer like she already owned him. Then, abruptly, she stood back, her eyes searching his. "You want me?"

David nodded. "Yeah."

"Then do me right, and you can have me." He laughed, unsure what to say, or even if he should take it seriously. Her fingers found the zipper on his jeans. She got on her knees and put her mouth on him, kept at it until they heard the rattle of a nearby bin and someone whistling from inside. She stood up and brushed herself off, wiping the back of her hand across her mouth.

"You better get back in there," she said. "Before the boss wonders why you're slackin' off." She walked off without looking back. By the end of the week, Maxine was gone, and Katherine Knight had her first real boyfriend.

To David, she was quieter than he expected. He noticed that she mostly kept to herself at work, her head down, her blade working steadily on the carcasses. But when she smiled—a proper smile, her head tilted to one side, like she was in on something no one else knew—his heart warmed for her. That was the first thing David noticed about her. That lovely smile. He'd seen her at the slicer's table, her glasses slipping down her nose, when a coworker stopped to tell her something, and she laughed. Something about the way she tilted her head made him want her.

When he was on shift in the boning room, he would call out across the floor to her and give her grief just to see the corners of her mouth curl. The other thing he liked was that she called him by his surname. "Oi, Kellett," she'd say, wiping her hands on her apron. "You gonna talk all day or actually work? Oi, Kellett, gimme a smoke, will ya? Oi Kellett!"

Soon after they became an item, David met her mother, Barbara, who seemed to like him well enough. She was a loud woman with a sailor's mouth, just like Katherine. When they decided to move in together—at Katherine's insistence—Barbara didn't protest. Katherine, who was only just eighteen, made it clear that she wanted to get out from under her parents' control. Barbara and Katherine had a complicated relationship, as many parents do with their children, and the truth was, Barbara was ready for a break from her daughter. Even so, on the day Katherine and David had packed his car up, Barbara had pulled David aside.

"She'll go off if you cross her," Barbara warned, holding a cup of tea, a cigarette burning between two fingers. "You better watch that, don't play up on her—she'll bloody kill you." Kellett just laughed it off at the time. "Yeah, all right."

"I'm serious, love. You better watch this one; she's crazy."

They rented an old farmhouse off a rancher that had worn lino floors, a leaky roof, and a front door that stuck as you opened it. It sat opposite a wheat silo, with paddocks stretching in both directions. On their second night in the house, Katherine stood on the veranda, her arms crossed contentedly across her chest as she watched the sky turn to dusk over the hills. David came up behind her, a Tooheys in hand.

"Told you we'd get the place," he said, nudging her shoulder.

"Yeah," she muttered, feeling like her dream of a stable, happy home was suddenly within reach.

Summer peeled the edges off everything—the paint on the veranda posts, the grass along the fence line, the skin on the tops of their shoulders. The days bled into each other. Heat, paddocks, beer in stubby holders, the buzz of blowflies against the screen door.

David got on well with Katherine's fraternal twin sister, Joy. She'd show up with a carton and something half-cooked from home, and the three of them would sit out back until late, bare feet on the grass, dust gathering around their ankles, smoking cigarettes by the fire, telling stories. For a while, wherever David and Katherine were, Joy was—sometimes laughing, sometimes quiet, but always there. Once, in town, David and Joy walked hand in hand down the main street. Just to stir the pot amongst the town folk. Heads turned. A few whispers passed between neighbors on the footpath.

"Don't everybody get your tits up," Joy would snicker, loud enough to be heard. David would squeeze her hand, grinning like a schoolboy. "There's never anything in it," he later told a co-worker at the pub. "Just fun. She's like a mate. And Kath don't mind."

The truth was, things were really good. They had fun together that first year, the three of them, playing records too loud, painting the house, making home videos. And through it all, David, always the show-off, never stopped being the larrikin. Anyone said, "I dare ya," and he'd do it. That summer, the dares were small: climb the town water tank, swim naked in the farmer's dam, tie a butcher's apron around a cow. The kind of silliness that made the days memorable. They became a kind of family—odd, untidy, loud, but happy. David would later say that Katherine "started off really wonderful, good as gold."

But as they approached the end of their first year together, cracks began to emerge. Katherine would line the kitchen shelves with wax paper, as her mum did. Hang the washing on the Hills Hoist the same way her mum did—knickers hidden in the middle behind the towels and the sheets—and she expected David to do everything the same. He found that she compared him to her parents, even though she couldn't wait to leave them behind.

"You don't do it right," she snapped at him one day while he was cutting up a roast. "Mum would lose her shit if she saw that."

Barbara's words began to echo in David's mind. *"You better watch this one, she's crazy…"*

They decided to throw a party around Christmas. They would invite a handful of mates from work, their siblings, some cousins. Joy would spin records on an old player and of course there would be a barbecue. David, ever the thrill-seeker, thought store-bought cuts of meat weren't good enough for the occasion. He drove out to a neighboring cattle farm the evening before the party, with a full moon lighting his way through the darkness. He found a stray cow in one of the paddocks, its large dark eyes staring at him sideways beneath the moonlight. He raised his .303 bolt-action Lee-Enfield rifle, pulled the trigger, and shot it dead.

The sounds of the outback were drowned out by the revving of David's chainsaw as he butchered the animal, blood soaking the earth around his feet. He returned to the farmhouse a few hours later, hauling the butchered hide over his shoulder. Katherine followed him out to the shed, and together they carved slabs of meat off the steer.

The party kicked off in the evening, as the barbecue hissed to life. "My Coo Ca Choo" blared through speakers. By then, everyone was in a raucous mood, with beers in hand and smoke curling into the gum trees. David got away with the theft for two days before dingoes found the buried carcass. They had dug it up and scattered the bones across the back paddocks. Noticing a missing head, the farmer followed the trail to David, who had forgotten all about it when the cops showed up a few days later.

"Bloody hell," he'd said, hands cuffed behind his back. "It was just an old cow."

But the charge—cattle rustling—had put him in violation of his parole. That meant five years' hard labor. He'd already done three months for a previous offence.

A week later, he stood in court with his shirt tucked in and his hair combed.

The prosecutor—an intense and serious-looking man who'd seen Kellett more times than he cared to count—glanced at the judge, then back at David with constraint. Or maybe it was mercy. Either way, he didn't mention David's priors. Didn't connect his name to the man the judge had indeed seen before on previous offences. It bought David some leniency.

He was fined fifty dollars—a slap on the wrist for a crime that could have ruined him—restitution, and a three-month bond. When he walked out of the courthouse into the hard sun, Katherine was waiting for him on her motorbike, squinting against the light. She hadn't missed a single court appearance.

She stood by him through it all, her loyalty unwavering. She even kept press clippings of his run-ins with the law.

"We weren't even married yet," David would recall years later. "But she stood by me. One hundred percent. Side by side."

On the morning of their wedding, David cracked open his first beer a little after eight. Katherine was too busy mending her gold minidress to notice. When it came time to leave a few hours later, David was unsteady on his feet. Katherine, irritated but determined, helped him dress in his best outfit: a purple paisley button shirt with matching flared trousers. She hooked her arm under his and ushered him out to the carport, where her motorbike was parked.

She kicked it awake with one clean stomp and revved it to life. "Get on," she called over her shoulder. By the time they hit the New England Highway, David was properly sauced. Wind sliced across his face as he held on to her waist and leaned in with the turns. They pulled into the Royal Hotel in Muswellbrook for another raucous round of beers, after which they crossed the street to the courthouse.

"What the fuck? Why we at the fuckin' courthouse? I...I hate this place," David slurred, blinking around in confusion.

"We're about to be wed, ya dumb cunt," Katherine reminded him as she adjusted the strap of her gold minidress.

"Wed?" he repeated, swaying as he furrowed his brow. "Who says?"

"I do," she replied with a wicked grin.

She had no veil, no flowers, no soft touches, just the gold minidress and some eyeshadow and lipstick. Katherine's brother

Charlie was there to walk her down the aisle. And David's best mate, Neville, was also there. No one else had been invited to the ceremony. It wasn't about the pageantry for Katherine—this was a statement, a claim, a tightening of the leash around David's chaotic, wandering existence. In her mind's eye, their future would unfold in warm, golden tones. They would have beautiful and perfect babies. David would cradle each one tenderly, his rough hands transformed by fatherhood. He would adore Katherine, his gaze soft with love as he brushed a curl from her face. He would call her beautiful, tell her she was the best mother in the world, and spin her around in the yard under a sky littered with stars while the children slept. It was a vision so vivid it made her dizzy.

Inside the courthouse, the celebrant barely looked up from the paperwork as the marriage license was signed. David fumbled for the twenty-dollar fee, spilling coins and a crumpled note onto the counter. Moments later, the celebrant, unimpressed by the spectacle, pronounced them husband and wife. Katherine let out a whoop, loud and triumphant, while David blinked at her, still catching up to what had just happened. He grinned and lit a cigarette.

"Didn't know I was gettin' married today." He laughed. There was no cheering, though. Just the shuffle of papers and the scratch of a pen on the registry. It was 1974. She was nineteen, he was twenty-three.

After the ceremony they rode back to Aberdeen to break the news to Katherine's mother. Barbara's reaction was as pointed as her personality. She again pulled David aside, careful to avoid her daughter's attention.

"Listen here, I hope you remembered what I told you," she cautioned, her voice low and firm. "Stir her up the wrong way or do the wrong thing, and you're fucked. Don't you ever think about playin' up on her. She's got something loose. She's got a screw loose somewhere."

David stared at her, dumbfounded, the haze of alcohol making it hard for her words to land. But when they finally did, he brushed it off again with a naive wave of his hand. "Ah, Barb, c'mon. She's a tough one, but she ain't that bad."

Barbara's sharp eyes didn't waver. "Hmmm," she replied grimly, her tone carrying the weight of eighteen years spent raising Katherine. But he could do nothing more than laugh it off, somewhat warily, and return to his bride.

Later that night, the temperature had cooled considerably, but Katherine was damp with a feverish determination. As soon as they stumbled through the door of the farmhouse, she wasted no time. She disappeared into the bedroom and emerged a moment later wearing a black negligee that clung to her curves. The boldness of her movements left no room for David to make any decisions. She drew him to the bedroom and climbed on top of him, her hands flat on his chest, her eyes flashing with intent.

David, still reeling from all the alcohol and the surreal impressions of the day, didn't protest. His body responded even as his mind lagged behind. Within twenty minutes, he climaxed, letting out a half-slurred groan, and then he passed out almost immediately, his head lolling back on the pillow.

Katherine wasn't finished, though. Not even close. She stared down at him, frustrated. *This wasn't how it was supposed to go— not tonight.* She nudged him, then shook him harder, finally punching his shoulder until he groaned awake. "Come on, you lazy sod, we ain't done yet."

David blinked up at her, bleary-eyed, but he obeyed. Despite the alcohol swirling in his veins and the weariness that pressed down on him like a heavy blanket, he rallied. Katherine got him going again, and after some time, he managed, against all odds, to climax a second time. But as he collapsed back onto the pillow, utterly spent, Katherine's frustration only deepened. It wasn't enough. She had expectations, standards to meet.

"Get up," she demanded not long after, punching and shoving him on his back again. "You keep passing out like a fucking baby. Mum and Dad had sex five times on their wedding night. Five. And we only done two." Her tone was sharp, accusatory, as if his inability to meet her demands was a deliberate act of defiance.

But David couldn't do it. He was too drunk, too tired, and too overwhelmed. The events of the day had left him in a mild state of shock, and her relentless insistence only made him want to retreat further into himself. He rolled away from her, his voice muffled against the pillow. "Go to sleep, Kath," he muttered, his words barely audible. "I can't. Not now. I'm wiped out."

Katherine glared at him. But he was already asleep, his body surrendering to exhaustion. She shook him awake once more. "Oi, Kellett, c'mon, let's go."

"Nah."

"You heard me, wake up!" He groaned, tried to roll away, but her determined hands were already making their moves on him. He couldn't get there again. As his mind drifted in and out of sleep, a faint, absurd hope fluttered at the edges of his thoughts. Maybe, just maybe, he'd wake up the next morning to find it had all been a dream. But deep down, some small, buried part of him knew this could become a nightmare. The shotgun wedding had been real, the rushed vows had been real, and so, too, was the crazed woman pounding on him and demanding more sex.

Finally, he woke with a start, his lungs screaming for air. Katherine's hands were clamped around his neck, her fingers digging in with surprising force. Her face hovered above his, flushed a deep, furious red, her jaw clenched tight. Her entire body seemed to tremble with madness, and yet her grip was terrifyingly steady, as though she were channeling every ounce of strength she had into this one act of squeezing his throat. David's head throbbed. He felt the blood pounding in his temples, the veins in his forehead straining as his heart slammed against his rib cage in wild panic.

Instinct kicked in. He clawed at her hands, scratching and pulling, desperate to loosen her grip. But Katherine was strong—unbelievably strong. Her weight bore down on him, pressing him into the mattress as they grappled. The room was silent save for the sounds of their struggle, his ragged gasps and the low, guttural noises she made, like some rabid, predatory creature. To David, it felt as though time had slowed, stretching each agonizing second into an eternity. And then, all at once, she let out a piercing scream, raw and animalistic, a sound born of pure, unfiltered rage. "Kellett!" she shrieked, her voice cracking under the strain. "How can we be properly married when you're only doing me twice on our fucking wedding night!?"

Her hands released him then, and she collapsed onto the bed beside him. Through the haze of her fury, Katherine saw it again—those visions of the life they were supposed to have. A happy home. Their children laughing. The two of them dancing in the yard beneath. As the images flashed in her mind, she told herself that this can't happen, this *rejection*.

David rolled away from her, gasping for air, his chest heaving as he tried to steady himself. He could still feel the ghost of her hands on his throat, the sting where her fingers had dug into his skin. He coughed and rubbed his neck, staring at her in disbelief. His wife, he thought, was gone, and this new person had taken her place. Even her eyes were different. A Jekyll-and-Hyde moment. He thought of Barbara's warning: *"You better watch this one, she's crazy."* It felt to him like the first note in a dark symphony that had just begun to resound.

After that night, the sheen of early love had begun to fade. By the middle of their second year together, the arguments came more frequently—not screaming matches at first, just sharp words in the kitchen, quiet digs over dinner.

"You didn't fold the towels right," she'd say.

"I folded 'em. That's the point."

"You folded them like a bloody child. And you hung the washing up so stupid. How many times I have to tell you, I want my knickers hung on the inside line. Behind the sheets and towels, so the neighbors don't see." David glanced at Katherine with a look of quiet disgust.

"Who cares if the neighbors see? They got knickers too!"

He stood up and walked out into the backyard with the washing basket and tipped it onto the grass. "Do it yourself, then!" he shouted as he walked off.

Katherine brought her mother's nagging standards into the marriage like static, pushing David to do more, fix more, be more. She'd compare him to her father—a man David couldn't stand—even while she claimed her parents' marriage was shit.

By late 1975, he was worn out by her. Her charm had gone, replaced by sudden and extreme mood swings. She ran sweet and loving one minute, hot and furious the next. There were days she wouldn't speak to him at all, followed by nights she'd seductively cling to him in bed as if she was afraid he'd vanish while she slept.

Katherine fell pregnant in October, and her mood swings became more devastating. Around that time, David met Susan, a woman in town who liked to have fun, and it didn't take long for an affair to kick off. Pretty soon, Susan fell pregnant, too. David stayed with Katherine through Christmas, about two months into her pregnancy—out of duty, perhaps. Or fear. Maybe both. By January 1976, he was done with their roller-coaster marriage. He had packed his car and headed north for Queensland with Susan.

Katherine was beside herself with grief and rage. She thought of nothing but revenge. The day her husband left, she called the police and told them he was running drugs. It wasn't true, but truth had never been her primary concern. The police pulled him over at the New South Wales/Queensland border. He watched as the officers rummaged through the boot of his car, and the glove box, and even through Susan's belongings. But of course, there was nothing. Just bags and boxes full of clothes.

Katherine gave birth to Melissa Ann Kellett on May 11, 1976, without David by her side. By then, it wasn't just her marriage that had dissolved—it was her world and her sense of self, and she didn't know what to do, where to turn, or how to cope. In her mind, she had given David everything. She had given him sex. She had given him love. She had given him a child. She had tried hard to be a good housewife, but it hadn't been enough.

Weeks passed, and the feeling of abandonment grew ever more suffocating. Alone with her baby, Katherine sank into a pit of loneliness and despair. The pain of rejection was searing. She could no longer distinguish between the days. Her mind ran wild with thoughts of David's betrayal. It was from within that wildness that she bundled Melissa into her pram one cold winter morning and ventured out of the house. As she walked the main road, the crushing need for revenge overcame her. She started to swing the pram wildly, her movements erratic, almost as if she were trying to push some invisible obstacle out of her way. The carriage rocked dangerously, threatening to veer into oncoming traffic. The sound of tires screeching and horns blaring rang around her ears. But it was of no consequence. Nothing mattered to her in those moments, not even her child.

People watched with grave concern. She could hear their gasps and stunned exclamations, feel their worried glances as she passed. But she cared nothing about that. She cared nothing of their judgements. All she cared about was her rage, and how to vent. It was the same rage that plagued much of her adolescence—that sense of compressed violence. She was on the edge now, teetering between reality and fantasy, between deep distress and clear-eyed vengeance.

The police were called, and Katherine was taken to St Elmo's Psychiatric Hospital in Tamworth. The diagnosis was postpartum depression. The dispensed medication didn't make things better. If anything, it numbed her, made her feel like a stranger to herself. She checked herself out that evening.

What unfolds after that would become one of those stories people told in hushed tones for years to come, the kind of scandal that belonged to a whole town rather than just one family. On a cold afternoon in July, Katherine walked out of her house with

Melissa and headed to the rail line near MacQueen Street. There, she jumped down the embankment onto the train tracks. She held the two-month-old baby in her arms the way some people carried their laundry. Her mind raced all the while with thoughts of making David feel her pain.

As she stood on the train tracks, she looked at the rails, stretching endlessly into the distance, and saw the speck of an approaching train. She looked at Melissa, held the child out in front of her, little bare legs dangling helplessly in the cold. She stepped over the ballast stones into the middle of the rails and placed her daughter, who had begun to cry, between the steel lines and walked away.

Ted Abrams, a pensioner who lived in the Aberdeen Hotel, was up near the ridge collecting scrap when he heard the faint cries of a baby. He looked up and spotted the bundle on the tracks and a twitch of movement. Then he saw a train about a mile or two in the distance. He heard the cry more clearly now and hurried down the embankment. Shocked to his core, he grabbed the baby off the tracks, his breath shallow from the horror of it. *Who would do such a thing?* Across the road, Lorna Driscoll stood outside the general store she owned, watching curiously as Ted carried the screaming baby into town.

Katherine was on Graeme Street, causing a scene with an axe she'd found by a woodpile in a neighbor's yard. She swung it around with hysteria, practically foaming at the mouth and threatening anyone who came near. A boy ran inside his home, terrified. An old couple watched, horrified, from their window. By nightfall, the police had Katherine in custody, and she was again sent to St Elmo's. The baby was unharmed and sent to stay with her grandparents. When she was released from St Elmo's two weeks later, Katherine picked up Melissa from her parents and went back home. Nothing had changed.

Until one morning not too long after that, she again stepped out of her front door, crossed the main road that split Aberdeen down the middle and walked the five minutes to Molly Perry's house. Molly had worked at the abattoir with Katherine for about a year, and they knew each other well. Molly answered the door in her slippers. Her sixteen-year-old daughter, Margaret, stood behind her, while her son Henry sat cross-legged on the living room floor playing with Matchbox cars.

"Mel's not looking so good, she's been crying nonstop." Katherine said. "Can you drive us to the GP?" Molly agreed and went to get her car keys while Katherine headed back to her house to get Melissa.

Margaret slipped on her shoes and followed her mother out. Henry tagged along too, and together the Perrys drove to Katherine's to collect her and the baby. Margaret went inside to help Katherine while her mother and brother waited in the car. She found Katherine in the bedroom standing above Melissa's cot. As she approached, Katherine's whipped a large boning knife from behind her back and without warning, she slashed Margaret across the face, a hot line of blood opening just beneath the girl's eye. Margaret screamed and tried to flee, but Katherine held her by the arm, and then it was all chaos.

"Get in the car!" she barked at the girl as she forced her into the backseat, holding Melissa in one arm and the knife against Margaret's throat with the other. They did as they were told. Because of the baby. Because of the knife. Because no one could believe it was happening. The Perrys were in a terrified state of shock as Katherine ordered them to drive north.

"Coffs Harbour! I need to see David's mother. She's gonna be the one to pay for him leaving."

Molly shook uncontrollably. Margaret sobbed as she pressed a hand to her face as she held tightly to Henry, who was deathly still, clinging to his sister. As they neared a petrol station on the opposite side of the road, Molly found her window. "We need fuel first," she said gently. "Let me fill up. Then we'll go to Coffs Harbour." Katherine agreed, but she jumped out and took the boy hostage, leaving Melissa, who was wailing, on Margaret's lap.

At the nearby police station, Constable Mackell and Sergeant Lyne had been talking about Katherine at that very moment—about the incident on the tracks and the axe—when Mackell caught sight of her through the station window.

"There she goes now!" he said, pointing at her. Then, just as soon as he said it, the phone on the sergeant's desk rang.

Inside the petrol station, the manager stood with the phone to his ear, quickly telling the police that Katherine was outside, holding the Perry boy hostage. Lyne and Mackell didn't have time to think. They bolted across the road, grabbed a couple of broomsticks leaning by the front entrance, and cautiously approached her. Katherine stood firm with the knife to Henry's neck.

In the car, his mother, sister, and the baby were hysterical. Several onlookers had gathered, gasping in shock.

"Put it down, Kath," Lyne said, edging forward, "and let the boy go." Her eyes flicked between the two officers. The knife hovered. Lyne jabbed at her wrist several times. Mackell poked her side, then swept the broom handle hard and fast at the knife. The handle cracked Katherine on the back of the hand and sent the knife clattering to the ground. Henry tore free and bolted for the car. The officers pounced on Katherine and cuffed her. They drove her to Muswellbrook Hospital, where a doctor wrote out a Schedule 2 under the Mental Health Act. This time, she was sent to Morisset psychiatric hospital for an extended evaluation.

Up in Queensland, David, who was now living alone after breaking up with Susan, got the call midmorning the following day while waiting for his meat pie to heat up in the microwave. The voice on the other end of the phone was flat and procedural.

"This is Sergeant Lloyd Lyne from the Aberdeen Police Department. We're calling to inform you that your wife's been committed to the Morisset psychiatric hospital."

David asked about Melissa and was relieved to hear that she was safe and being looked after by Katherine's parents. He hung up without further questions and immediately rang his mother, Jean. By sunrise the next morning, he was on the highway pushing south past cane fields and truck stops, making the long drive to Morisset.

The hospital was a single-story tan brick building, set back from the road and surrounded by a large parking lot. The grounds were clean and tidy, the sort of place that looked calm on the outside but held something else entirely on the inside. David and his mother signed in at the front desk. A nurse walked them through the corridor to meet with Katherine, who sat behind a locked glass door, barefoot and in hospital blues. Her arms were folded across her chest, and her hair hung limp around her shoulders.

"I still love you," she told David when they had a moment in private.

David didn't answer. He sat there, his hands clasped and resting on the table, eyes fixed on her, the realization dawning on him that he would have to stay and look after her, for Melissa's sake.

At the tribunal hearing six days later, the three of them sat side by side—Jean, David, and the woman who'd once tried to strangle him on their wedding night, who had attempted to kill their child, and who had abducted and assaulted a neighbor. Katherine's eyes were half-lidded from the medication, her voice quiet but lucid. The board asked questions. Kathrine answered them. David watched the panel exchange comments in low voices. Forms were signed, and Jean reluctantly offered to take Katherine in and care for her.

"Until she gets back on her feet," she reminded them.

Katherine said she still wanted to be with David, and David— caught somewhere between guilt, habit, and the weight of her breakdown—said he'd take her back. A psychiatrist handed Jean a small white box before they left. Inside was a supply of lithium and chlorpromazine. To dull the edges.

"She'll need these every day," the doctor said. "Make sure she takes them. She doesn't get to skip doses." Jean nodded. She took the box and slipped it into her handbag. Afterward, they set off south for Aberdeen to pick up Melissa from her grandparents. From there they would have a six-and-a-half-hour drive north to Jean's house in Coffs Harbour.

Katherine sat stiffly in the passenger seat as David rolled into Short Street, where Katherine's parents lived. The light had already begun to thin. The house looked just as he remembered it: fibro, peeling in patches, rust along the guttering, a couple of folding chairs on the veranda. A cluster of Katherine's family stood there now, tracking the car as it slowed to a stop out front. While Katherine went in to get Melissa, David stayed behind the wheel with the engine idling. Jean shifted uneasily in the backseat, hands tight in her lap.

Suddenly there was Barbara, moving across the yard like a predator, quick and determined. Her mouth was already going, words spilling out like sparks. Before David could work it out, Barbara was at the driver's window, grabbing him by the scruff.

"You bastard!" she snapped. "You fucken' cunt! You did this to her!"

She got both hands around his throat. Her grip was strong and she pulled him toward her with a snarl. "I warned you! I warned you and now you've gone and broken her! You left her for some bloody cunt and now look at her, you bloody useless, stupid piece of shit!" She tightened her grip around his neck.

David clutched at them desperately while also trying to roll up the window. Jean screamed and scrambled out of the back seat, running across the dry grass to the neighbor's for help.

"Somebody call the police!" she shouted as she banged on the door. "Please, someone, help us!" But no one came.

Back at the car, Barbara was still latched onto to her son-in-law. David's face had gone a desperate red with blotches on his cheeks and forehead. His jaw moved, but nothing came out. And then Katherine emerged from the house. She came down the steps past her bemused relatives, the baby tucked in the crook of her arm. She didn't yell. She just reached out, grabbed her mother by the shoulder with her right hand, and swung. Her fist connected square with Barbara's temple, and down she went, her knees giving way cleanly beneath her, no stumble, no sound. She just crumpled onto the grass like a marionette puppet whose strings had suddenly been cut.

"Don't you ever touch him again!" Katherine shouted at her mother, who was just barely able to sit up. Barbara reeled back, stunned, but was soon on her feet, touching the side of her head where the blow had landed. Up on the veranda, no one moved. They merely watched, with hands on hips or arms folded, wry spectators. David coughed hard, regaining his breath. Katherine stood between them, the baby on her hip and a wildness in her face that didn't seem to know whether it was protecting or destroying. She went to the car, opened the back door, and buckled Melissa in. Barbara stepped away, muttering obscenities. Jean got back in the car and David started the engine. No one said goodbye.

It was late when they arrived at Jean's house. For the next two weeks, Katherine moved from room to room with the baby in her arms, a soft, medicated glaze in her eyes. She took her pills morning and night as the doctors had instructed, Jean made sure of it. David didn't say much. He helped with Melissa and did small repairs around the house to stay useful. He still loved Katherine—or maybe he just remembered what it felt like to love her because she seemed gentler now, docile even, and easier to be around. She let Jean brush Melissa's hair without snapping. She didn't shout when David hung the washing up wrong.

But that gentleness didn't last. By the end of the second week, she was growing restless and started pacing the house more and more. David worried that she'd stopped taking her medication. He knew they couldn't stay much longer with his mother, so they soon packed up and went north to Queensland, landing in a rental in Woodridge. It was a squat little home with warped fly screens and a letterbox full of other people's mail. David picked up trucking work, and Katherine eventually got hired at the Dinmore meatworks in Ipswich as a slicer. Melissa, now close to six months, went into daycare. Things seemed to settle for a while. Katherine rode her motorbike to work through the back roads. She liked her job and said so often. It brought her peace. One evening after her shift she brought home her tools—two curved slicers, handles worn smooth from use—and asked David to mount them on a board and bolt it above the bed.

"I want them here," she said, pointing to a space above her pillow.

"Why on earth?" David asked.

"In case I need them." He wasn't terribly happy about it, but he did it anyway. Best not to upset her, he decided. He cleaned and sharpened the knives first, as she'd asked him to do, then fixed them on a mount so they could be removed and put back with ease, also as Katherine had requested. He screwed the mount into the gyprock right where Katherine had pointed, above the pillows on her side of the bed.

She would hand the knives to him every few days. "Sharpen them for me, will ya," she'd ask sweetly. He did what she asked because he adored Melissa. She was the soft center of a life that was quickly hardening. If keeping Katherine calm meant playing along, he would do it. And for a while, it worked. But her moods would inevitably darken. She snapped when the bin hadn't been emptied. Slapped plates down too hard. Slammed the door on her way out, kicked it when it got stuck. David would be out on the road for two days and come home to find the bed unmade, or something smashed in the laundry. It was clear to him that she couldn't help ruminating on his affair with Susan. Her anger grew more sharp-edged as time went on, and would be followed by fists, thrown objects, and violent threats. David never hit her. He said it again and again over the years. He never laid a hand on her. She was the one who hit him. Flat-palmed slaps. Scratches. Punches. Sometimes just words that felt like being stabbed. Jean rang often. She could tell within seconds whether it was safe for him to talk.

About six months after they'd moved to Queensland, Jean visited for the first time. She had a little scan of the place, at the crumbs on the kitchen bench, at a painting askew on the wall. Then she saw the knives above the bed.

"Katherine," she said softly. "Why do you keep knives by the bed?"

Katherine didn't look up. "Just in case I need them," she muttered, busy with her knitting.

Jean decided not to press the issue. Weeks later, David came home early from a haul to find a stranger's work boots by the door. He heard laughter and a man's voice. He walked into the bedroom and found Katherine with a meat worker from Dinmore. David roared. The man bolted, diving through the window in his jocks. Katherine just lay there smiling, one leg crossed over the other, watching the curtains flap where her afternoon lover had just vanished. Despite the payback, David tried to make the marriage work, for Melissa's sake. They had another child. Natasha Maree Kellett was born in Nambour on March 6, 1980. They bought a weatherboard house in Landsborough that had a bigger backyard. The place had a sloping tin roof and a Hills Hoist out the back that leaned slightly to the left. David wanted to believe things would be better this time, but he couldn't help worry.

To take his mind off his troubles, he threw himself into darts. He played competitions most Friday nights at the Maleny Club Hotel. It wasn't serious—just a cold beer in one hand and his darts in the other. Sometimes he won, sometimes he didn't. Mostly he liked the feeling of being with mates, of not being glared at from across the kitchen table or followed from room to room by mood swings he couldn't make sense of. Then Katherine started encouraging him to go. "Go ahead," she'd say, sweetly. "Have a few. Unwind, you've earned it."

But one night, as David was chalking up for his last game, the phone behind the bar rang. It was five minutes past ten in the evening. The barman called out, "Kellett, phone, it's the missus."

He picked up the receiver, expecting a request to grab some milk or a pack of smokes on the way home.

"Get your arse home, Kellett, I'm waiting for you," Katherine commanded. No hello, no pause.

"What do you mean, waiting for me?"

"I want you, so get home. Now."

"I'm on me last game," David said, turning his back to the bar. "I'll be home when I'm done." Fifteen minutes later, he was pulling into the driveway. The porch light was off when he reached the front door. He stepped into the hallway and dropped his keys into a bowl by the door. That's the last thing he remembered.

He woke up to harsh bright lights, and sheets that felt stiff and rough and tucked in too tight. A monitor beeped from somewhere behind him. A nurse stood near the foot of the bed scanning through a folder of medical notes and forms.

"You've had a pretty bad concussion, Mr. Kellett," she explained. "You're at Maitland Hospital. Do you remember what happened?"

David blinked. He touched the side of his head. A lump the size of a golf ball had formed, tender to the touch. He didn't know what Katherine had hit him with. Could've been a saucepan. Could've been a lamp, a bottle. But she had clearly hit him with something. He looked up at the ceiling and tried to recall what had happened after he'd walked in the door.

A young constable came by on the second day. He stood near the side of the bed with his notebook.

"Mr. Kellett, can you tell me what you remember?"

David exhaled through his nose slowly. "She must have been waitin' by the door when I got home and hit me with something on me head," he said.

"What for, why'd she hit you?"

David hesitated. Scratched his eyebrow with the tip of his thumb. "I told her I'd be late home from the pub," he said. "Ten or fifteen minutes."

"And then?"

"She didn't like that." The constable tilted his head, unsure. "So, are you telling me she assaulted you because you were ten or fifteen minutes late from the pub?"

David looked at him, then to the window where a Jacaranda bloomed with vivid lavender petals. "Yeah, you could say that. I defied her," David said. "And you don't defy Katherine Knight."

"Do you want to press charges, Mr. Kellett?"

David shook his head without looking up. "We've got two kids," he said. "They need their mum. And I need to get back to work."

"All right, but if you change your mind, give us a call." The constable closed his notebook and left it at that. Later, when Jean called, David told her not to come, that he was fine. He told her it had just been a fall. He could tell that his mother didn't buy it.

He stayed in hospital for four days. The nurses were kind but held a thoughtful bearing, the way country nurses do when there's domestic violence involved.

Sometime later, when he was back home and fully healed, David woke to the weight on his chest before he felt the knife on his throat. The bedroom was dark but for the dim glow of a streetlamp bleeding in through the curtains. Katherine sat astride

David's chest, her knees pressing into his arms. One of her boning knives was held beneath his chin. His breath caught in his throat. He didn't dare move.

"Is it true," Katherine said, her voice a tight menace, "that truck drivers got a girl in every town?" Her hair fell in wisps around her face, her eyes locked with his. The knife didn't tremble. It rested against his skin with just the right amount of pressure to mean business without breaking the skin.

"That's bullshit," David protested. He kept his voice even. No anger, no fear—at least not in the tone. He knew better. Katherine looked at him as if trying to read his mind, to scrape out the truth somehow. Outside, a dog barked. And then rain began to patter against the tin roof.

"You'd better not be lying to me," she warned.

"I'm not," David said. "You know I'm not." He saw in that instant something flash in her eyes, a flicker of rage, as if the thought of dragging the knife across his throat had landed in her mind but then flew off. She pulled back slowly and climbed off him, the mattress sighing beneath her weight. Soon she was in the kitchen lighting a cigarette. David heard the kettle start to boil. He stayed where he was, staring up at the ceiling fan, listening to the sound of the rain. A clap of thunder boomed suddenly, startling him. He heard Katherine react to it with glee. "Oi, Kellett, listen to that. That was a big one!"

Later, she came back to bed and curled up beside him like nothing had happened, whispering that she was dead tired and needed to sleep. David lay awake for hours afterward, listening to the rain as it battered the house.

20

THE FORENSIC PSYCHIATRIST[9]

June 21, 2000. Mulawa Women's Correctional Centre. Mum Shirl Psychiatric Wing. Day 1.

Katherine leaned back. Her arms were crossed tightly against her chest as usual.

"Why did you ask your neighbor to drive you to Coffs Harbour?"

Katherine cast her eyes down. The light through the blinds made dull stripes on the floor. "Because I thought…. I wanted to kill Jean. And then kill meself."

"Why?"

"To get Kellett's attention. I knew he'd come back from Queensland if I did that."

"You were going to kill his mother, and then yourself, to get your husband's attention? How would you know if you were also dead?"

"That was the plan," Katherine said. "Doesn't mean it wasn't stupid."

---

[9] *Speculative reconstruction inspired by documented psychiatric interviews.*

Dr. Martin noted the absence of remorse, or regret in her voice. "How long had you been thinking about that plan?"

"Not long, a day or two. 'Cuz he left me, he betrayed me, running off with Susan to Queensland, when I was pregnant."

Dr. Martin made another note, then turned to a fresh page in his notebook.

"And what about leaving your baby on the train tracks? Can you tell me more about that and how that plays into it?"

"Not really. I didn't leave her, that's what people say. I went back for her."

"Hmmm. Okay." Dr. Martin made a note, then paused for a moment to gather his thoughts. "Katherine," he continued, "when you talk about David, and Jean, the words you use are the same you used when you talked about John Price."

Dr. Martin watched her for a moment. "They betrayed you," he said. "Left you. Or tried to. You've said before that you gave David everything. Loyalty. Time. Children. Money. Sex."

"I did, and the bastard didn't appreciate any of it."

"Same with Price?"

She uncrossed her arms and sat forward slightly. "Yeah, I'd say so."

"And when they didn't want you sexually, how did that make you feel?"

She leaned back again. "They always wanted me. I told you, me and Pricey were engaged."

"But they all tried to leave at some point."

"They didn't leave, they just got angry sometimes, so what? They all said I was the best they'd ever had."

Dr. Martin was quiet once again. Then he leaned forward, resting his elbows on the table. "As I said earlier, it seems to me that sex is like a tool you use to keep them in the relationship, would that be fair to say?" he asked.

Katherine narrowed her eyes. "It's called being a woman."

"It can also be a form of control. Did you think perhaps you used sex to control these men?"

She scoffed. "You think that's what this is all about? Sex?"

"I think," he said slowly, "you used it to try to stop men from walking away. And if they rejected you, you punished them for it."

21

THERE IS A GOD SOMEWHERE

1984. Landsborough, Queensland.

Katherine watched David from the kitchen window as he walked to the carport, hauling a crate of empties to the bin. He stopped to say something to the neighbor's kid—a skinny blonde girl with a tiny waist and smooth legs. Sixteen, she was, maybe seventeen. Always in her school uniform. Katherine often saw the girl leaning out of her bedroom window, brushing her hair behind her ear, laughing at whatever dumb thing Kellett was saying.

She asked him straight when he came back in. "You screwin' that girl?"

David looked at her like she'd spat in his face.

"What are you going on about? *She's a kid.*" But the suspicion remained in her, as heavy and unforgiving as dead weight. She started tracking his movements. That Friday, she'd again encouraged him to go out so she could test him. "Go play darts," she said. Her voice was light, almost sweet. "Get outta here, clear your head a bit."

David looked at her sideways, understandably wary. "Really? You mean it?"

"Yeah. I'll put dinner in the oven now so we can eat before you go."

"All right," he said brightly, "thanks. It'd be nice to see the fellas." They ate dinner together in front of the television. Then David left for the pub. "I'll be back at half ten."

She watched him go. And as she had anticipated, saw him look toward the little bitch's bedroom window as he got in the truck. By ten o'clock, the oven was cold and Katherine was on the phone. It was almost an exact repeat of last time.

"Get home, Kellett. Now. You hear me?" She hung up without another word. He sighed deeply and turned back toward the dartboard, but he could already feel that sick pull in his gut. Something awful would be waiting for him at home, he knew it. He threw one more dart and decided he'd better get going, lest she come to the pub, dragging chaos in with her. As he was heading out, the bar phone rang. He heard the barman shout for him.

"It's the missus again, mate." Katherine's voice was low and calm. "Your clothes are in the bathtub, on fire, Kellet." And she hung up.

David drove fast. He pulled up out front where smoke was already curling out of the bathroom window. He ran inside, and there it was like she'd said—his shirts and jeans, his boots, his socks and underwear, his belt and hat—piled into the bathtub in a smoldering heap. The only clothes he had left were the purple paisley shirt and flared trousers he was wearing—the same outfit, in fact, that he wore on their wedding day. Even in those wild moments, the irony was not lost on him.

Katherine appeared at the bathroom doorway, watching him watch the smoke. "Next time you think to fuck that schoolgirl," she said coolly, "it'll be more than your clothes that's burned." David said nothing. He turned on the bathtub faucet and watched the heat evaporate into wafts of smoke. He stood there for a moment, looking at the crude pile that were once his belongs, thinking of the life he'd regrettably stitched together with her, and he wept.

A week later he stumbled through the front door one night, his head buzzing with the aftereffects of too many pints. He didn't hear her at first. Not until the sound came: a sharp, metallic whoosh of air as something heavy swung toward him. The steel came down hard, cracking against the back of his skull with a dense, grotesque thud. The force knocked him forward. He barely caught himself on the doorframe before the pain exploded inside his head. He staggered, touching his skull. Blood dripped through his hair in a warm, yolky little stream.

Katherine stood behind him, a sharpening steel in her hand. "You were out with her again, weren't you?" Her voice was controlled, like it was just another night, just another thing to be angry about. David could barely form his words; the pressure behind his eyes made everything spin. He wanted to say something, anything, but he couldn't speak. Everything was fractured—the world felt far away, and soon the floor came rushing up to catch him.

Paramedics wheeled him out to an ambulance. Flashing lights, multiple voices. They wrapped his head up, careful not to anger the blood-soaked wound on his scalp. They spoke to him slow and clear, told him he needed scans and stitches. Told him Nambour Hospital was only a short drive away.

He was kept for longer this time. He could've pressed charges, he could've walked out of that hospital and into a court-room. But again, he chose not to. For the girls, he told himself. After that, he started spending more time on the road, hauling goods across the state and interstate. He would routinely be gone for week-long stretches, then back home for a week, sometimes less, then gone again. He felt it gave him some sort of balance with Katherine if he wasn't around too long. And it bought him much-needed respite. Plus, he could see that Katherine was taking good care of the girls. Somehow that mercurial, moody, and violent side of her never surfaced when it came to the children, and for that he was grateful.

It was just after midnight when he returned from a week-long trip, and he was looking forward to seeing his daughters. The screen door creaked on its hinges as he stepped into the darkness of the house. He reached for the light switch by the door and flicked it on. Nothing. He tried again. Still darkness. He fired up his cigarette lighter. The flame held steady, trembling at the edges, throwing faint light across the room. That's when he saw that the house was hollowed out. Emptied of life. The old couch his sister had given him was still there. And a few pieces of Tupperware sat in the sink. But everything else—the curtains, the rugs, the rest of the furniture, the lightbulbs even—all of it was gone. Even the power tools, he later discovered, had vanished from the shed. He found a note from Katherine on the kitchen counter, misspelled and scrawled so badly it looked as if one of the kids had written it. The note said they had gone back to Aberdeen to live with her parents. That she was done waiting for him. That he could "fuck off." David stood there, letting his eyes adjust to what was left. Strangely, he felt no panic or anger. Only stillness. And in that stillness, something unfurled in him—not grief, not resentment. Just the cool space of freedom. After nearly ten years of hell, he was finally free. "There is a God somewhere," he whispered to himself as he held the note.

22

DAVE SAUNDERS

1984. Aberdeen, New South Wales.

When Katherine left David in Queensland and moved back to her parents' place in Aberdeen, it was the last place she wanted to be. She couldn't wait to get out of that house when she was eighteen, but now, ten years later, she was back—older, angrier, divorced, with two little girls—Melissa, eight, and Natasha, four—to raise on her own.

It wasn't easy. There was not much room for them at her parents', and no money to go anywhere else for the time being. Her father drank too much. Her mother talked too much. They all argued too much. Katherine slept on the fold-out in the living room, while the girls shared a bed in the room that used to be hers.

She enrolled Melissa at Aberdeen Primary. And Natasha went to the local preschool. Katherine returned to work at the Aberdeen meatworks. And it was like she'd never left, like Queensland hadn't happened, like the years with Kellett had never unfolded. She was back in the boning room, back under the strip lights, back in the rhythm of the line. Each morning, she tied on her apron and sharpened and cleaned her knives. Muscle memory. Shoulder to shoulder with the other workers, her blades flashed as the carcasses came down the line. Not much had changed.

There were new faces, but some of the old ones remained. She could tell by the way they looked at her—sideways glances and guarded nods—that her reputation had followed her home. But no one asked questions.

She was busier now, not just at work but at home—cooking, cleaning, ironing school uniforms. In the evenings, she sat outside with a smoke and a cup of sweet, milky tea, listening to the kids argue or play nearby. Sometimes she drove down to the servo just to get out of the house.

She wasn't pining for Kellett—not exactly. But the size of the hole his absence left was confronting. She didn't like being alone. A few weeks in, and she started dating again. Not seriously at first. Just blokes she met at the Top Pub or the RSL Club—men who hadn't heard about her or said they hadn't. It didn't matter anyway. None of them lasted long. A few drinks, a fumble in the car, dinner at the RSL. Then it would fizzle.

For a while, she managed to keep things steady, bringing in some income. The girls had what they needed, and the routine gave her purpose. But before the year was out, Katherine dislocated a vertebra in her back while working. It began with a nagging ache—deep and dragging—and worsened every time she lifted or twisted the wrong way. A sharp pain would catch her breath, and she would have to stop what she was doing to let it settle. She tried to push through it. But back pain, once it sets in, was hard to ignore, and hers was becoming a real problem. In 1985 it seized up badly. Her GP signed her off for a couple of weeks and told her to rest and not overdo it. But when she went back to work, she aggravated it again, lifting a side of beef she shouldn't have touched, and the pain got worse. More time off. Then she was back, trying to manage, then off again. By August that year, the plant had had enough. Her employment was terminated. She received a severance package, enough to cover groceries and bills while she waited for a compensation payout from insurance.

The following year, she was finally able to move out of her parents' house. She packed up and moved into a two bedroom in Segenhoe Street with her daughters. It was a single-story brick house with a veranda, and a small backyard. The local school was only a few blocks away. Melissa and Natasha could walk themselves, which freed her up in the mornings.

The house wasn't great, but it was closer to town. There were three pubs and two clubs within walking distance; if she wanted company, she could usually find it. Tall and still slim, and pushing thirty, she felt comfortable in her skin. More than that—she knew how to walk into a room and make it hers. She didn't mind turning up on her own, she didn't mind standing at the bar and ordering her own drinks. The praise and validation of others was never her goal.

In a town like Aberdeen, you didn't have to wait long for someone to shout you the next one. That's how, in November 1986, Dave Saunders came into her life. He was at the Aberdeen Bowling Club, knocking back a couple of Tooheys with a mate, when Katherine walked in. She'd been at the back bar, watching a game of footy, when she wandered into the main bar for another drink. He noticed her straight away. His mate knew her through a friend and that was enough of an opening. Dave bought her a round and she joined them.

He was from neighboring Scone, a town about fifteen minutes' drive north of Aberdeen, and he was seven years her senior.

A bit shorter too. He worked in one of the Hunter Valley mines. He had big hands, Katherine noticed, and a lean frame.

It was early evening. Drinks were on the table. Conversations drifted in and out. They played three-handed Euchre. Katherine sat between the two men, slamming her cards down with more force than finesse, laughing loudly, having a good time. Saunders liked that. She was different from the women he usually met. There was nothing coy or sentimental about her. He found that intriguing. Later, he walked her out to the parking lot, where her red Toyota LiteAce was parked.

"You heading home?" he asked.

"Yeah."

"You right to drive?"

"Yeah, I'm right," she said, digging the keys out of her purse. He hesitated, not ready to end the night. "You want to go out sometime, have a drink, play some cards?"

She looked at him. "You asking me on a date?"

"What do you think?" he said jovially.

"All right, yeah, we can date."

They started meeting up regularly after that. He'd come around to hers after work and they'd head to the pub, or she'd meet him at the Bowling Club. She told the girls he was a friend, though Melissa figured out what was going on. Which was fine with Katherine. She liked Dave. He was steady. He had a job. And he didn't talk too much.

Being from Scone, David Saunders knew little about Katherine, and she didn't offer much. She came across to him as easygoing—quick with a joke, relaxed in a way that made the first few outings feel casual and unfussed. Dave liked that she wasn't shy about eye contact. And she asked him questions. He was used to women talking around things, or over him, but Katherine listened, and when she spoke, she did so plainly and directly. She told him on their second date that his shirt didn't suit him.

"You've got a good build," she'd said, "don't dress like you're hiding it."

He laughed. "You always this bluntly honest?"

"Blunt, yes, honest, no."

He laughed again. "Well at least you're honest about being dishonest." They met for drinks a few more times after that. The intimacy came one weekend when Dave offered to drive a friend to Sydney airport. He had asked Katherine if she cared to join him; they could enjoy the sights of the big city together. It was offhand. He hadn't expected her to say yes so quickly.

They left early on a Friday morning. Katherine packed a thermos of tea and some snacks for the trip. On the drive, they talked about work and kids, and family. And mundane little details about the towns through which they would pass.

They dropped Dave's friend off at the airport by early afternoon and checked into a cheap motel near the Cross. That night they took a tour of the city, watched the ferries motor across the harbour, shared chips from a paper bag outside the Opera House. At the hotel, Katherine stripped off and slid into bed next to Dave and gave him the night of his life. The next morning, he approached her in the bathroom, while she brushed her teeth and put his arms around her waist. "You snore," she said to his reflection in the mirror.

"You talk in your sleep," he shot back.

"What'd I say?"

"You said I was the most handsomest guy in the world."

She laughed. "Guess I only tell the truth in me sleep." Dave felt puffed up and aroused by the compliment. He squeezed Katherine tight and pressed himself against her. They went back to bed before checking out.

The drive home was leisurely. They stopped for breakfast, then for petrol even though they didn't need it. Their relationship took off after that weekend. Katherine started referring to them as "we." She called him "love." He left a toothbrush and a few other items at her place. She made him casseroles, mashed pumpkin, and shepherd's pie, to fill up his freezer in Scone. "Don't you go forgetting how to cook, though," she told him after she gave him food, packed neatly in Tupperware. "What's 'cook' mean?" Dave joked. She laughed again. He liked their dynamic and how she handled herself in the relationship. She didn't pry. Didn't ask about his ex or about his past and he didn't ask where she'd been before him. He figured if it mattered, she'd say. She was intense and he liked that about her too. She had a big laugh, a hard grip, and she was something divine in the bedroom. Everything about her was immediate and uninhibited. He wasn't used to that. Most of the women he'd dated shied away from or withheld sex. Katherine owned her sexuality unapologetically. Things were good.

But it wasn't long before things started to change. An angry edge came over her one night at the pub when a woman looked too long in his direction. There was a bite in her voice when he took too long to answer her call. One night she grew irritated when he didn't notice her new earrings. "You don't look at me like a woman needs looking at," she'd said.

"I'm looking at you now." In the end she dropped it, but her mood lingered. Dave put it down to passion.

One day in early December, Katherine was in the kitchen at Segenhoe Street, peeling potatoes for dinner, when the phone rang. She wiped her hands on a tea towel and answered. Her face quickly soured as she listened. She stood still for a long time after she hung up. The potatoes sat in the sink, half-peeled. The radio kept playing in the background, but she didn't hear it. The girls were in the living room with the TV blaring, but it all felt far away. Katherine stood there, holding the edge of the counter. When Dave came over about an hour later, she was still in the kitchen, smoking a cigarette and staring out the window at the late afternoon sky, which had started to go soft, bathing the hills beyond Aberdeen in an orange, dusky glow. Dave could tell straightaway that something was wrong.

"What's wrong, love?" he asked.

She turned toward him. "Mum's gone."

He stepped forward, unsure. "Gone where?"

"She dead. She died this morning of a heart attack."

He didn't know what else to say. He reached for her and Katherine let him hold her. She was rigid at first, but after a moment, she pressed her face into his chest and let herself sink. Her breath caught. Her shoulders shook and she began to sob like she hadn't sobbed in years.

Dave held her tight and rubbed her back. "I'm sorry, love," he said. "I'm so sorry." Katherine didn't talk much about her mother in the days that followed. She didn't want sympathy or platitudes. And she didn't want to cry anymore. It was too painful to think about. She just went quiet. Dave didn't push. He made the dinners the week of the funeral. Got the girls to school. Let her be. And for that, she was grateful.

In the months after her mother's death, things between them settled into an easy rhythm. They got on well—no fireworks, no dramas, just steady company. Their laughter filled the rooms, the kind that came from small jokes shared over cups of tea or a late-night cigarette on the back porch. And their sex life was healthy and uncomplicated. David felt lucky to have found a woman like Katherine, and she, who had known more pain than pleasure in the past, felt more confident. It was a relief, in a way—the rough edges of her life seemed to be softening out. David still kept his flat up in Scone. It was a modest place, nothing fancy, but it was his space, and he wasn't ready to let it go. Still, as the months passed, the visits to Katherine's home in Segenhoe Street grew longer. Weekends spilled into weekdays, and evenings stretched lazily into mornings. Eventually, it became easier to just move in.

He brought his bags one afternoon, arriving with a smile and a quiet resolve. "Thought I'd save myself the trips." Katherine was glad for the company, glad the girls had someone around who wasn't just their mother—someone who could step in without demanding things change. Melissa and Natasha, young and still cautious, took their time adjusting. But Dave was gentle with them. He didn't try to force affection or play dad. Instead, he joined their games, helped with homework, and made the odd silly face to draw out a giggle. He knew what it was to be a father, having a daughter from a previous relationship. He was divorced himself and carried scars from that life, but it made him patient with Katherine's girls and gave him an understanding of the ties that bind a mother to her children.

It wasn't perfect, though. There were days when the noise of the kids' fighting filled the small house with chaos, when the mess piled up and tempers frayed. But those moments didn't undo the progress. They were just part of the daily grind of an intimate relationship—a relationship that both Katherine and Dave had longed for.

But then one day, almost overnight, things took an alarming turn. David couldn't quite put his finger on why, but Katherine seemed like a different person. She became possessive and her mood seemed to drop to a dark, fretful low. She grew jealous, slicing David with one accusation after another, claims that he was seeing other women, whispers of betrayal that weren't there.

Around mid-January 1987, the tension finally snapped. They had a terrible row, her anger spiraling out of control, and David packed his things and fled back to Scone.

Katherine wasn't ready to let him go. Before long, she was pounding on his door, begging him to come back. And he did. She wore him down with sex. When she was herself—or at least the version of herself that could be gentle and warm—Katherine was truly something special. Those moments held a kind of magic for him. Yet just as quickly, things would turn again. She'd slam the door shut in his face and lock him out without warning, leaving David confused and uneasy. He never knew when the tides would turn, but he recognized the pattern—the cycle of closeness followed by chaos, affection followed by fury. And so it went, up and down, a tumultuous dance neither could escape.

As their relationship evolved into this new pattern, which only they seemed to understand, David learned to expect the cycle. When Katherine kicked him out, he packed a bag and retreated to his flat. He'd keep his distance for a couple of days, long enough to let the storm pass, until the knock came on his door. It was always the same: Katherine, her voice soft but insistent, asking him to come back to Segenhoe Street. Then her seductions, followed by the fights.

One evening in May, Dave was at a mate's place, nursing a few beers after yet another rough night at home. He'd lost count of how many times Katherine had ordered him out that month. He was tired, but the alcohol gave him a numb kind of courage. When the clock nudged past midnight, he left his mate's place and walked the familiar route back home, leaving his car parked safely outside the friend's house. The street was empty and peaceful, lit only a few streetlights.

But the peace was short-lived. There was a knock at his door not long after he got home. Dave opened it to find Katherine standing there, eyes sharp. "Come home," she said. "I want to talk about us, about what's gone wrong." Her voice held a mix of vulnerability and steel.

He hesitated but nodded. "All right." The ride back to Aberdeen was largely silent. Katherine stared out the window, her mind churning. No sooner had Dave stepped through her door than the tension began to boil over again.

"You've been seeing someone else, I know you have."

Dave shook his head, firm but weary. "No, Kath. I haven't. How many times do I have to tell you?"

She didn't believe him. Her eyes narrowed as she pressed her lips tight. The tension quickly heightened. Then, suddenly, she pushed him. He stepped back, hands raised, trying to defuse the situation. She pushed again, harder this time.

"I'm pregnant you idiot!" she yelled. Dave's eyebrows shot up. At first, he thought this was meant to be her way to announce the news, and he was about to show his elation. But then she screamed, "And you kicked me in the bloody stomach!" The accusation hit him like a slap.

"*What!?*" He was shocked, holding up his hands, wondering what she was talking about. "Kicked you? Why would you say that? I never touched you!"

But Katherine was caught in her own vortex of reality. Her voice rose. Her shoves turned into frantic blows, turned into a full-blown struggle.

"I'll show you what I'm gonna do with you!" she hissed. Without warning, she grabbed a carving knife from the kitchen bench—long and sharp, and glinting under the overhead light. Dave barely registered the blade before she stormed out the back door. Moments later, Katherine returned, blood dripping from her hands and her clothes. "There's your dog out there," she said flatly. "That's what I think of you."

"What did you do?" But he didn't wait for an answer. He rushed out to the yard, where he saw his eight-week-old pure bred dingo pup lying on the ground. Its throat cleanly sliced open, blood pooling out onto the grass. Dave's stomach churned while Katherine stood in the doorway, still gripping the knife. Once his initial shock subsided, he called the police.

When they arrived, the officers examined the scene but took no formal action. Whether it was because it was just a dog that got hurt, or because it was a woman who had committed the act, they chose not to escalate things further. The night ended with Dave once again retreating to his flat.

The following morning, frustration gnawed at him. He went to retrieve his car, which he'd left parked outside his friend's house, and found the windshield wipers had been bent out of shape. The radio aerial, too, was twisted and mangled. Most glaringly, the interior rearview mirror lay shattered on the passenger seat. When he confronted Katherine, she didn't deny it. "Yeah, I did it," she said without a trace of remorse. And then she dropped a bombshell. She wasn't pregnant after all. He realized then that the accusations, the fights, the destruction—they were all part of a darker game. A calculated charade of sex, control, and revenge.

23

THE FORENSIC PSYCHIATRIST[10]

June 21, 2000. Mulawa Women's Correctional Centre. Mum Shirl Psychiatric Wing. Day 1.

"Katherine," Dr. Martin began gently, "the incident with the dog. Can you tell me more about that? What was running through your mind when you decided to…end this dog's life?"

Katherine leaned back in her seat and let out a breath. "He laid his heavy steel-cap boots into me when I told him I was pregnant." Her voice was flat but carried the weight of arrogance. "So, I went out and cut his dog's throat."

Dr. Martin's expression remained neutral, inviting more.

"I ended up having my nerves treated," Katherine continued. "But at that time, I just lost mum…. So, I lost it."

Dr. Martin studied her quietly.

"It was a clean cut, they said," Katherine offered.

"And did you say anything to Saunders at the time?"

Katherine's gaze hardened, recalling the fury of that moment.

---

[10] *Speculative reconstruction inspired by documented psychiatric interviews.*

"He told me to kill him." There was a brief silence before she added, "So I threw the knife away and picked up a frying pan. I hit him in the head with it."

"That must have been a very intense moment," Dr. Martin offered.

Katherine let out a bitter little laugh. "He asked for it."

24

THE COTTAGE

1987. Aberdeen, New South Wales.

They were heading south from Wingen, the paddocks running green and wide on either side of the road. Dave was behind the wheel. Katherine sat quietly in the passenger seat, arms folded across her chest. A friend of theirs, Wayne, mid-thirties, was in the back seat. They'd picked him up to give him a lift back to Aberdeen after his car broke down. The atmosphere had been quiet for the first twenty minutes or so of the drive before Katherine started in on Dave. It seemed to him that her mind had been building up a fury all that time, telling herself stories that fed on themselves.

She said, "I know you've been rootin' someone."

Dave, feeling embarrassed and tense all of a sudden, did not respond, hoping to give her the hint to shut the hell up.

"You think I don't know? You think I'm some kind of fool?" Still, he said nothing. His jaw tightened, but he kept his eyes on the road. So, Katherine punched him in the shoulder.

"You cunty piece of shit, admit it."

Wayne sat forward from the back seat. "All right you two, come on," he said gently, "let's just get home."

But Katherine had other ideas. She started clawing at the door handle as if to jump out of the car. Dave reached out to stop her, but she had already pushed it open, her body half leaning out, the car moving at speed. Wayne lunged forward to grab hold of her where he could. "Jesus Christ!" he yelled. Dave eased the car onto the shoulder as quickly as he could without careening into traffic and slammed on the brakes. He pushed the gear into park. "What the hell are you doing, woman!?"

"Get off me! Get off me!" she screamed, her cheeks flushed with heat.

Wayne let her go and she stumbled out onto the gravel and began pacing in circles. Dave approached her gently. He kept his hands in his pockets and just stood there, by the side of the road, with the traffic whizzing past, and let her anger burn out.

They dropped Wayne off and Dave asked the next-door neighbors, who were babysitting Melissa and Natasha for the afternoon, if they could keep them an hour or so more. "Just have a couple of things I have to square away with Kath," he said by way of an explanation. They chatted for a few minutes while he settled the girls in front of the television, told them he'd be back soon to collect them. When he returned to Katherine's, the place was eerily still. The hallway light was off. He could hear the faint tick of the clock above the stove. He walked toward the lounge, where he found her lying on the floor. There were pills scattered around her—white, blue, and yellow. A glass of water on the coffee table.

"Kath?!" He knelt beside her and shook her roughly. She didn't respond. He quickly ran to the neighbors for help. Within minutes they had her loaded into the back seat of Dave's car and were speeding toward Morisset hospital. She was unconscious when they arrived. The nurses moved quickly, and Dave stood back, watching as they placed an oxygen mask over her face and began their triage. She remained unconscious through the night. Dave waited in the corridor, his jacket rolled into a ball under his head.

By morning, she was stable. They admitted her for observation. Her family came to visit—Joy, her brother Charlie, and one of the cousins from Muswellbrook. No one said much. They sat around her hospital bed in shifts while she slept.

When she woke, she didn't mention the pills. No one pushed it. Dave reckoned it was grief over her mother's death. It had been less than six months earlier. She hadn't really talked about it. Just kept a photograph on the kitchen counter, near the phone. After a few days in the hospital, she was discharged. But that wasn't the last of it. She did another two weeks in Tamworth hospital, this time under psychiatric care. Dave drove her there after another breakdown.

She saw the psychiatrist every day. Spent most of the time resting or smoking in the courtyard. Her chart read "reactive depression." The nurses said she was cooperative, quiet, and polite. When she returned home, she seemed calmer. She cleaned the house, rearranged the kitchen drawers, threw out some of the girls' old toys. Dave came over after work. She made him tea, and they sat at the table for a long time talking and not talking.

The same patterns continued: peaceful stretches, sharp exchanges, long silences, breakdowns, and in between it all, sex. In October 1987, Katherine fell pregnant with her third child. The following June, in the cold weeks that signaled the start of another New England winter, she gave birth to Sarah.

Dave was there for the birth. The nurse handed him the little redheaded bundle, and he grinned at her like he'd won the lottery.

"Look at her," he said, full of paternal sentiment and awe. "She's got your hair."

Things were good for a while after that. Katherine was attentive and tender with the baby. She'd lift Sarah from her cot in the middle of the night without complaint, rocking her gently against her chest in the dark. Melissa and Natasha started calling Dave "Dad." The house on Segenhoe Street was noisy and warm. For the time being, everything held.

Not long after Sarah was born, Dave bought a small timber house on MacQueen Street. It was a practical decision. It gave them somewhere new to begin again. Somewhere neutral and close. Six months after the baby's birth, they packed up the flat on Segenhoe Street and moved the family into the MacQueen Street cottage. The house was squat and blunt, a cream-colored weatherboard set on the footpath of MacQueen Street, a busy main thoroughfare that funneled interstate travelers through the town. There was no front yard. The dark timber door opened off the sidewalk. If the wind blew in from the west, a swirl of dust would ride in with it, collecting on the floors of the lounge room.

There was only one square window on the house's façade, its frame peeling and dented. The green corrugated iron roof pitched low across the top, pocked with patches of rust. An awning reached out toward the street, propped up by two wooden posts painted red, a splash of color that stood out like lipstick on a tooth.

She didn't say it out loud, but the house seemed to offer Katherine a new kind of leverage—one that didn't rely on pleading or seduction. Sometimes, during their arguments, she'd stand at the front door, one hand on a red post, and declare the cottage hers.

"Get out of my house," she'd say. And he would do it. But then he'd come back. He always came back. What he didn't understand—or maybe just refused to see—was that the house on MacQueen Street wasn't just four walls and a roof. To Katherine, it was an anchor. A place she could ultimately control.

By then, Dave had begun carpooling with a few colleagues from the mine—four, sometimes five of them crammed into an old Holden Commodore that rattled all the way down from Aberdeen to the site. On those early morning drives, the sun still tucked beneath the hills, he'd sometimes shift in his seat to ease the bruises along his ribs, or wince when the seatbelt pressed against his collarbone. At first, the other men said nothing. A busted hand here, a split lip there—these things could have been chalked up to the job. But Dave hadn't been injured on the job. They all knew that. And before long, the silence broke into jokes.

"What'd you do this time, mate—burn the chops?"

"Forget to put the bins out again, eh?" He laughed along with them, but it never reached his eyes. One morning, as they pulled into work, someone asked him straight: "Is it Kathy?"

Dave nodded. "Yeah," he said quietly. "Yeah, it's her." It wasn't the kind of thing a bloke like Dave was supposed to admit. Not out here, not among men who measured pain in silence. But things at home were getting worse, and he couldn't keep pretending they weren't. One Saturday, he and his mate Brian—an old friend from Muswellbrook—had been out most of the day running errands, then a few beers at the pub. They got back to the cottage just before sunset. Dave hadn't called ahead. He didn't think he needed to. Katherine knew he was out with his friend and had seemed unfazed when he left. She was in the lounge, ironing, when he came in with Brian. A game show was playing in the background. She didn't look up when he walked in. Just pressed another sleeve flat beneath the hiss of steam.

"You're late," she said.

He glanced at the clock. "Late for what?"

She stopped ironing. Her shoulders stiffened, and she turned toward him with the iron still in her hand. "You think I slave over dinner so you can waltz in whenever you bloody feel like it?"

"There's no need to carry on," Dave said, trying to keep his voice level. "We just got stuck in traffic."

"Yeah, right," she snapped. "You don't care, and you never did!"

Brian stepped forward, his hands raised slightly. "Hey, Kath. We didn't mean anything by it."

She moved fast. Too fast for Dave to dodge out of the way. She swung the iron at his face. The blunt edge struck just below his cheekbone with a dull crack that made Brian wince as if he had been struck. Dave staggered backward, one hand holding onto his cheek, and stared, unblinking, at Katherine. The iron clattered to the floor with a spittle of steam.

Brian shouted something—maybe her name, maybe Dave's—and she suddenly turned on him too. Shoved him hard against the wall, then swung her fists. Brian darted out of her reach and bolted through the front door. Dave didn't even stop to grab a jacket. He followed Brian out, blood already dripping down his cheek.

They stood in the front yard, catching their breath. Katherine didn't follow.

"Jesus," Brian muttered. "You okay?"

Dave nodded, even though his face had turned purple. He wiped the blood on his sleeve. "I can't go back in there," he said. "Not tonight."

Brian hesitated, then said, "You can crash at mine."

In late 1988, Katherine was in the kitchen spinning her wheels when Dave came home late from work. "You don't care about anyone but yourself," she told him.

He didn't answer. He opened the fridge and grabbed a beer.

"You think you can come and go as you please?"

"This is my house, Kath. In case you forgot. I paid for it. And I'm not doing this tonight, so just stuff it." She was barefoot on the linoleum, and before he could step back, she was on him. A sharp jab—low, sudden, pierced his abdomen. His breath left him in a grunt. He looked down. The handle of a pair of nail scissors stuck out of his left flank just under his ribs. "What the fuck!?" She laughed at him. And he reeled back against the counter, then hurried for the door. One hand cradling the scissors, the other reaching for the door. His parting words: "You're fucking insane!"

He drove straight to his mate's place outside of Aberdeen, blinking through the pain, one hand pressed firmly to his side to keep the scissors from moving or, God forbid, snagging on something. When his mate opened the door, Dave said, "Can you help get these out of me guts?"

The scissors weren't long—just a pair of nail scissors. But she had plunged them into his abdomen with a driving force. Dave pulled up his shirt in the bathroom, and they both stared at the wound.

"Jesus, mate," his friend said, pulling a face. "You wanna go to the hospital?"

"Nah. She didn't get anything vital. Just a nick."

"You sure?"

Dave shook his head. "No. But I'm not going to hospital. We'll be there for hours."

Through Dave's wincing resignation, they pulled the scissors out slowly, cleaned the wound, and wrapped his midsection in gauze and a clean tea towel.

"Why the hell are you still with her?" his friend asked in bewilderment.

Dave just dropped himself on the couch, exhausted. He stayed there all night but got little sleep.

Two days later, there she was, at his door, begging him to come back, telling him that she only did it because she loved him so much. He could've said no, but she had that look in her eye. The same look she had the night they first met, that switch she flipped when she wanted something. And Dave, like always, stepped back and unzipped his pants.

And then, in 1989, Katherine received the compensation payout she had long been waiting for—money for the injury she'd sustained at the abattoir. She used it to pay off the cottage, and by doing so, the house became hers. It wasn't much, but it was hers, and she could walk a little taller after that. She had a roof that couldn't be taken from her. She had three girls and a man who, despite everything, had stuck with her.

Dave's father had passed away from cancer, and in the weeks that followed, his mother had handed down to Dave his father's clothes and bowls gear. He and his father were about the same size—it was a small, but sentimental inheritance. Dave wasn't given to sentiment easily, but those things mattered to him more than he let on. One evening, after a few drinks at the pub, he returned home to find the front door locked. It didn't make sense—she'd been happily watching him play bowls earlier that afternoon.

He put his shoulder to the door and forced it open. She was inside knitting. He confronted her and she unleashed her violence on him. Blood ran quickly from his lip after a sudden blow; a bruise swelled on his cheek from a volley of punches. They tussled, and then, all of a sudden, Katherine ran off to the kitchen and called his mother.

"Come pick up your bloody no-good son!"

His mother arrived soon after and found Dave out front on the sidewalk black and blue and bleeding.

A few days later, when things had sufficiently cooled, Dave returned to pick up his father's clothes and gear. "Well, where's me clothes?" he asked her.

"What clothes? There's no clothes," she replied nonchalantly.

He'd later found out that she'd cut them up and thrown them away. Dave was deeply stung. Those clothes were more than just fabric to him; they were a connection to his father. Losing them pained him more than any physical wound. That night, he decided that was the proverbial straw. He called his boss the next morning and arranged to take a long service leave. He left Aberdeen and Scone behind and headed for Newcastle, a city large enough to disappear in. He found work as a panel beater and kept his head down for a while.

While Dave was lying low, Katherine was calling around to his friends, asking where he might be. No one knew, or if they did, they didn't say. She looked for him at the pubs—the Thoroughbred and the Willow Tree. She looked for him at the RSL Club. But when he reemerged months later, she had moved on. An Apprehended Violence Order stood between them. And the cruelest cut: Dave found out that Katherine had told their daughter, Sarah, that he had died.

Over the next decade, the cottage would become well and truly hers, legally and completely. She would transform it into a kind of death den—a reflection of what appeared to be her happy place. It was chaotic, cluttered, and disturbed, but it was also intentional. Everything was placed exactly where she wanted it. The walls were crowded with skins, meta, and chains. A full cowhide was stretched taut across one side of the lounge room. Mounted above it were the treated skulls of a water buffalo, a steer, and a deer, their faces long gone, their horns communicating a brutal warning.

A taxidermized fawn stood on a side table near the window. A peacock with its feathers flared was positioned beside the television set. Cow and sheep skulls hung beside an old collection of iron animal traps fastened in a row down the hallway wall.

Though she never rode horses anymore, a single black riding boot was fixed to the wall above the small fireplace, alongside a crop and a saddle she picked up secondhand from a man outside Tenterfield. A giant wooden fork and spoon hung diagonally across the kitchen wall. An old rake and a bent pitchfork dangled from a ceiling beam above the dining table. In one corner sat a glass cabinet brimming with mismatched crockery and porcelain figurines: dogs, cats, birds, ballerinas, and cherubic angels. The rest of the walls were decorated with cake tins, meat cutters, and rusty farm and gardening tools. One pan still had flecks of congealed fat on it.

25

THE FORENSIC PSYCHIATRIST[11]

June 21, 2000. Mulawa Women's Correctional Centre. Mum Shirl Psychiatric Wing. Day 1.

She crossed one leg over the other, slowly, like someone with time to kill. Her arms were folded, as always. He noted that, as always. She met his eye for a moment before looking past him, toward the corner of the room where the paint peeled slightly at the ceiling joint.

"I don't see why we're going back through all this," she said. "It was years ago."

Again, Dr. Martin didn't answer straightaway. He let the silence carry its own weight. But Katherine held his gaze this time, as if she'd worked out his technique. "Why do you think Saunders kept coming back, even after all that you'd done, with the dog, and the scissors, the assaults. Why?"

"Why do you think? He came back because he knew I loved him."

"Loved him?"

"Yeah," she said. "'Course I did."

"You were aggressive toward him. Friends of his gave statements to that effect. The scissors," he said. "The frying pan. The iron. How can you call that love?"

"He was no angel," she said quickly. "He'd get up me too. No one ever talks about that part."

"You're saying he hurt you?"

"Yeah! I had to defend meself," she said.

"Is that why you sought an AVO against him?"

"I'm telling ya, he wouldn't leave me alone."

"Or you wouldn't leave him alone, because again, according to witnesses and police reports, you come off as the primary abuser. What do you have to say about that?"

Her eyes spoke volumes as they narrowed behind her eyeglasses.

Dr. Martin made a note.

"You were pregnant around this time?"

"Had me second daughter. That's why I let him stay as long as I did. I wanted to make it work."

"But in the end, he left."

"If you mean he ran off like a coward, yes. He wouldn't face me. He said nasty thinks about me. He hid from me. Like I was the problem."

Dr. Martin looked up from his notes. "I'm sure he had his part to play. But I want to know, Katherine, is it possible for you to take some responsibility for your role in the breakdown of your relationship? Can you see your half in any of it?"

She stared at him blankly but not blankly, like an animal suddenly stunned by a piercing light.

"There's a pattern here. Of possession, control, retaliation, abuse. Do you see it? As we've been talking now for a number of hours, have you come at all to recognize your role in any of this?"

"You'd be surprised what a woman's role is when she's being beaten up."

Dr. Martin looked again at his notes, aware there was a sentence waiting to be written and emphasized: *"Escalation consistent with borderline pathology; capacity for violence increasing over time; projected control onto others to stave off perceived abandonment. Unwilling and or unable to take responsibility for her actions."*

26

CHILLO

1991. Aberdeen, New South Wales.

She saw him one afternoon, leaning against the bar, laughing loudly with his friends. John Chillingworth, or "Chillo" as he was known. He looked like Paul Hogan in Crocodile Dundee. Broad-shouldered, sunbaked skin. He had that flushed, easy look of someone halfway through his fourth beer. She walked straight up to him. "Fuck, you've got a cute arse." Chillo was speechless for a moment. "Oh, thanks," he said, boozily. "You're not bad yourself."

It was trite, but that was all it took. Before the night was out, Katherine had taken him home. He was a body, a drinker, someone warm who laughed easily. But they didn't see each other for the better part of a week after that first night. He'd gone to stay with his mother in Scone. It was a warm evening when he saw her again. He happened to be walking past her house on MacQueen Street and decided to drop in.

From then on, they were an item. Like Dave, he didn't move in, but he spent at least a few nights a week there. There was no conversation about it. It just happened. One night early on, they lay in bed together. Katherine lit a cigarette and turned on her side to face him.

"You'll piss off eventually," she said.

Chillo laughed. "What are you talking about?"

"You blokes always do."

He stretched, folding his arms behind his head. "Not all of us."

"Nah. All of you."

"Well, not me." She tapped her ash into a coffee mug on the bedside table. "I can't be on my own, Chillo. Not for long. Makes me go funny."

"Funny how?"

"Like I start seeing things wrong. I can't sleep right. I start thinking thinks." The cigarette flared as she took another drag. "Even if I hate someone, even if they're no good, I'd rather have them here than be by meself. If anything happens with us, I would just find someone else."

"Bit early for that kind of talk, isn't it?" he scoffed.

"I'm just saying."

He reached over and brushed a piece of hair from her cheek. "Look at me. I'm not gonna piss off."

They lay there a while longer. The fan kept spinning round. A magpie called out through the bedroom window. Katherine took another drag of her cigarette, dropped her butt into the mug. Then she rolled on top of him and they started to kiss.

There were days when she went quiet for no reason, and other days when she was full of motion, cleaning the house top to bottom, hosing down the driveway, checking on the kids, stacking kindling in the shed. He never knew what version he'd get.

He recalled the first time he'd seen her. It was two decades earlier, when he'd done a few shifts at the Aberdeen meatworks. He was twenty-two. It was 1971 and he saw her on the kill floor, flirting with Kellett, and watching the pigs get stunned. He thought it odd, this young girl, being there of all places, staring at death happening over and over. He remembered she looked barely out of high school, and he remembered that flaming red hair. There was something carnal about the way she carried herself. Like she'd maybe seen too much too early.

She was pregnant within two months with her fourth child. When she told Chillo, she was pleasantly surprised by how thrilled he was.

"Mate, I'm forty-three, I thought it would never happen for me, this is the best news all year!" He grabbed her by the waist and hoisted her up off the floor in celebration.

"It's gonna be a boy, I can feel it in me waters!" he teased. Katherine glowed in the early weeks. She bought bibs from the Vinnies in Muswellbrook and folded them like little treasures in the top drawer. He watched her with a kind of serene disbelief, thinking perhaps the rumors about her had been just that: rumors.

But then one night, a different Katherine emerged. This Katherine didn't like how long he'd been at the bar. She didn't like the way one of the women touched him on the back as she squeezed past him, and she didn't like the way he smiled at her when she did so. Katherine had said nothing when he returned to their table from the bar with another round. She kept it bottled up and filed away in her mind, and it angered her even more that he didn't notice.

"I'm ready to go," she said to him when they were halfway through their drinks.

"What, already? The night's just getting started."

"Nah, I wanna go." And she got up, started walking. He followed her out, fully expecting to stop and talk her out of it. But when they reached the car park, she got in the car and took off without him.

Furious and confused, he ambled back into the pub realizing that he would likely have to walk home. He ambled along past the servo, after another hour spent at the pub. Past the empty lots, and rows of squat suburban houses. It was after midnight when he reached MacQueen Street and knocked on the door. The porch light turned on. Katherine came to the door and spoke behind the locked screen.

"You've had enough, huh?"

"Kath, what the fuck? Why'd you leave me there?"

"Get fucked." She shut the door. The porch light turned off.

"Wait, what the fuck, Kath!? What'd I do?" But she wouldn't let him in, even after his frantic banging, which stirred up the neighborhood dogs.

He hitchhiked to Scone none the wiser. But he was back in Aberdeen three days later, begging *her* to forgive him for whatever it was. And that was how it went. On again. Off again. Silent spells. Big blowups. Followed by sex and dinners at the pub.

When the next big blowup ignited, he fled to Newcastle and she took up with her now-ex, Dave Saunders. They spent the weekend together. Nobody needed to spell out what that meant. When Chillo returned, sunburned and hollow-eyed from two days of drinking, she told him straight, "I was with Dave all weekend." She could see the hurt in his eyes.

"I want nothing more to do with you," she said. "I'm getting back with him."

Chillo was crushed. *"But you're having our baby!"* Katherine shrugged. *"So!"*

"Kath," he continued, "don't do this."

She leaned in close. "It's David's anyway. Or could be someone else's. I don't really know for sure." She had no interest in how much it hurt him—just the satisfaction of the blow. It wasn't true and she knew it. So did he, which only made it worse.

Melissa, who was fourteen, had started keeping her distance whenever Chillo was at the house. If he were around for dinner, she'd eat on the couch, with the TV on. Or she'd stay in her room. She didn't like Chillo and she felt anger toward her mother for bringing him around. Since leaving her dad, Kellett, Katherine had cycled through a number of men.

"Want some more, chippies, Mel?" Katherine called out from the dinner table one night. "Come, join us."

Melissa shook her head without turning around. She gave a surly, "No thanks." Then she turned up the volume on the TV a couple of notches, enough to underline the message: *not interested*. It made Chillo furious, even more than it did Katherine. He was very close with his mum, loved her to bits, everyone knew it. He saw his mother several times a week and would never dream of treating her that way. He found the behavior offensive. "Oi, don't be rude to your mum. She's just trying to be nice."

Melissa snapped her head around to Chillo. "You're not my dad, so shut the fuck up." Then she got up, leaving her dinner plate on the coffee table, an episode of *Home and Away* playing on the telly, and started for her bedroom. Chillo rose quickly—too quickly—and stopped her. His open hand caught her on the side of the head, a sharp clip above the ear that made her head stumble forward slightly before she made it into her bedroom and slammed the door. He whipped around to find Katherine lunging for him.

"She was out of line!" he said in his defense.

"Don't you fuckin' ever touch my kid again, or I'll cut your throat!"

Later, Chillo drank a few more beers and fell asleep on the couch. When he woke the next morning, hungover and sore, he went for his dentures, but they weren't on the coffee table where he'd left them the night before in his beer glass. He rose painfully and started checking under cushions, beneath the coffee table. Behind the couch. Then he saw them—on the floor by the kitchen doorway, smashed to pieces.

"What's this?" he said when he confronted Katherine.

"Oh, you found them," she said, looking at the clattering mess in his hand.

"What happened to 'em?"

"I smashed them, what does it look like?" she said, walking past him into the kitchen.

He followed her in. "What for?"

"You hit Melissa."

"It was a clip! She was mouthing off."

"You hit her," she repeated. "So, I hit back."

"You think this is funny?"

"No."

He waited there, his gummy mouth making him look decades older, not sure what he was expecting her to say or do.

"You shouldn't have done that, Kath. These are me teeth."

She shrugged. "You shouldn't have touched my kid."

He stared at her for a moment, wanting an apology, but resigning himself to the fact that he would never get one. He went back to the living room. He was hungover, and now he looked like an idiot. He got dressed and slammed the door behind him. He traveled to his flat in Scone to get his backup pair of dentures. When he returned to Katherine's a few days later and spent the night, he awoke the next morning to find his backup pair had also been smashed to pieces.

Katherine gave birth to their son, Eric, in fall 1991. He was full-term and healthy. She told the midwife the boy would be christened within the month. Chillo bought her a secondhand Mitsubishi van. It was meant as a gesture—something useful, to make life with four children a little easier. Katherine's youngest brother, Shane, travelled with them to Newcastle to collect the car. Shane drove the van back to Aberdeen. Katherine and Chillingworth took his car. They were near MacQueen Street when Katherine turned on him, full of stored-up resentment.

She called him a drunk. "I'm taking you home. You're not staying with me tonight."

"Oh bullshit, I'm not," he said, brushing it off. "Don't be ridiculous."

"I'm fucking serious. I've had enough of you." As she said this, she reached over and grabbed his glasses and snapped them in two. "I'm taking you home to your whore of a mother." He slapped her in the face. Katherine retaliated by pounding him on the head repeatedly. He struck her with another backhand. She drove straight to the Scone police station after that and dropped him at the curb. She told the officers what had happened and pressed charges.

At the hospital, she gave a statement. Her injuries were photographed: swelling to the cheekbone, bruising beneath the eye. They gave her Panadol, pressed an icepack to her face, and sent her on her way. The next day, she took out an Apprehended Violence Order against Chillo and they split up. The separation lasted less than a week because Eric was due to be christened. They got back together again. Katherine showed up to the christening with a black eye. Chillo was back at the house within in a matter of weeks. A blanket on the couch, clothes in a plastic bag in the laundry. The pattern had once again been set: separation, reentry, violence. In between it all, she was fond of saying: "If I love ya, I love ya. If I hate ya, I hate ya." That's how it always was with her: go to war, then have a party.

He stayed longer than he should have. He knew she was capable of harm. Not just in theory. Real, deliberate harm. Years later, he would say that he always knew she would do something serious. That it was only a matter of time.

27

THE FORENSIC PSYCHIATRIST[12]

June 21, 2000. Mulawa Women's Correctional Centre. Mum Shirl Psychiatric Wing. Day 1.

The tea she'd asked for remained untouched. Her arms were still folded high up on her chest in a vaguely defensive posture, hands tucked into her armpits, her eyes darting anywhere but at him. The body language was never lost on Dr. Martin.

"I've been going over your statement about Chillingworth," he said. "You mentioned the AVO. You were the one who took it out, correct?"

She shrugged. "He hit me. I got a black eye. My cheek was swollen this big." She gestured to show him how big.

"And yet you were back together shortly after."

"For the christening. Eric had to be christened, didn't he, and his father needed to be there."

Dr. Martin made a note.

"What are you writing?"

---

[12] *Speculative reconstruction inspired by documented psychiatric interviews.*

"Just that you returned to the relationship soon after reporting him. That this wasn't a unique pattern."

She leaned forward. "What's that supposed to mean?"

"It means we've seen this before. With David Kellett. With Dave Saunders. And with John Chillingworth, and, by the sound of things, with John Price too. The order changes, but the ingredients stay the same. Violence. Distance. Reunion, then back to violence again. The cycle continues and you seem to want it to continue."

"I wasn't the one causing the cycle," she said adamantly. "They pushed me. You talk like it's all me." She began to grow red in the face.

"I'm not saying that," Dr. Martin replied gently. He was more than aware of her ability to suddenly snap, and not for the first time, he was grateful for the two security guards waiting just outside the door during their sessions. "But you were the common denominator." He let the silence draw out once again, watching as she pretended not to be turning this over in her mind. She sighed a heavy breath and looked away, reached for the tea, and took her first sip. Dr. Martin thought he sensed fatigue, and the briefest flash of remorse in that sigh, or maybe it was a mourning for the loss of control.

"Why did Chillingworth go to Queensland?"

She thought for a moment, recalling the details. "For a job with the Salvos. He was going for two weeks, but then he, um… he decided to stay there. He asked me to come up with the kids 'cuz he wanted to get us a place, all of us together. So, we went up and seen him."

"Were you hoping things would be different?"

"I was hoping he'd stop sulking and act like a proper man."

Dr. Martin put his pen down and steepled his fingers beneath his chin.

"You mentioned earlier that he came home from work one day to find you with another man?"

"Yeah, we weren't doing nothing, just laughing and having some tea. But Chillo came, and when he saw Pricey he lost it, and he hit me."

"And what did you do after that?"

"I left back to Aberdeen. I never saw him again. I started seeing Pricey for real."

"Did you meet Mr. Price after your trip to Queensland?"

"No, before that."

"Around when was that?"

"I don't remember; before."

Dr. Martin looked at her squarely. "Just to be clear, before you went to see Chillingworth, you had begun a relationship with John Price, correct?"

"Yeah." She leaned back in her chair, slouching a bit, as she thought about it. Dr. Martin made some notes. "Relationship was already in motion," he said without looking up from his writing. "That helps to clarify the timeline."

Katherine reached for the cold tea and took a sip.

28

JOHN PRICE

October 8, 1993. The Top Pub, Aberdeen, New South Wales.

The night she met John Price was the night Chillo left for Queensland. He would be away for a couple of days. Katherine decided to go out with her friend Cheryl at the Top Pub, for drinks and a good time. She wore a pair of skin-tight black jeans and a backless Glomesh top that glittered under the pub lights. At the bar, Cheryl ordered a gin and tonic. Katherine ordered her usual: Cadbury's chocolate liqueur in a snifter with one ice cube.

While they waited for the drinks, she adjusted her top in the bar mirror. That's when she caught sight of him, holding court at a table behind her while his drinking buddies and several women surrounded him. She recognized a few of the men, roughnecks from the mines, but John was the one who held her attention. He had them all laughing at his jokes; his voice was loud and unguarded, his arms gesturing wildly, occasionally spilling his beer as he burst into another story. His curly mullet looked roughed up and matted from a long day under a hardhat, and his shirt was wrinkled and stained with sweat. Must have come straight from work, Katherine thought as she watched him. There was something magnetic about the way he didn't try to impress anyone, just laughed and drank and took up space with glee. When their drinks arrived, Katherine motioned to Cheryl.

"That one over there is going to be mine tonight."

Cheryl scoffed. "Good luck. He's got half the women in here wrapped around his middle finger, if you know what I mean." She gave Katherine a knowing look.

"All the more reason." Katherine took her drink and cut through the crowd to John's table. She threw a pointed stare at a woman who'd been hanging off his shoulder. The woman murmured something in John's ear and moved off. Katherine took her place, nudging John with her shoulder.

"Didn't I meet you a while back with Saunders?"

John took a second. "Oh yeah, Kath. Kath Knight, right?

"In the flesh." She tilted her head as she smiled coyly at him. "John Price."

"Yeah, that's right, Pricey. Where you been hidin' yourself since then?" she teased.

John looked at her with eyes a little glazed but bright with that easy charm.

"Workin' like a dog, love. You know how it is." She tilted her head again and looked him over slowly.

"You look like you've been workin' all right. Time to clean you up." John barked a laugh. "Oh, mate, don't even get me started."

Katherine leaned in closer, dropping her voice. "Oh, I'll get you started, Pricey, 'cause I'm not lettin' you out of my sight tonight."

They drank together the rest of the night. The longer they talked, the more Katherine pressed up against him, her body language unmistakable. When Cheryl finally grew tired and left, Katherine stayed, keeping John in stitches with her crass jokes and flirtatious jabs. By the time the pub was thinning out, they were sitting close together in a dim corner, her hands wandering over his chest. She whispered something filthy in his ear, and he nearly choked on his beer.

They stumbled outside, John half drunk and swaying as she guided him around the side of the building. The only light came from a single bulb above the parking lot. She pushed him back against the brick wall and dropped to her knees right there in the dark of the lot. And it made John's blood rush to watch Katherine, as she looked up at him with that glinting hunger, dirty and reckless. When she was done with him, it took him a minute to catch his breath. He helped her up, grinning. "You're bloody wild, fucking hell."

Katherine wiped her mouth and shot him a wicked smile. "You like that, huh?" It was more of a statement than a question. But he answered that he did. Very much. It was her lack of pretense—the way she came at him without filters, unashamed of what she wanted.

They went out together most nights after that, drinking at the Top Pub until the noise got too loud or they got too drunk. Katherine would dance with him, hugging him around his neck while he laughed and swung her around like they were the only ones there. When the mood hit, they'd sneak out the back and go at it behind the pub, just like that first night, because Katherine liked the idea of pleasing him where anyone could find them. It was proof that he was hers.

By mid-1994, they were inseparable. Katherine and her two youngest, Sarah and Eric, stayed at John's house most nights. She took over the kitchen almost immediately, cooking elaborate meals and packing his lunches for work. When he came home, there was always something simmering on the stove, the smell of meat and gravy thick in the air. She liked to be useful, liked him to see how much she could take care of him. It gave her a renewed sense of purpose.

John grew fond of her kids too. He never tried to be their dad. One weekend, he took six-year-old Sarah and four-year-old Eric fishing at the dam. He showed them how to bait hooks and cast lines. When Sarah struggled with her rod, he knelt down beside her, guiding her hands.

"Gotta be gentle," he said, grinning. "Fish don't like it rough. See? Just like that." Sarah beamed when her line shot out across the water. Eric watched as John unhooked a bass he had caught. John showed Eric how to hold it without getting finned. "You're pretty good at this, mate," he said, ruffling the boy's hair. "Maybe next time you'll catch a real whopper."

Later, he fixed Melissa's car when the engine started knocking, spending most of his Saturday lying under the hood while Katherine handed him tools.

When he got the car running again, Melissa flung her arms around him. "You're a legend, Pricey!"

Katherine had watched the moment from the doorway, feeling deeply content, so much so that it began to frighten her. What if he left her? What if she lost him to another, younger woman? She was nearly forty, still technically a single mother of four. Unemployed after her back injury. Uneducated. Living in that dusty old cottage. What were the chances of her finding another John Price?

And just as the terror had begun to grip her, so too did the cracks start to appear in their relationship. In September 1995, they had their first real fight. It happened at the Top Pub. Katherine had noticed how the barmaid kept laughing at John's jokes, touching his arm when she served him drinks. She didn't say much to him for the rest of the night. When they got home, John noticed the shift. "What's the matter with you?" he asked, frowning.

"You were too friendly with that cunt at the bar," Katherine snapped.

He blinked. "Who?"

Katherine exploded; it seemed that she had been waiting to all night. "The bloody barmaid! You think I didn't see her makin' eyes at you!?"

He was caught off guard. "She's just being nice, Kath. Don't get your knickers in a bloody twist," he said jovially. That did it. Katherine slapped him hard across the face, hard enough to leave a fiery mark. John stood there, stunned.

"What the hell, Kath!?" he shouted, clutching his face. She stood there glaring at him with anger, her chest heaving, her eyes wild with untold grievances. A great shift had taken place, and John was at a complete loss as to why. *What just happened?* he wondered. Before he could react, she turned and marched out of the room.

He stood in the kitchen, staring at the spot where she had been. He didn't follow. A few minutes later, the sound came—soft and metallic. He turned just in time to see her reemerge, holding one of the knives from the display she insisted on mounting in the hallway. The knife wasn't raised at him, nor was it pointed at him. It was simply held by her side.

"I'm not going to hurt you," she said, flatly. "But you should know what I feel like sometimes."

His mouth went dry. "Put the knife down, Kath."

"You don't understand. You never have." Her voice was eerily calm now. "When I see you laughing with other women, I feel like I'm vanishing. Like I'm not real anymore. I've felt that way my whole life."

"Katherine—"

"I don't want to be like this," she whispered, tears forming suddenly, betraying her steeliness. "But it's like there's something inside me that breaks loose, and I can't, I can't always hold it in." She looked down at the knife, then back at him. "I love you so much it makes me sick."

Though he wanted to, he couldn't speak. After a moment, she put the knife down. Delicately. As though it were a living thing. And then, just as quickly as she had boiled over, her demeanor softened. She stepped closer to John and placed a hand on his chest.

"Listen to me," she murmured. "I just...I love you. I just had too much to drink. It can do that to me sometimes." John hesitated at first but let her guide him outside, to the back of the house, where she dropped to her knees and unzipped his jeans. It was rough and sexy, and when it was over, he leaned against the wall to catch his breath once again. As he did so, a chill moved over him—like a gust of wind that stirs up out of nowhere.

His heart thumped. In his gut was a new feeling—of fear. Not for his safety—but for her. Later, he sat alone on the porch, drinking a beer while she slept. The town lay quietly around him. He wondered if it was just jealousy with Katherine. Or if there was something darker at play? Something he didn't understand yet but could feel creeping in around the edges. He drank his beer, staring out into the night. A few lights glowed in the neighboring windows, blinking through the gum trees. His mind kept circling back to the way she'd exploded and then erased it with sex, like wiping a slate clean. *What was that about?* He tipped the bottle back, draining the last of it, and decided to push the thought out of his mind.

INTERIM FORENSIC NOTE 2[13]

June 21, 2000. Mulawa Women's Correctional Centre. Mum Shirl Psychiatric Wing. Day 1.

Dr. Martin flipped back a page in his notebook, underlining a few words, then pressed record on his device.

"Interim note two. Recorded during day one, afternoon session. Dr. Robert Martin speaking. Forensic psychiatric assessment for the prosecution brief. Subject: Katherine Mary Knight, forty-four years old, currently remanded for the murder of John Charles Thomas Price. Location is interview room 3B, Mum Shirl Psychiatric Unit, Mulawa Centre. Time is 1:17 PM, during a break in the session.

"Subject continues to present anecdotal evidence of a personality structure centered on dominance, control, and retaliatory violence. There is no overt psychosis. Affect remains largely neutral and contained. She is verbally cooperative but reframes events to preserve her internal logic—namely, violence as justified. The wedding night incident with David Kellett—the attempted

---

[13] *Speculative reconstruction inspired by documented psychiatric interviews.*

strangulation when he refused a third round of intercourse—is the earliest documented example of her sexual coercion fusing with violence. She interpreted his refusal not as physical limitation, but as rejection, humiliation, and personal injury—he was apparently very drunk and could not perform. Her response to this was impulsive, punitive, and set the pattern.

"By the second year of marriage, the relationship had begun to devolve into verbal abuse, manipulation, and betrayal. Kellett's affair was met with retaliation bordering on the psychotic. Placing their infant daughter Melissa on the railway tracks and walking away was a chilling strategy: if she couldn't punish Kellett directly, she would inflict pain through shared grief or public shame. The child survived by chance. What followed was escalation: public outbursts, armed threats, psychiatric confinement. While a diagnosis of postnatal depression was plausible, it does not explain the calculated nature of some of the acts. The attempted kidnapping of neighbors to facilitate murder reflects not stupor, but goal-directed rage.

"Her violence is reactive, theatrical, and instrumental. She wants to be feared, noticed, obeyed. When love fails, fear is acceptable currency. Kellett's return from Queensland to support her recovery was telling. It allowed Katherine to reassemble the family structure she seemed to crave. For a time, she was compliant. The medication helped. But the cycle resumed: abuse, hospitalizations, retaliatory infidelities. Notably, Kellett never pressed charges, just as John Price had chosen not to do. His explanation—that the girls needed their mother—echoes a pattern among her partners: grim tolerance, helplessness, and in some cases, real fear. I wonder if this is a personality type that she targets, whether consciously or not.

"Katherine was regarded as a good mother to her children. When she eventually left Kellett and returned to Aberdeen with the children, his reaction, as reported by witnesses, was relief. Indicating perhaps that he remained with her for so long, not out of love per se, but out of a lack of a safe exit. Earlier, she described an incident at the abattoir involving a coworker, Vince, who threw a piece of animal fat at her during a shift. She responded by seizing him by the throat and threatening him with her knife. The foreman had to intervene. Strikingly, she linked the event to an earlier memory, age thirteen. A group of boys taunting her and her friends. She held a knife to one of them—someone she implied she'd been sexually involved with. Her recollection was unemotional: 'I wasn't afraid.... I was angry.' This framing reveals a cognitive structure in which violence is not only permissible, but stabilizing. A common dynamic in trauma-linked power reversals found in individuals with entrenched borderline or antisocial traits." Dr. Martin paused, glancing at his notes.

"I received crime scene photographs of her home in MacQueen Street, Aberdeen. The absence of any kind of domestic warmth is striking to say the very least. The decor centers on violence and death: animal skulls, skins, knives, rakes, pitchforks, rusting tools, mounted on walls and ceilings—like a museum of animal remains. These are not decorative flourishes, but symbolic. They represent both her occupational identity and her psychological alignment with death, control, and ritual.

"I believe it's a significant reflection of her personality. It's a place, to me, of death and destruction," he continued, scanning the photographs. "She is not in the garden growing things. I am not aware there is a pet budgie there or something like that. It is a theme of death, and some writers in psychiatry have made a lot of significance of this. They have given it a term in fact, *necrophilis*, and it literally means a love of death. Erich Fromm defined it as the antithesis of *biophilia*—the love of life and living things. She is surrounded by death. And she enjoyed her work at the abattoir. Why did she keep visiting the man who kills the pigs? These are all important signs. And back to the wall hangings. The theme of death, necrophilis. These things are all just so significant.

"It leads one to ask: why would someone seek that environment day after day? What internal structure finds such proximity to death not just bearable, but gratifying? The answer lies not only in economic necessity but in a deeper psychological architecture. The site of slaughter became, for her, a space of power and competence. Returning to her home—with its dead decor and absence of life—we see a personality in which death is central, even nurturing. Not incidental but foundational.

"From a forensic perspective, her abusive episodes indicate a pattern of targeted, affectively charged violence that is not necessarily impulsive, at least not all of the time, but driven by perceived betrayal. In other words, I don't believe her actions are detached from reality—they are more than often hyper-attuned to relational dynamics, particularly rejection. If she is guilty of the crime we are now investigating, it will not have been madness in the strict sense. It will likely have been a form of punishment.

"I will now return to the period after the Howick Mines incident, when she resumed her relationship with John Price, as well as the events leading up to his murder. End interim note two. Time is 1:26 PM."

PART THREE

29

AND YET...

February 1999. Aberdeen, New South Wales.

When Katherine started turning up at St Andrews Street again, John's youngest daughter, Jackie, fourteen at the time, confronted him about it. So did his son, Johnathon, who was in his early twenties and living with his wife just a few blocks away. They begged their father not to let her back in and called him a fool for even considering it. John's mate, Laurie, and a few of the others also tried to reason with him.

"But I love her," John told them. "I miss her."

"For God's sake. After everything she's done?" Laurie couldn't believe it. No one could. John's decision to take her back unsettled his mates. Some wouldn't speak to him. Most wanted nothing to do with her. They barely tolerated John when he brought her around. The Howick Mines scandal had marginalized them both. He stopped going to the RSL Club and only went to the Top Pub, where people would still associate with them, mostly because they didn't know the whole story or they didn't care.

John and Katherine would often sit at the bar, chatting up whoever was closest. The mates he'd leaned on were largely gone.

John had taken her back, but he would not allow her to move in, honoring a promise he'd conceded to his children. Even so, Katherine came and went as she pleased. She still had the key.

There wasn't a cupboard or room that she didn't still lay claim to. Her kids' pajamas went back under pillows in the spare bedrooms, neatly tucked away for the next sleepover. Some of her clothing went back in the drawer next to John's, and her knitting and sewing kits returned to their usual spot on the floor next to the lounge.

A few months later, John landed a job at Bowditch Mines, doing much the same as he'd done at Howick. But this time the pay was better. When he had come home from work after his first day, he'd found Katherine waiting for him in bed, naked, with a sheet pulled up to her waist. She'd lit one of the good candles that she kept stashed in the laundry cupboard, the one with the vanilla scent. Her hair was brushed, and she'd applied a bit of blush to her cheeks. She patted the mattress beside her when he came in, her intentions clear. While they were having sex, she squeezed him tight, pushed him deeper still, and kissed him on the lips.

"See? Things are better."

And yet…even though John had forgiven her, Katherine's need for revenge continued to plague her. One afternoon, while John was at work, she'd brought two girlfriends over from the meatworks for tea. John's daughter, Jackie, who was staying with her father for the week, was in the living room watching television when they all came in and started up their gossiping. They sat around the coffee table with their mugs and Anzac biscuits, talking about the people they didn't like, casting judgments and aspersions. Jackie had to keep turning up the volume. But Katherine's voice rose louder each time, and the women with her.

When they finally left, Katherine walked into the lounge, wiping biscuit crumbs from her shirt, still glowing from all the wicked table gossip. She stood behind Jackie.

"Jackie," she said.

Jackie didn't bother turning around. "Yeah?"

"I've got to tell you something."

"What?" she said with mild disgust as she flipped through the channels with the remote.

"I just thought you should know, your father's not really your father." The words came out matter-of-factly.

Jackie whipped her head and squinted at Katherine. "What?"

"Well, that's what I heard. Your mum played around. The whole town knew it."

"You're lying," she exclaimed, her disgust mounting.

Katherine just shrugged. "Go ask your mum."

Jackie sprang up from the couch. "Why would you say something like that?"

"Because it's true," Katherine said. "Might as well know." It wasn't true, but it got into Jackie's head and stayed there. She was fourteen. Old enough to doubt things she once took for granted. She marched into the kitchen and called her mother. When Colleen heard what Katherine had said, she demanded to speak to Katherine.

"Yeah, Col?" Her grin widened as she listened. Colleen was shouting loud enough that Jackie could hear it through the receiver.

Two hours later, Colleen pulled up John's driveway. It was just after 8 PM. She had come straight from work to collect Jackie, who no longer wanted to finish out her week at her father's. John came home from work as Colleen was in the driveway with Jackie, about to leave.

"Hey, what's going on here?" John asked when he jumped out of the truck.

Colleen brought him up to speed, and John was livid. He tore inside and confronted Katherine immediately.

Colleen started the engine while she waited for John to return with Jackie and her things. She glanced at the front door to see Katherine hurrying toward her. Quick steps. No pause at the threshold. She marched straight to the car and leaned into the driver's side window. As she did so, she lightly touched Colleen's hand, which was resting on the window frame. They both felt an electric shock pass between them; Colleen shuddered. There was something in Katherine's touch that caused a tremor in her. Just as quickly as she felt the charge, a vision flashed in her mind of John's body, limp and injured. She saw blood, and she felt a surge of dread well up in her.

"Col, can I ask you something?"

"Uh…yeah," Colleen said cautiously, her fingers lightly on the ignition key.

"Did Pricey ever hit you?"

Colleen scoffed in a way that signaled how absurd the question was. "What!? Of course not. John doesn't hit women. He barely raises his voice. Who told you that shit?"

Katherine tilted her head. "A bloke you gave a ride home from the club one night."

Colleen glared at her, incredulous. "What bloke?"

"You know," Katherine said. "When you used to go to the raffles. One night you gave some bloke a lift."

"For a start," Colleen snapped, "I have never given any bloke a ride home from the club. Ever." She unbuckled her seatbelt and stepped out of the car. She stood eye to eye with Katherine. "Who told you that? Go get him. I'll come with you. I'll say it right in front of him—that's a load of bullshit."

Katherine shrugged. "Oh. I might've got it wrong then." Soon John was coming out to the car. He noticed Katherine's satisfied little grin as they crossed each other on the lawn. Jackie hopped into the car with bags. John leaned in through the passenger window and kissed Jackie on the cheek.

"Darling. Sorry about all that nonsense. Kath's just being… well, she's being, Kath. Talking rubbish. There's no way I ain't your pop. I'll even take a test to prove it to ya if you want."

"I know, Dad." Jackie didn't say anything more. She just wanted to be done with the whole business.

"I'll see you in a couple of weeks, poppet, yeah?" he said.

Jackie gave him a half-smile. "Yeah, maybe."

John looked at her; it was a small but sharp sting. Colleen walked over to John. "Can I chat to you for a sec?" They stepped a few paces away from the car, out of earshot. Colleen's voice dropped. "Listen to me. Look at me." She caught his arm. "She's gonna do something to you."

"Who?"

"Kathy, you fool."

"Oh, come on, Col—"

"Nah, I'm telling you. Look at me. She is gonna do something to you, mate. I don't know how bad it's going to be, but she's going to hurt you."

John glanced at Jackie, who waited patiently.

"Listen to me. I'm telling you now, she's going to do something to you, Pricey. I can see it. I actually seen it. She put her hand on me and said, 'Can I ask you something?' And she tapped me on the hand and no sooner had she done it, I seen it. I actually got a shock. Like an electric shock. And straight away, I saw it—just like flashes. You were hurt. It was like a picture in my head. And I knew. She's going to do something, John. I'm telling you now."

John's jaw tensed. The dread he already felt suddenly gained more layers. Colleen stepped back. "You can brush me off, but you know it too. I can feel it. That woman's got something wrong in her."

30

HIS HEAD ON NOW

March 1999. Aberdeen, New South Wales.

Katherine's sweet side reemerged again, showing up wherever she went, whenever she needed it: at Bingo in Muswellbrook, where she played on Tuesdays and Thursdays. At sewing class every Wednesday night, where she made her own clothing. During her knitting group, where her lace quilts were the envy of all the gals, and at the Community Centre, where she sometimes took her kids on weekends. She helped out when friends or relatives needed a lift to the mall or a doctor's appointment. She'd offer to mind her granddaughter and the kids of friends, take them to the park for the day. She behaved with a heart of gold. And she and John were getting on great. They'd go to the Top Pub and have a laugh, or they'd go camping.

And the sex. It flowed like water. John couldn't get enough. She would do it anywhere, anytime, and anyhow, even with anyone, if he asked her to. But that still didn't ease his underlying sense of dread. He knew her patterns all too well. He knew it was only a matter of time before the other Katherine returned.

Thankfully, his job kept him occupied, and he was grateful for that. After just nine months at Bowditch, he'd been put in charge of the scraper crew, which gave him more responsibility. He took pride in that. He even looked different. He had stopped drinking like he used to. He was leaner. Healthier. His beer gut had pulled back some. The lines around his eyes were still there, but softer. He was even learning how to use computers. For a man who'd never finished high school, who fumbled through forms and letters, and who was not a reader, learning to read progress reports, log hours, and track maintenance orders on a computer was a big deal. His foreman trained him up. Then one of the younger guys showed him a few shortcuts. John listened, and he learned. He took notes in a little dog-eared notepad he kept in his shirt pocket.

He started mentoring some of the younger crew as well. His friends saw the change in him. At the Top Pub, they'd nod and say, "Pricey's got his head on now." And he did. He was working hard, earning good money, spending weekends with the kids. He looked clean-shaven and clear-eyed. But whenever anyone brought up Katherine, the edge would come back into his voice. Just a flicker. Or he would glance down at the floor and pause before answering.

"Yeah, nah. She's still around." He never said much more than that. But his friends, the few he had left, could see he was worried.

31

SCAR TISSUE

August 1999. Six months before the murder.

One day in August 1999, the other Katherine returned. John got an angry phone call from Colleen. Katherine had antagonized Jackie again, bringing up the business about his paternity. Colleen was still bruised from the first time, and now Katherine had gone and told Jackie more lies. And after the "vision" Colleen had had, she was more certain than ever that something terrible was going to happen.

"You've got to get her out of your life, Pricey," Colleen had told him over the phone.

Katherine was up to her wrists in suds at the sink, scrubbing pots in hot water, when John came in and confronted her once again. "I was talking to Colleen on the phone," he said. "She reckons you had no right saying what you said to Jackie. And I agree with her."

Katherine didn't look at him. Just kept on with the pots, clattering another into the drying rack. "You're nasty sometimes, you know that?"

John felt anger rising in him. "You cause trouble. And you stir shit up that's none of your fuckin' business." Now she looked at him, a tea towel bunched in her hands. "You calling me nasty now?"

"I'm saying you went too fuckin' far. That stuff with Jackie—what the hell were you thinking? Everything was going so well, then you go and ruin it. Like you always do."

Her mouth tightened. "I told her what she deserves to know."

"She's a kid!" he snapped. "You don't get to just poison people like that. You're twisted, Kath. It's like you…"

Before he could finish his sentence, Katherine drove a knife into the hollow below his left shoulder. John staggered back, clutching at the wound.

"You fuckin' stabbed me!?" he shouted in disbelief.

She stepped away. "Don't say I didn't fuckin' warn you!" She tossed the knife, stained with John's blood, into the sink and walked out of the kitchen. Blood soaked through his shirt. He stood there for a moment to get his bearings. His heart raced; sweat was beading on his forehead. He went to the sink and turned on the tap and cleaned the wound. Then he went into the bathroom and grabbed a large Band-Aid from the first aid kit in the cabinet. The same one Katherine had accused him of stealing, the same kit that got him fired. The irony, John thought as he patched up the wound. He didn't think to go to the hospital. And he didn't think to go to the police. All he wanted to do was go to bed. He wanted the day to be over.

A few days later, he was at the RSL Club with Laurie and Fran Lewis. He drank his beer with his right hand only, his left arm still stiff and painful from the injury. Laurie noticed. "What's wrong with you, mate?"

"Ah, you know, the usual."

"Katherine?" Laurie asked, taking a sip of his beer.

John set the glass down and undid a few buttons on his shirt. The edge of the large Band-Aid peeked from beneath. He peeled it back, showing the shallow stab wound, bruised purple and green around the edges. "She took a knife to me," he said flatly.

Laurie shook his head, almost laughed, not because it was funny, but because it was getting absurd.

"Mate, we've been telling you that for ages! It'll be worse than that next time." Fran leaned forward, her voice coarse and unforgiving. "She took your job off you and everything else, and you're back with her? What's it going to take, John?"

John shrugged. "I've got nothing else to lose."

Fran stared at him in shock. "Yes, you have, Pricey. You've got your bloody life to lose!"

No one spoke after that. "Scar Tissue" by the Red Hot Chili Peppers played on the sound system. Once again, the irony… John left without finishing his beer.

32

THE FORENSIC PSYCHIATRIST[14]

June 22, 2000. Mulawa Women's Correctional Centre. Mum Shirl Psychiatric Wing. Day 2.

"It could've been a fork," she said. "Or a spoon. Could've been anything in my hand."

Dr. Martin made a note in his file. Katherine watched him stiffly from across the table. Her voice was steady—not defensive, but not apologetic either.

"It just happened to be a knife. You know, one of those ones you cut your meal with. And I aimed it at him, yeah, but he was leaning closer than I thought."

Dr. Martin made another note.

"My eyesight was bad back then," she added. "I've only had these glasses for a couple of months. You can ask anyone." She glanced at Dr. Martin, who remained silent. "It was an accident," she continued. "Just an accident. I even went to the police and reported it the next day. Told them exactly what happened—I

---

[14] *Speculative reconstruction inspired by documented psychiatric interviews.*

said, 'I had an accident.' That's what happened." She leaned back and folded her arms.

"You reported it the same night?" Dr. Martin asked.

"Of course," she said. "Soon as I realized he was bleeding more than I thought he would."

"You didn't take him to the hospital?"

"He was fine. He already cleaned himself up and put a Band-Aid on it. He didn't want to go to the hospital." Katherine smoothed her hands down the front of her dress. "He shouldn't have come at me like that. He was all stirred up. Arguing with me about Colleen. I just wanted it to stop."

Dr. Martin tilted his head, studying her carefully. "Are you saying you didn't intend to harm him?"

"Yeah. I didn't. Like I said, it was an accident."

"And yet, the fights continued, did they not? The violence, the arguments?"

"Pricey would get angry about losing his job at Howick. He was still remembering that all the time, and he'd start yelling at me when he was drunk and hitting me. I had to defend meself."

"Right," Dr. Martin said as he made another note in his file. "And what did you think about him getting angry over losing his job the way he did, due to you?"

"It made me mad. 'Cuz his new job was better pay. He was higher up than he was at Howick. He should have been thanking me, when you think about it."

33

ANGRY RED LINES

Sunday, February 27, 2000. Two days before the murder.

Katherine's nephew, Jason, who was staying with her at her cottage for a couple of weeks, came in through the back door one afternoon, wiping his boots on the mat. Katherine was at the kitchen table smoking, a stubbed-out collection of butts crowding the ashtray. She gestured for him to sit.

"You sleepin' all right? All good?" she asked, blowing smoke through her nostrils. Jason, who was nineteen, shrugged as he took a seat. "Yeah, all good."

She tapped ash into the tray. "You like staying here with your aunty Kath?"

He nodded and smiled warmly. "Yeah, Aunty Kath."

"Good. 'Cuz I need your help with something."

"Sure, anything you need."

"I want you to steal John's truck and burn it."

Jason blinked and laughed aloud, completely taken aback. "Are you serious?"

Katherine sat back and crossed her arms, looking him square in the face for a moment. "Yeah, I'm serious as fucking cancer, mate."

"Why would you want to do that?" Jason asked, screwing up his face with bewilderment.

"Because I don't like the way he treats me when we're out. Because he calls me a slut and a moll in front of people at the pub. Then he goes and buys drinks for the other sheilas. I'm sick of it."

Jason shifted uncomfortably in his seat. "Aunty Kath, I'm not sure I…um…"

"Plus, his car has no insurance," she added. "He told me so. I want to hurt him financially, in his wallet." She reached into her purse on the kitchen table and pulled out a handful of one-hundred-dollar notes. She laid them out. "Five hundred. Yours if you do it."

Jason looked at the money. Then at her, stunned.

"And do something else for me, while you're at it." She paused for a moment, taking a drag on her cigarette. "Maybe you could throw battery acid in his face?"

Jason was speechless, almost like he was holding his breath. "No way, Aunty Kath," he said finally, shaking his head steadfastly. "I'm not doing that, Aunty Kath, no fuckin' way."

Katherine darkened in that moment. She reached for the money on the table, folded it, and slipped it back into her purse.

"Right then. Get out."

"'Scuse me?"

"You heard me; get your sorry ass out of my house."

He stared at her again, his mouth slightly open, trying to process what was happening.

"You're not gonna help me? Then you're not stayin' here, end of story."

Within the hour, his bag was packed, and he was walking out the door for the last time. When he was gone, Katherine lit another cigarette while she gathered her thoughts. Then she changed clothes and left the house.

The Top Pub was already noisy when she pulled into the lot. She killed the engine and left the keys in the ignition. She reached for her bag in the front passenger seat and rummaged through it. Her hand found what she was looking for: a metal fork. She scanned the car park—no one was about. Then she took the fork up and dragged it across the side of her neck a few times on both sides. Not hard enough to bleed, but enough to leave angry red lines.

Inside the pub, John was at the bar, halfway through a pint with a couple of the crew when he saw her come in. She stood just inside the doorway first, close enough to be seen by the bar-man. He clocked the marks on her neck; so did John, so did the others. She kept touching them lightly, like she was agitated and in pain. She moved through the bar slowly, not quite looking at John, but not quite avoiding him either.

With alarm, John knew she wanted everyone to see the bruises on her neck. He knew. He caught her eye as she moved across the room toward the back, then he turned back to his mates, laughing a little too loudly at something one of them said. He wouldn't give her the satisfaction of seeing that he was afraid. Even as Colleen's warnings ran through his mind.

34

IT JUST WOULDN'T SETTLE

Monday, February 28, 2000. One day before the murder.

John's boss, Geoff Bowditch, was in the site office when John arrived for work on Monday morning. Peter Cairnes was standing by a filing cabinet and going over some invoices; they had been discussing the replacement of some equipment when Geoff looked up and saw John near the lockers, putting on his hi-vis jacket. Geoff knew right away something was wrong. For one thing, John was late. That was unlike him. John was never late. And he seemed unsteady as he stood there quietly, buckling his vest, doing up his sleeves, one boot partly unlaced, a sheen of sweat on his brow even though it was early and still cool out. Geoff watched him, and something about John's demeanor made him stop talking and sit back in his chair. Then he noticed the scratches and bruises on John's face.

"What's going on, Pricey?" Geoff asked.

John looked out the window toward the yard at the dozers lined up in the sun and took a deep, weary breath, almost as if he was relieved someone was asking.

He sat on the other side of Geoff's desk, and before he knew it, everything came pouring out—the years of Katherine's mood swings and abuse. He explained to Bowditch about last night at the pub, and how when he had arrived home, he had told Katherine they couldn't keep going on like this, that he was done and wanted her out of the house. Geoff gave a short nod. He thought that much was obvious and a step in the right direction.

But, John said, Katherine refused to go, and they had gotten into a terrible fight. He told Geoff that Katherine had attacked him, punching and scratching him in the face.

"The police had come. It was just a mess," John said. "And get this, as I'm leaving for work this morning, I get served with an AVO on her behalf. Like I'm the one that's been bashing her, when it's been her the whole time. Even though she's the one who won't leave. She's living in my house! And I have to keep away from her!? What a fucking joke. And look at this." He pulled down the collar of his shirt to show his boss the puckered scar under his left shoulder. The wound had healed, but the shape was unmistakable. A knife. Deep enough to injure but not enough to kill.

Geoff stared at it. "Jesus, mate," he said. "That's something, John. Wow. When did that happen?"

"About five, six months ago," he said. "I didn't want to make a big thing of it. But now I'm worried, mate. She won't leave, and I don't know what the fuck to do."

Geoff didn't like what the scar implied. He'd known people, mostly women, who got stuck too long in violent situations. It never ended well. John would be only the second male he'd encountered in such a situation. He told John that maybe he ought to hide out for a bit, head north to Queensland. Let things fade. But John shook his head.

"Can't. What about me kids? She could do something to them if I'm not around. I can't let that happen."

"Then you need to get the law involved. You need to get this all documented. And get your own AVO against her. I'm amazed you haven't done it already. Listen, tomorrow, take the morning off. Go down to the courthouse in Muzzie and get yourself sorted. Take all the time you need."

Through the office window, Geoff watched John as he climbed into his truck and drove off toward Bayswater to check on his crew. Bowditch stayed in the office for a while after that, looking at the chair where John had been sitting, picturing the scar on his shoulder, the bruises on his face, and the fear in his eyes. He just shook his head. Something about it all gave him a bad feeling and for the rest of the day, it just wouldn't settle.

While John was heading to the site in Bayswater, Katherine was at his house, still moving through it as if it were her own, waking the children for school, giving instructions, gently prodding them on in her practiced morning routine. Eric and Sarah had breakfast at the table while she packed their lunches.

She drove Sarah to school in Aberdeen, then took the highway out to Muswellbrook to drop Eric at preschool. By mid-morning she was back on the road again, heading south to Scone, where she would meet with her solicitor to show him the scratches on her neck and the other bruises on her body. Then she made an unplanned visit to an old friend, again showing off the bruises. She said they were still sore. She lifted her sleeve, exposing another bruise. Her friend gave them a look with much sympathy.

Later, she saw another friend. This time she pulled her shirt to the side to show the bruise on her breast. "The bastard's not gonna get away with this," she told her friend. "I'm gonna bloody get him."

By lunchtime, she was back in Aberdeen, visiting her sister Joy. She didn't stay long, just enough to show and tell what happened. She drove back to John's house. She moved from room to room, straightening up, rearranging things. On the surface, it looked like a normal Monday. A bit of driving, a few errands, just your average domestic routine. But the shape of the day, in hindsight, was not average for Katherine. Too many roads. Too much circling. She told more than one person about the fight with John on Sunday. She made sure they had all seen the bruises and the scratches. And she got her solicitor to document them in a statement. She was laying down a story—placing markers, subtle as they were, like someone rehearsing not just what she was going to say, but what she would need others to remember.

35

APPREHENDED VIOLENCE ORDERS

Tuesday, February 29, 2000. Twenty-two hours before the murder.

John Price, a forty-four-year-old estranged father of three, walked into the Muswellbrook courthouse at around 8:00 AM. He waited an hour before a clerk appeared and called him through to the chamber magistrate. The room was small and chilled by air conditioning. The magistrate nodded for John to take a seat and begin. John spoke plainly. He said he was there because he wanted to end things with Katherine Mary Knight. The relationship had been on the rocks for some time. They'd been together, off and on, for six years, he said. Over the last few years, she had grown increasingly volatile, controlling, and violent. Their fights usually revolved around getting married (she wanted it, he did not), the house (he was leaving it for his children and not her), and jealousy (she was convinced he would leave her for another woman). It hadn't been easy, John said, and he hadn't always made the best choices, but he was done with her now because he no longer felt safe.

He undid the top buttons on his shirt and pulled the fabric aside to show the knife wound. The magistrate leaned forward. The scar was still a little pink. John even told him something he'd told no one else: that Katherine had threatened on more than one occasion to cut off his penis. He wanted something done as soon as possible, to be documented on paper, so that the abuse would be known. He had realized that he'd been silent for far too long. If something were to happen to him, she could claim self-defense. He needed to make up for years of inaction, he told the magistrate, for which he was now kicking himself.

The magistrate explained the process. John would need to provide details, dates, a sworn affidavit. He would be the applicant. She would be served notice. John listened carefully. By mid-morning, an interim Apprehended Violence Order had been issued on behalf of one John Charles Thomas Price, for the purposes of preventing one Katherine Mary Knight from entering the applicant's home or workplace. The terms were clear. But as John left the courthouse, with the paperwork tucked inside a manila folder under his arm, he wondered if the order would even be followed.

He walked across the courthouse parking lot briskly. The sky had that bright, colorless glare that could be blinding and warned of high temperatures. Back in the ute, he turned the ignition, cranked the AC, and drove to work, hoping that today would mark the beginning of a new life without Katherine.

As John was making his way to Bowditch, Katherine was walking into the Muswellbrook police station, furious over receiving John's AVO while she was at John's house, which meant she had to leave the property immediately. She spoke to an officer at the front desk, a policewoman, who lodged her domestic violence incident report. Katherine showed all her bruises, told the officer about the fight on Sunday, when John tried to kick her out of *their* home. The policewoman took Katherine's statement and advised her to see a doctor right away, to have the bruises documented.

Katherine left the station and drove to her daughter Natasha's house to see her two-year-old granddaughter, Angela. While she was there, she rang the doctor's office and booked a late afternoon appointment in Scone for 4:30 PM.

She then had a cup of tea and watched a television show with her granddaughter crawling across her lap. For the next hour or so, she was the matriarch again. Three generations of women in the same house.

Just before three o'clock, Katherine left her daughter's house to collect Sarah and Eric from school. From there she went to her sister Joy's house to retrieve her video camera—Joy had been holding on to it since John forbade it in the house after the Howick Mines incident. Katherine said she wanted the camera now to capture her granddaughter's affection for her. "She was giving me heaps of kisses and cuddles," Katherine had said. "I want to get it on tape."

By 4 PM, with Sarah and Eric parked at Joy's for the afternoon, Katherine was back in the car, driving to Scone. The GP's office was cool comfort. She didn't complain of any ailments. She didn't want any painkillers. She only wanted the doctor to make a note of her bruises and photograph them. By the time she left the clinic, the sun was inching toward dusk. She had the camera; the kids were at Joy's. And dinner was still to come. Followed by the night ahead.

Around 6 PM Katherine quickly dropped in to her cottage on MacQueen Street to collect some money for the "special dinner" she had promised her kids. She dropped John's AVO, torn to pieces now, on the dining table. She grabbed a bottle of perfume from her bedside table and some movies on DVD before heading back out into the evening.

Outside, the heat had broken, but the air was still warm. She got into her red van and drove back to her daughter's house. John was inside the Top Pub with a beer in front of him when Katherine drove past in the red LiteAce. If she had had a sixth sense, she might have felt it then—her name carried in the mouths of the patrons, her presence alive in the conversation unfolding between them around the bar.

John was not in good shape. He was telling the few around him, including the bartender, that he'd gone to the courthouse that morning, where he had secured an interim order against Katherine. But it hadn't brought him the peace he had hoped for. The bartender listened while she poured another pint. John was well-liked at the Top Pub. He never caused them any trouble, and he was always cheerful. But today, he was off. Slouched and slower than usual, his eyes darting when the pub door opened, expecting it to be Katherine.

Frank walked in not long after and slid onto the barstool beside him. He noted the bruises straightaway. "Oi, the red hen's been at ya?"

"You're not the first one to comment," John replied, smiling thinly.

Frank leaned in a little. "Mate, you ought to be real careful. She's gonna get you one of these days."

John shook his head. "Nah. Not if I can help it." But his tone didn't quite match his demeanor. Frank could feel the anxiety emanate from him like a vapor. John was not just worried or stressed—he was genuinely scared. And that fear had sunk into him, into the way he spoke, the way he moved.

Eventually, John said it. "But, if you see me vehicle there in the morning, don't bother coming across. Ring the police." Frank didn't laugh. There was no comeback for that. They sat in silence for a few minutes after that, watching the bubbles rise in the beer.

Katherine arrived at her daughter Natasha's house just before 7 PM with Eric and Sarah. She had the video camera with her and made a deliberate show of setting it up, gushing about the kisses Angela had showered on her that afternoon. She wanted to capture a maternal version of herself—the devoted mother, the doting grandmother.

She fussed over the angles, made sure the children were close, affectionate, clean, and smiling. The resulting footage showed Natasha's toddler, Angela, bouncing on Katherine's knee as Katherine sat back in the lounge chair, smiling, cooing, crooning in grandmotherly tones. Sarah and Eric played nearby, unaware or uninterested in the camera's gaze. There was laughter and soft talk, but also something more strained running beneath it. Off-screen, a woman's voice—possibly Natasha's—could be heard complaining about housework, about being tired, about the long, unrelenting strain of the past few months. Then came quiet sobs in the background.

Katherine turned her attention to her youngest daughter, Sarah, who was now curled beside her on the lounge. She pulled her in close, brushed the girl's hair with her fingers, and spoke quietly, like a mother passing down something sacred. She told Sarah to make sure she kept the pram—the one her own mother, Barbara, had given her when she was about Sarah's age. A thread of legacy, handed from grandmother to mother to daughter.

"I love you very, very much, my darling girl," Katherine told Sarah. Later, when no one else was in the room, Katherine turned the camera on herself. "I love all my children," she said, looking straight into the lens. "And I hope to see them again."

When she was done with the filming, Katherine took them all out for dinner at the Chinese restaurant in Muswellbrook. They sat at one of the booth tables, plates of sweet and sour pork, fried rice, and honey chicken passed around between them.

While they were still eating dinner at the Chinese restaurant, John had turned up at his neighbor Anthony's door with two longnecks of Tooheys in hand. He was barefoot, Anthony noticed. His gout had flared up again. John went inside, and they sat and talked for a while. Anthony asked how things were going with Katherine following the blowup on Sunday and the AVO he'd taken out.

"I think it might be good. Yeah, haven't seen her all day. They told me she had to leave the house straightaway. So, yeah. I have no idea where she is."

A bit later, Geoff Bowditch dropped in on his way home. He didn't stay long, just enough to check in on John. John told Geoff he'd gotten the AVO and thanked him again for the time off.

It should have felt festive, one of those rare nights when Katherine played the role of provider and nurturer. But Natasha could sense that something was off. She watched her mother closely. Katherine seemed unstable in herself, as Natasha would later testify. When they were done with dinner, Katherine paid the bill and the family left.

The red Toyota van returned to Natasha's house sometime after 9:30 PM. All five of them climbed out and made their way inside to get Angela ready for bed. Katherine sat down in the lounge while Natasha busied herself with their bedtime routine. She rewatched the video she'd recorded earlier of her children and her granddaughter, the moments preserved like an echo from earlier that day. When the video ended, Katherine asked Natasha if Eric and Sarah could stay the night while she went to John's.

"It's late. No sense in driving them home now." Natasha agreed, even though it struck her as odd. Her mother had never before left Sarah and Eric on a school night without notice, or without a clean change of clothes, their school bags, and lunches. It was uncharacteristic of her, and it made Natasha nervous. She walked her mother to the front door. Katherine was already halfway down the step when Natasha blurted out what she was thinking, words that came more from the gut than the mind.

"You're not going to kill Pricey and yourself, are you?" Katherine waved her off with a laugh and got in her car.

Around 9:30 PM, John decided to head home from Anthony's. He was tired, he'd said, and wanted to go to bed. Both Anthony and Geoff tried to dissuade him. Stay the night, Anthony offered. There were spare beds. No rush to go back to St Andrews Street tonight. But John wouldn't hear it. "Nah," he said. "I want to be there when Johnathon comes home in the morning." They told him they'd wake him early, drive him over if he wanted. *Just don't go*. But John's mind was made up. He rose and made for the door. Before he disappeared into the night, he called out, "Love youse forever," and then he was gone.

At home, John found himself sitting on the edge of his bed, unlacing his boots with the slow clumsiness of someone both exhausted and a little drunk. The rest of the house was dark, with only the kitchen light on, which he'd forgotten to turn off after dropping his things on the kitchen table. He had opened a drawer and taken out a blister pack of pills. Sleeping tablets or painkillers—whatever, he didn't care. He swallowed two with the last warm sip of beer from a bottle he'd left on the counter the night before.

The past two days had left him running on nerves and habit. The fight with Katherine on Sunday had shaken him. She'd hit him, clawed at his face, and threatened to cut off his penis. And having to relive it all with the magistrate, all so he could draw his own line in the sand, had wore him out. The folded manila envelope in his possession did little to quell the fear; it didn't undo the fact that Katherine was relentless in her violence, and still out there somewhere. And that he was alone.

His thoughts turned to Colleen. He'd been thinking a lot about his past lately. About a version of his life that had worked once. He'd been thinking about asking Colleen to come back. Earlier that evening, he had almost rung her to float the idea. They had been married for fifteen years and separated for twelve; they shared three children and a lot of history. Maybe there was a way back? He hoped so. He missed her terribly. And the regret that came with his longing flooded his heart with pain. If only he'd paid her more attention, spent more time with her, instead of always hanging out at the pub with his mates. That was all she'd asked of him, just a bit more time together. And he had loved her so much, as he did still, so why had he not given her what she wanted? He struggled to understand his patterns, which meant he couldn't answer the question. But he knew that he wanted to answer it. Before it was too late. He lay in bed, staring at the ceiling. It was his house, his room, his silence. He should have felt safe. But the weight of everything that had happened in the past two days—the past few months, the past few years—it all hung over him.

The beer and the pills had worked their way through his bloodstream, softening the edges of everything. In time, his breathing settled. The tension in his shoulders eased, and he drifted off to sleep, thinking to himself that he had made it through the day—a leap year of all days. A day that would not exist this time next year.

36

THE FORENSIC PSYCHIATRIST[15]

June 22, 2000. Mulawa Women's Correctional Centre. Mum Shirl Psychiatric Wing. Day 2.

"Let's stay there for a moment," Dr. Martin said. "You told the police you didn't remember anything about the murder."

"I don't," she said.

"Nothing at all?"

"No." She looked at him briefly. "All I remember is going to bed."

Dr. Martin watched her closely. "It's interesting, because you remember details from years ago. From your time with David Kellett. From when you were fifteen. You remember how people looked at you. What they said. What your reaction was. But you don't remember what happened that night?"

She stared at the floor. "I had a breakdown."

"Were you angry with him?" Dr. Martin waited. After a moment, "You told your brother Charlie that you were going to kill John."

"That was just talk."

---

15 *Speculative reconstruction inspired by documented psychiatric interviews.*

"You said you'd make out like you were mad so you could get away with it."

She looked up now. Her eyes were flat. "Well, maybe I am. Maybe it's 'cuz I know I am already."

"Let's go back to what you remember. Going to bed, correct? What side of the bed did you get into?"

"I don't remember."

"You remember having sex with John, is that correct?"

"Yeah."

"And I believe you said you remember him going to the bathroom; it's in my notes here."

"Yeah, he went for a pee after we had sex." She looked at the window again, and this time her voice cracked a bit. "He was leaving me."

"That night?"

"Well, he served me with an AVO, so yeah."

"When John came back from the bathroom, what happened next?" She didn't reply. "What happened next, Katherine?"

"All I remember is he had sex with me and I had sex with him. He went off for a pee. I remember him coming back. I don't remember anythink after that."

Dr. Martin crossed his legs and leaned back. "I received information from Detective Wells about things you did after that." Katherine looked at him, waiting. "Do you remember showering?"

Her eyes narrowed. "Not really."

"Do you remember dressing again, into your denim shorts and blue shirt?"

A shrug. "I might have. I don't know."

"And taking John's wallet from the kitchen bench?"

Her lips pressed together. "If you say so."

"Do you remember driving to Muswellbrook?"

A flash of irritation crossed her face. "Like I said, I don't remember much."

"You can't recall standing at the bank machine at 2:32 AM, putting in John's PIN, withdrawing five hundred dollars?"

She shifted in her seat. "I don't know. Maybe. I can't keep track of times."

"You can't recall doing it again three minutes later? Taking another five hundred? Money that I'm told has never been found."

Katherine crossed her legs and arms and held the doctor's gaze.

"And the receipt? The one that shows exactly how much was in Mr. Price's account. The one left in your van. You don't remember that either?"

Her hands gripped her knees as she grew more irritated. "I don't need to sit here and argue with you about scraps of paper."

He paused, then spoke slowly. "Katherine, these are not scraps of paper. These are records. They show a woman who remembered his PIN and knew exactly how much she could take. That isn't nothing. That seems to me to be calculation."

"You can twist it however you like."

Dr. Martin's gaze remained steady. "I don't need to twist it. It's right there. You just don't want to say it out loud." He watched her and waited. But she looked off and started biting her nails and jiggling her legs. He could tell she was growing more agitated the closer they came to the murder. He tapped his pen on the paper.

"All right," he said finally. "Let's take a coffee break." As they left the room, Katherine with prison guards, Dr. Martin on his own, he paused in the corridor and scribbled these words in his notebook: *She remembers everything.*

37

THIRTY-SEVEN TIMES

February 29, 2000. 84 St Andrews Street, Aberdeen, New South Wales.

While John was asleep, Katherine parked outside his house just after eleven. Both of his vehicles were parked where they always were—the truck with the Bowditch logo in front, the white Mondeo by the side of the house. She walked up and sat on the steps of the veranda and lit a cigarette. Winfield Blues. One long drag after another, listening to the sounds of crickets and frogs. A bat whispered across the sky and landed in a fig tree just behind the house. She could hear its particular shrieks and rustling of leaves as it fed on the figs. When she finished her cigarette, she flicked the butt into the lawn and let herself in with her key.

In the kitchen, she found his wallet and keys exactly where they always landed on the counter, beside an empty Tooheys bottle. His work bag was open on the table. Two bowls were in the drying rack. A beer mug upturned in the sink. There were soft drinks in the fridge. She took one.

In the lounge room, she flicked on the TV to channel nine. *Star Trek: Deep Space Nine* was playing. It barely held her interest. She turned it off after about ten minutes and went into the bathroom, where she showered, dried off, walked the hallway barefoot, and padded into the bedroom. She slipped into a black nightie that she'd bought earlier that day at Vinnie's. She got into bed next to John.

He woke up. The air conditioner still murmured. He shifted toward her under the covers and asked, gently, "Where's the kids?" She told him they were with Natasha. He settled back.

There had always been a strong sexual connection between them, even in their worst moments. Fights didn't mean the intimacy stopped. If anything, it became its own kind of bridge—flesh forgiving what words couldn't. Even now, with the weight of restraining orders and final warnings, their bodies still reached for comfort where they once found it. Neither resisted the other. The act itself didn't last long. It didn't need to. No declarations, no softness beyond what was desired.

When it was over, John got up to go to the bathroom. Katherine lay still, listening. The flush came, then the sound of the tap. She reached for her bag beside the bed. Her hand found the handle without searching. The knife was within easy reach. She drew it slowly from the scabbard, cradled it under her forearm across her abdomen, the edge angled inward, and waited.

He came back into the room, unaware. He didn't say anything as he climbed back into bed. The mattress shifted under his weight. The air conditioner kept humming. He lay flat on his back, breathing slowly, and closed his eyes. The room was cool and comfortable, the sheets loose around his waist. His chest rose and fell with the heavy calm that often follows sex. Familiar skin. A familiar bed. It was easier, for now, to believe things were normal. John might have even told himself—if only in some dim, unspoken way—that the last two days had been a mistake, or at least something temporary. He didn't feel her watching.

And then, Katherine rose up and made her move, bringing the knife down into his chest with an immense pounding force. The first jolt took his breath. Shock arrived before the pain. The second jolt didn't allow him time to scream. The third triggered a surge of adrenaline and launched him out of bed. A well-placed knife can slip between layers of flesh before the body knows how to react. But the knowing comes quickly. The sting, the weight, the rupture. The fourth jolt was in his back as he ran for the door. From there, the blade came down again and again. It landed a fifth, a six, a seventh, an eighth, ninth, tenth…fast, pounding, practiced. The knife struck deep. Blood hit the wardrobe in streaks. It spattered the wall and slid down slowly. John stumbled forward, leaving behind his blood-stained side of the bed as he fled the room.

Survival instinct propelled him down the hallway as Katherine followed close behind, bringing the blade down again and again. A trail formed in his wake, streaks of blood across the carpet. His hand reached out for the walls, leaving smears. He found the hallway and plunged toward the light switch. His fingers sliding, leaving a smear of blood across the switch, which remained out of reach. Blood sprayed and dripped from his wounds in steady bursts, arching across the wall.

His breath came short and fast. He turned left and pushed down the hallway, heading for the front door. She followed, keeping pace, driving the knife into his back again and again and again and again. Between the shoulder blades, down through the spine, then his buttocks. The blade sliced through him cleanly and quickly. Twelve, thirteen, fourteen. He didn't cry out. There wasn't enough air for it anymore. Just the sound of the air conditioner humming distantly, his frantic dragging footsteps against the floor, and the ghastly cries of a woman committed to finishing him.

Blood spread everywhere, soaking the runner along the hallway. There was no real chance of escape, though he tried. His shocked, adrenaline-fueled body refused to surrender. It kept him upright. It kept him moving. The front door was in sight. Just beyond it, the cool night air of Aberdeen and a possible escape.

But Katherine didn't let up. The rush of the blood, the noise of his feet dragging, the wet sounds he made as he tried to breathe—it compelled her forward. The blade found the space between his ribs and drove deep. He gasped. It made a hollow, leaking sound—an internal rupture, air pulling through where it shouldn't. She'd pierced a lung. He would have felt it instantly: a pressure blooming under his sternum, the sudden inability to breathe properly. His chest cavity filled with air that had no exit, pushing down into the diaphragm, pressing hard into the organs. He slammed against the wall, leaving a smear of blood on the white paint as he tried to keep moving. By now each breath hurt worse than the last. The air trapped inside him crushed inward— his own breathing working against him. The front door swam in front of him, the exit…it was just meters away.

She stayed with him. Not frantic, not wild. Just moving forward, knife in hand, stabbing him repeatedly. The blood flung from the blade and traced arcs across the walls—sweeps of red as Katherine closed in behind him. She struck with great force, connecting along the back and side of his torso. Miraculously,

John was still on his feet, pushing his body toward the door. His lungs struggled painfully. He could hardly breathe. And he could not scream.

One of his legs began to fail. His right buttock, he realized, had been opened clean. How long had it been since she first attacked him—one minute? Two minutes? He felt the blade sink into his side and split tissue clean through to the lower lung. Blood shot forward from the wound and spattered the wall beside him. He gasped, coughing once, and dropped to the floor. His hand reached the doorknob. He tried to turn it, making it partway. The door open slightly to the night air. But she caught him, drew him back with force, and slammed him into the hallway. Then she stabbed him again—front this time. His abdomen took the blow. She pulled the knife back and stabbed again and again. He was still upright, holding onto the door frame. She stabbed again. Thirty-five. Thirty-six. Thirty-seven.

Her nightdress was wet, the fabric dark and clinging. Her arms were streaked. Blood dripped from the edge of the knife in her hand. John made one last attempt for the door, leaning against the frame. He left a bloodied print on the edge of the timber. Then his body twitched as he took his last breath.

She stood above him, breathing rapidly, her shoulders rising and falling. Her hair had come loose. Her arms ached. The knife was still in her grip. Part of the handle had cracked. She looked down at the mess, at the blood smeared everywhere—on the floorboards, the wall, the doorframe, her hands. Bits of his flesh clung to her. She looked at John. There were no defensive wounds on him. He hadn't fought back at all. Had only tried to flee.

Katherine left the hallway and went into the bathroom, where she peeled off her black nightie, draped it over the tub, and got in the shower. When she was done, she dressed in her denim shorts and sleeveless blue shirt. She went into the kitchen, grabbed John's wallet and her car keys, left the house at around 2:15 AM, and headed for the bank in Muswellbrook.

She returned to St Andrews Street just before four in the morning. She stepped into the kitchen and retrieved her sharpening steel from a drawer. Then she stood over John's body and dragged his corpse into the lounge. There she began to sharpen the blade of her boning knife as she kneeled beside his body.

Her father's voice came to her, as it often did when she got down to work, as if he were close behind, watching her with that same flint-eyed patience he had when she was young, guiding her hands, one large, callused palm over hers, correcting her grip and the pressure.

Katherine paused for a moment, the knife resting in her hand. Her breathing slowed. She imagined the steel rail above her in the slaughterhouse, the chain hooks swinging gently. Imagined herself back in the boning room with the tiled floor sluiced pink and steaming. Her father's words echoed in her mind as she knelt in the lounge, the blade cool and sure in her hand. There was no anger. No wild fury. This was a task like any other. A procedure. Like the work she performed at the abattoir—precise, deliberate, masterful. And always, her father's voice guiding her: *After the slaughter, you dress the corpse….*

38

TWO PLATES

March 1, 2000. 84 St Andrews Street, Aberdeen, New South Wales.

The knife sliced through the flesh of John's corpse—a sharp whisper of steel parting skin and muscle. She worked methodically. Her hands moved with quiet authority. There was no hesitation, only the lucid focus of someone who knew exactly what had to be done. The world shrank to the space between the blade and the body. The scent of blood rose strongly, coppery and sharp, transporting her with its essence. She had experienced this sensation many times before, in the routine and repetition of industrial slaughter.

Her mind turned over the fractured pieces of her life with John. The laughter and the insults, the promises and betrayals, the tangled mess of love and hate. This was the end of all that. She moved with practiced ease, slicing through his flesh to expose the structures beneath. The ribs, the muscles and tendons, the arteries, the soft tissues that gave way beneath her hands. Her thoughts were focused not on pain or remorse but on the control she wielded in that moment. The fragments of herself settled into place—the parts that demanded respect, the parts that would not be hurt again, the parts that transformed rage into ritual. The house felt still around her, time suspended in the low light of early morning and the muted hum of the air conditioner. She paused for a moment to think, the blade resting against John's skin. Then she cut several thick chunks of flesh from his buttocks and set them aside.

At the kitchen counter she reached for the potatoes first, peeled them, then halved each one before quartering them again. The skin curled into a pile at the corner of the cutting board. She pushed them aside. Next, the carrots. She cut the ends off, sliced each one lengthwise, then halved them again. Pumpkin followed. She cut through the rind with both hands on the knife, worked it down the center, then across. She scooped out the seeds and discarded them. The beetroot stained the board as she diced it. She wiped the handle of the knife and went on to the zucchini, then the squash, then the cabbage. She worked in order, not hurrying. When she was done, she arranged the vegetables onto a tray lined with foil and drizzled oil across the top. She rolled the tray slightly to coat the pieces evenly, then she slid it into the preheated oven and closed the oven door.

Next she filled a large pot with water, placed it on the stove, and turned the burner on high. She went back into the lounge where she had posed John's body with his legs crossed and a hand holding the soft drink bottle she had been drinking the night before. She picked up his head from off the floor and went back into the kitchen, dropped it into the pot of water, shifted it to make room for the remaining vegetable scraps, then replaced the lid and left it to boil.

At the stove, she took another pan and began to stir together the ingredients for the gravy. Stock powder. Water. A spoonful of flour. Stirred until it thickened. The mixture darkened and started to bubble. She returned to the counter again and took the cuts sliced from John's rear end and placed them in a frying pan and turned the flame on high. The meat sizzled and browned slowly. She turned each piece until it was cooked through. She checked the head in the pot, pressed a fork into a cheek. The water began to boil. She turned the burner down to low and left the lid half off.

With the meat done on the stove, she lifted the tray from the oven and used tongs to portion out the vegetables—first the potatoes, then the carrots, then the others in order. She arranged a cut of meat beside the veggies, then spooned gravy over the top, letting it run across everything. Two plates. She wiped the counter. Rinsed the board. Dried her hands. At the small table in the kitchen, she placed the two dishes with a set of cutlery. On a pair of folded paper towels, she wrote the names of each recipient: Johnathon Price and Jackie Price, John's children. They would be greeted by the meal when they got home. She took a third chunk of meat and set it on a plate in front of her as she stood at the kitchen counter. The light outside was brightening. She looked at the clock; it was six thirty. John would have been heading off to work now, with the packed lunch she would have made him. She looked down at the meat in front of her, cut away a small piece and tasted it. Then she threw the rest out the kitchen window. Afterward, she took some pills, then took her rest in the bedroom.

INTERIM FORENSIC NOTE 3[16]

June 22, 2000. Mulawa Women's Correctional Centre. Mum Shirl Psychiatric Wing. Day 2.

"This is Dr. Robert Martin with my third forensic summation on Katherine Mary Knight. We are at the Mum Shirl Psychiatric Wing, interview room 4D, Mulawa Centre, approximately two hours into day two, midday break now at 12:35 PM. Today is twenty-second June 2000. This interim note is recorded during a lunch recess.

"Regarding the homicide of John Price, the subject does not exhibit markers of acute emotional dysregulation, or dissociation typically consistent with a spontaneous, emotionally driven act of violence. Instead, the evidence suggests a retaliatory homicide—premeditated and shaped by a psychological trajectory that consolidated after the Howick Mines incident, during which the subject perceived Price as disloyal, humiliating, and ultimately ungrateful, which is shocking to say the least, given what she had done. His refusal to marry her, combined with the revelation that

---

[16] *Speculative reconstruction inspired by documented psychiatric interviews.*

he intended to leave his estate to his former wife and children, appears to have triggered a prolonged campaign of retribution.

"What emerges on further examination is not only a pattern of impulsivity and rage but of something more deliberate. The subject shows, at key moments, a conscious awareness of social optics, legal exposure, and the narrative she wants to control. Her decision to describe the first stabbing of Price as an "accident," for instance, is not suggestive of a dissociative state or psychological break. Rather, it reflects a measured effort to manipulate the perception of events—evidence of strategic thinking, not loss of contact with reality or diminished responsibility.

"This is consistent with a broader behavioral profile that blends emotional volatility with manipulation and cruelty. In her relationships, the subject cycles rapidly between idealization and devaluation—often within the same interaction. While professing love or dependence, she has shown an ongoing impulse to punish those who disappoint or abandon her, and often in ways that are sustained, personal, and calculated. These are not heat-of-the-moment reactions. They are retaliations stored up and executed when the opportunity allows.

"A particularly troubling example occurred in the days leading up to the homicide. The subject enlisted her nephew in a plot to harm the victim, offering him five hundred dollars to steal and burn Mr. Price's car. She later encouraged him to throw battery acid in his face. This incident is significant in several ways. First, it demonstrates the degree of premeditation behind her aggression. Second, it shows her willingness to involve others—especially those vulnerable or easily influenced—to carry out her objectives. There was no indication of remorse regarding the boy's exposure to serious legal risk. Nor did she express concern for the possible harm such an act might cause him. That absence of empathy, combined with her persistence in pursuing revenge through proxies, suggests a deeply ingrained need for control and domination.

"From a diagnostic standpoint, the working considerations include borderline personality disorder with psychopathic features, or alternatively, complex trauma manifesting through maladaptive personality traits—chiefly entitlement, rage, and control-based aggression. Additional assessment is required to clarify the extent of Axis II pathology, particularly Cluster B features. The possibility of co-occurring trauma-based personality dysfunction and psychopathy should not be overlooked.

"During our sessions, the subject claimed several times to have been physically and sexually abused by several members of her family during childhood. She states that this conduct persisted until approximately age eleven. While the veracity of these claims remains unverified—there are no police records—that doesn't mean it didn't happen. Some accounts have been generally supported by information obtained from other family members. The clinical consensus, based on available testimony and interview data, is to accept the claims as substantially credible within the context of her developmental history. In cases of chronic, early childhood trauma, there is often a deeply embedded pattern of rage, mistrust, and distorted intimacy. The subject described her early sexual experiences as coercive and degrading, involving multiple older men. Whether entirely accurate or not, these memories appear to have shaped her internal model of relationships: love as possession and sex as a means of power and control. We know that trauma can leave a person stranded in time. Katherine's adult life certainly bears the marks of something unhealed. I will seek to get more clarity on this matter during the final hours of our session. End interim forensic note three. Time is 12:45 PM."

PART FOUR

39

CHILDHOOD[17]

Late October 1965. Tenterfield, New South Wales.

Katherine and her twin sister Joy sat on the couch in the lounge room one Saturday afternoon in October. It was like any other Saturday, except this was two days before their tenth birthday. Katherine sat cross-legged on one end of the couch, eating an apple. Joy was sprawled lazily on the other end. In between them was a pile of unfolded laundry and the laundry basket was turned on its side under the coffee table, on which were scattered a few stubbies of Tooheys and an ashtray filled with butts. It was one of those Saturday afternoons where the kids would be left in the care of the television for as long as they wanted, which was typically a couple of hours before they got bored and ran outside to see what else was going on.

Mr. Squiggle and Friends was on the ABC. It was a warm afternoon. Sunlight poured in through old frilly curtains, illuminating a small universe of floating dust in the air. Katherine watched intently as Mr. Squiggles, in an episode titled "The

---

[17] *Fictionalized scene inspired by documented claims and research.*

Moon," began to interpret a "squiggle" drawing sent in by two young viewers out of Noble Park, Victoria. Two semicircles and a squiggly line, evidently. Katherine wondered briefly if she should send in a squiggle to be fleshed out by the puppet, with his giant pencil for a nose, but quickly decided against it. She was woeful when it came to anything pencil-and-paper-related, whether pictures or words. No sense in drawing more attention to that.

Mr. Squiggle drew two straight lines beneath the pair of joined semicircles, then he connected those two straight lines with a crude triangle, as you'd find on a sharpened pencil tip, only this pencil was big and had two balls where the erasure would be. It looked remarkably like a penis. Mr. Squiggle declared the drawing finished. Rebecca, the woman in the show who delivered and held the submitted squiggles for the puppet, looked stunned.

"It's finished?" she asked in high-pitched surprise.

"It's a rocket, rocketing past the moon!" Mr. Squiggle shouted with glee.

"Oh…! Oh…" said Rebecca with a hint of concern as she stared at the rocket.

Bollocks, thought Katherine, giggling to herself. It was undeniably a penis. Mr. Squiggle had drawn a penis. She knew what penises looked like. She'd seen her father's in the bath, her brother's when he did a wee out in the yard. And she'd seen her cousin's too. Plus, there was always some defilement in the school textbooks. So, this so-called rocket, lying horizontally as Mr. Squiggle had drawn it, looked nothing like a rocket and everything like a penis. Its tail fins were round, for heaven's sake.

Just then, she heard shouting from her parents' bedroom. Katherine froze, her gaze shifting from the television to the hallway, at the end of which violence was quickly escalating. Joy glanced at her. *Not again.…*

Within seconds, Barbara and Ken erupted into the living room, shouting and shoving each other fitfully, Barbara trying to get away as the girls darted behind the couch. Barbara screamed at Ken, "Get the fuck out!" But he cornered her in the dining area, undoing his belt with his left hand, while grabbing her by the scruff of the neck with his right. He proceeded to slam Barbara against the wall so hard that a school photo of Katherine fell off its nail and crashed onto the floor.

Barbara's face, flushed and bruised, trembled with a defiant rage. She resisted, but mostly with words, a torrent of expletives. *"Fucking bloody cunt…you sorry fuck, nothing but a big bloody hole…!"* Both were oblivious to the girls hiding behind the couch, staring anxiously at this nightmare of domestic violence.

Ken unzipped his pants as he restrained Barbara, his erection poking out. He clamped her wrists together tight, kicked her legs out from under her, and slammed her to the floor. It wasn't until he was thrusting into her in a drunken frenzy on the linoleum that Barbara caught sight of the girls hurrying past and making for the back door.

Outside, Katherine and Joy watched the lounge room rape through the haze of curtains as they stood in the garden bed beneath the window. They would wait for the right time to enter the house again, for the right time to act like nothing had happened—again. Katherine watched her mother give in to Ken, as she would later advise the girls to do many times, to just get on with it until it's done.

The image of Ken's rough hands on Barbara's wrists, his drunken assault, her futile resistance. It rooted itself in Katherine's young mind and body, twisting and knotting with a fearful curiosity. Ken collapsed on top of Barbara with a heavy postcoital grunt.

"There," he said. "That's what you get for mouthing off." He rolled onto the floor beside her and wiped himself with the hem of her skirt. "You oughta know that by now." He got to his feet and grabbed a beer from the fridge, popped it open, and swilled the entire bottle in a few gulps. Barbara lay frozen for a moment, her hands balled into fists at her sides, her skirt torn. The door slammed as Ken left the house. Mr. Squiggles gibbered on cheerfully in the background.

The girls stayed by the side of the house while Ken got in his car and drove off. Joy clung to Katherine's arm, her fingers pressing into her flesh. They watched their father's car disappear up Mount Street. To the pub no doubt. Where else was there to go?

Inside, Barbara sat up on the floor with her legs out in front of her, attempting to light a cigarette with trembling hands, but the match refused to ignite. Finally, she rose stiffly, clearly in pain, her cigarette at last glowing red, and inhaled. She wiped her nose, tidied her hair, patted down her clothing, putting herself back together. She muttered something under her breath as she dragged again on her cigarette, then she ambled stiffly down the hall to the bedroom and shut the door.

Joy reached for Katherine's hand, tugged her away from the window. A light breeze swept through the surrounding eucalyptus. Everything was dead quiet.

"You look just like Mum when you're mad," Joy whispered.

Katherine locked eyes with her sister. In an instant, a tempest took shape inside of her. White-hot and visceral, it churned with alarming speed. It was like a foreign entity. Her eyes changed, and without warning, she slapped Joy hard across the face.

That night, Barbara put dinner on the table for the girls: meat with vegetables and gravy. She sat with them. "You know what your father's like," she said, her voice tinged with something vaguely like pride. "Couldn't get enough of me. Even when I didn't want it."

Barbara talked as if nothing untoward had happened. But she told them how she hated sex, how she never wanted it, how men were filthy and always wanting things from you. She said their father was no different. She said you just have to get through it. You never let them see you break. She said things like this often. Sometimes late at night, standing barefoot in her nightdress, waving a hand in the air like she was in court. Sometimes at breakfast. The details came without warning. What their father liked. What other men wanted. What she put up with. She told them she was done with all of it. That men were only ever out for themselves. A few years later, when Katherine told her mother that one of her boyfriends pressured her to do something she didn't want to do, Barbara didn't look up from her cooking. "Just put up with it and stop complaining," was all she said.

40

WHAT SHE LEARNED

Rural Australia, circa 1950s and 1960s.

The Hunter Valley in early summer was a pleasant place to be. The hills were green from spring rain, horses grazed along the fences, and the vineyards and orchards ran in quiet rows across the lower slopes. The scent of eucalyptus and cattle dung often trailed through the dry wind. The small towns dotting the valley mostly contained fewer than two to three thousand residents. Life typically revolved around cattle farming, mining, slaughter, and pubs.

Katherine was born into this rural tableau on October 24, 1955, in Tenterfield, New South Wales. The abattoir loomed large over her family's history. Her mother, Barbara, née Thorley, was married to Scottish-born Jack Roughan. They had four sons together. Jack moved the family to Aberdeen in the early fifties, where he took a job at the Aberdeen meatworks as a slaughterman. That's where he met Kenneth Knight, and the two became fast friends. A year in, Barbara began an affair with Kenneth, who revealed himself to be a foul-mouthed and violent alcoholic, much like her husband, Jack, whom she left because of his drinking and gambling addiction. The scandal forced Barbara and Ken to flee to Moree without her sons. Barbara had four more children with Ken, including Katherine and her fraternal twin, Joy.

Their house was set back from the road on the edge of town, where the trees thinned out and the grass turned brittle in high summer. A Hills Hoist leaned crookedly in the backyard, its arms tangled with pegs and fading, tattered rags. Inside, everything felt cluttered. Barbara had grown up knowing that her great-grandmother had come from Moree and was a Kamilaroi woman who had married an Irishman. Her Indigenous heritage had not been passed down openly. It was told quietly, inside the house, in whispered fragments. Barbara was proud of it. She identified as Aboriginal, though she understood the consequences of saying so publicly. The region had long held its own codes about race.

Within the household, Barbara's Indigenous roots became a point of conflict. Katherine and her siblings had not been raised to claim any one heritage outright, but the knowledge existed, and it worked its way into things. At school, some of the children said horrible things about Aboriginal people. Katherine didn't talk about it, but she listened. Her mother's identification became a kind of static in the background—present but mostly unspoken.

Outside of her sister, Joy, Katherine didn't have many people she trusted. The only adult in her orbit she seemed to look to with any steady feeling was her uncle, Oscar Knight. He lived just outside town. He broke horses, worked on stations, took contracts that moved him across the Hunter and the northwest. He taught her how to hold the reins and ride, and how to move alongside a horse without startling it. He also taught her to hunt, a skill she took to readily, bringing home skins, skulls, and other souvenirs from her kills. She carried herself with a kind of focus in the bush, moving quietly, deliberately, hardly wasting a shot. The kills weren't just for food. She loved the souvenirs, the bones, pelts, and horns. She loved arranging them in her room like trophies. It was an activity she continued throughout her adolescence, and much of the macabre décor that filled her home years later could be traced back to those early days.

When Oscar took his own life in 1969, something in Katherine came apart. She was thirteen. The news reached her late in the day. There were no explanations given. The adults spoke quietly about it, and her mother made a few calls from the kitchen phone. Katherine didn't ask questions. She stayed in her room for most of the afternoon, sitting on the bed with her back against the wall. She refused to eat dinner. Later she lashed out at Joy and the two went at it in the yard. Blood was drawn and bruises were raised.

In the weeks that followed, she insisted that she had seen her uncle in the paddock behind the house. Sometimes she'd walk out the back door barefoot, down the slope toward the gum trees, and stand still for minutes at a time, looking out toward the fence line, seeing her uncle in the distance, standing perfectly still and somehow conveying restraint and gentleness all at once. Her sister told her not to be stupid. Oscar's name would come up in the house from time to time, mostly from Barbara. She kept a photo of him in the top drawer of her bedside table. Katherine took it once and put it under her mattress.

That same year, the family left their house in Moree and moved back to Aberdeen. Barbara said it made more sense to be near her own people, where the children could walk to school and where they could get help if anything happened. Ken found work again at the abattoir. There were other things going on with Katherine by that time. She had begun fighting a lot. She argued with her teachers. She struggled to sit still in class. Her mother brushed it off as just a phase. It was the move that unsettled her, Barbara said. Still, there were notes sent home. Katherine was suspended for a week after kicking a classmate in the yard. When she was asked what had happened, Katherine said she couldn't remember.

Some things were spoken openly in the Knight household. Some were not. What passed for parenting had little to do with nurture and everything to do with control. Katherine learned early to keep her ears open and her mouth shut—except when she didn't. Even as a child, she had a temper that came on without warning.

There were times late at night, the girls would find their mother in the kitchen while their brothers slept. Barbara would light a smoke, pour a glass of sherry, and start talking. About things Katherine and Joy were too young to be hearing. About Ken. About men in general. About how shit life could be. About sex—violent, loveless, or strange. She described what Ken was like in bed. What he did to her. What he made her do. She spoke of it not with shame, but bitterness. Katherine would sit on the edge of the vinyl chair, her bare feet tiptoed against the floor. She said nothing. But she remembered everything.

Other times, the girls woke to find Ken in the hallway, standing just inside the bedroom door. Or there'd be the sound of the kettle boiling at two in the morning and Barbara screaming at him to *get the fuck off me!* Barbara later warned her daughters about the things men were capable of. "They'll use you up and leave you broken; believe me, I know."

At school, Katherine didn't do well with sitting still. She had the look of someone always waiting to explode. One teacher described her as "high-strung with flashes of brilliance," though nothing ever came of that brilliance academically. She could barely read or write. She picked fights without a clear cause. Sometimes because someone looked at her too long. Sometimes because they didn't.

There were days when she came into school sullen and stone-faced, and then she would crack a joke that would have the other kids rolling. And then there were days she flipped a desk over out of rage. Once, a boy from year five tried to grab her by the hair in the playground. She bit his ear and tore through cartilage.

Unlike her sister Joy, who was more outgoing and confident, Katherine moved through the corridors of childhood more shyly. She wasn't popular, though people knew who she was. The other kids told stories about her—how she could fight like a boy, how her mother was mad, how her old man drank too much. No one said these things directly, but they hung in the collective minds of their peers. Her father was known to whip and beat her with whatever was close at hand: a dog leash, an electrical cord, or his belt.

Once, when she was eight, she had refused to come in from the yard. He dragged her inside by the arm and lashed her across the back until the welts rose in dark ridges. She didn't cry. She held her breath and waited for it to end. Even then she seemed to understand that the one who did not flinch, the one who absorbed the blow without breaking, held a different kind of power. At school, she replayed the lesson. She held a younger girl's face down in the gravel until her cheek split open.

What she learned at home carried into adulthood. The same patterns would emerge years later with the men in her life. The weapon might change, the setting might change, but the logic never did: to control was to frighten, and to frighten was to win.

Her body changed early. She grew tall and slim. A once-unattractive redhead became desirable. Curves drew the eyes of men. She learned to walk faster past the pub on her way home from school. Still, some men called out to her, older men who knew exactly whose daughter she was.

At home, Barbara began warning her more often. "Don't let them in." Or "Keep your legs shut or you'll end up like me." Sometimes, it was colder than that. "You're already ruined. Might as well use it." There was a boy once—lanky, and cocky—who worked at the feed store and was three years older than Katherine. He would do things to her in the bathroom. She told one friend—a girl who moved to Aberdeen from Muswellbrook—that another man had done the same things. The friend said nothing, just stared off, unable to imagine it.

By fourteen, Katherine's name was on the lips of every teacher and half the parents in town after she'd thrown a desk through a classroom window. When asked why, Katherine said, "Because I felt like it." On her last day of school, she came home with her uniform torn and her knuckles grazed. Barbara didn't ask. Katherine sat in front of the television, watching a game show through the static. She felt older than fourteen. She dropped out of high school after that.

With that behind her, she went to work. She wasn't interested in typing pools or cashier work. The abattoir was where she wanted to be. At fifteen she followed the sound of the siren to the slaughterhouse gates and applied for a job. Her father had worked there, and his name still carried weight.

She was hired first as a general laborer, then as a slicer. They said she took to it unnervingly fast. They said she liked the knives, felt their balance and weight like they were extensions of herself. Blood didn't bother her. The smell didn't either. There was something calming about the work and the routine, about the cool sharpness of the air inside the boning room. She felt in control. Her mother, who had also done her time at the meatworks, called it "men's work," but not with disapproval. There was something almost proud in the way she claimed it.

"You'll never be nobody's fool," Barbara joked, "not with skills like that."

PART FIVE

41

THE PRE-TRIAL HEARING

Monday, October 15, 2001. East Maitland, Supreme Court of New South Wales.

The courtroom was full but quiet. A late-morning sun filtered through the high glass, streaking the timber panels with light. Katherine sat at the defense table with her solicitor, Peter Thraves. She wore a dark blouse and blazer, her hair neatly brushed back into a ponytail, her eyes focused behind prescription lenses. She had not looked toward the public gallery once. Her hands remained folded on the table in front of her.

To the right, the Crown prosecutor, Mark Macadam, held his notes in a plain manila folder. He nodded as Dr. Robert Martin took the stand. Dr. Martin had spent nine hours across two days interviewing Katherine. He took the oath, sat, and adjusted his chair slightly as Justice O'Keefe motioned for the proceedings to begin.

"Dr. Martin, can you share your professional findings as to the matter of the prisoner's culpability?" Macadam asked.

"Based on my clinical observations, in sum, Katherine Knight presents with a complex psychological profile shaped by early trauma, disordered attachment, and personality pathology. She exhibits many features consistent with treatment-resistant borderline personality disorder and psychopathy, marked by volatility, obsession, and retaliatory aggression." He paused for a moment to let that register.

"She also displays a cold, instrumental style of manipulation that complicates any simple diagnosis. This is not a case of transient psychosis. Nor are we looking at the disinhibited violence sometimes observed in acute affective episodes. She was not delusional. She was not confused. There is, in my view, a core pattern of punitive control. What I mean is, the subject does not merely react. She remembers. She stores slights—real or perceived—for a long time and acts upon them with a degree of calculation that speaks to premeditation." He glanced briefly toward the defense table, but not at Katherine, who remained still.

"I believe the homicide of Mr. John Price was not the result of diminished responsibility. In my professional opinion, it was a premeditated act of revenge. Her borderline personality disorder had nothing to do with the murder. What she did on the night was part of her personality, her nature, herself, but it is not a feature of borderline personality disorder. It is not even significantly connected. The evidence, combined with my interviews, supports the conclusion that Miss Knight was fully culpable at the time of the offence."

Macadam looked at his notes briefly. "And just to clarify, did the accused exhibit any signs of dissociation or acute emotional dysregulation at the time of the interviews?"

Dr. Martin shook his head. "No, she did not. In fact, her demeanor was controlled. She was lucid, responsive, and, at times, even strategic in how she framed events. There were a couple of moments of anger and impatience, but no indication of psychotic thought processes or major mood instability during the interviews."

"Very well. Thank you." Macadam sat down. The judge turned to the defense.

"I understand your client intends to enter a plea of not guilty, Mr. Thraves?"

Thraves stood, adjusted his glasses. "That's correct, Your Honor."

Justice O'Keefe nodded again, then leaned back slightly in his chair. His eyes moved from the doctor to the woman seated quietly beside her solicitor.

"Having reviewed the psychiatric assessment and heard the expert testimony, I find that the accused is fit to stand trial. I accept Dr. Martin's opinion that Miss Knight was of sound mind at the time of the alleged offence and that she bears full criminal responsibility. Accordingly, the matter will proceed to trial. Jury selection will commence as scheduled. Court adjourned."

He brought the gavel down and everyone got up to leave.

42

WHAT IT WOULD FEEL LIKE[18]

Monday, October 15, 2001. Mulawa Women's Correctional Centre Visiting Room.

Katherine didn't stand up when the door opened. She merely blinked as her siblings, Joy and Shane, entered the visitors' room. It was early morning in spring, a chill to the air. The room was large and had many tables and stools situated throughout, bolted-to-the-floor furniture, at which inmates sat with people who had come to visit.

The small, round lenses of Katherine's new glasses gave her a slightly pinched look, more schoolmarm than murderer. She wore the standard-issue overalls of the correctional center. After a few minutes of small talk about the kids, and how they were doing, it was on to the elephant in the room.

"They say they're taking it to trial," Katherine told them without ceremony.

Joy nodded. "Yeah, I heard."

---

[18] *Fictionalized scene for dramatic purposes.*

"That shrink, Martin, he said you knew what you were doing. Did you?" Shane asked. Katherine's eyes flicked between them, resting on Shane a beat longer. His gaze was one of deep pain and sadness. "They'll put it all out there," he said. "The photos. What you did." He inhaled, almost choking on the words.

Joy said, "We'll have to sit in that courtroom while they go through every detail. I don't know if I can do it, Kath. And the kids, they'll hear about it all."

"I don't want to talk about it," Katherine interrupted, coming the closest to showing remorse than she had to date.

"Well, you won't have to, 'cuz they'll be doing that for you at trial," Joy said. "Everyone will be talking about it. They're already talking about it. It's all over the papers, the TV news. They even got it covered *overseas*. So yeah, fine, don't talk about it. Thanks. We gotta live with this now."

Shane reached for Joy's arm, a gesture to keep her calm. Katherine sat back, her expression vague. She looked at the scratched steel tabletop and traced the line of an old gouge with her finger.

"I didn't think it would come to trial," Shane said softly. "I thought for sure they'd realize you weren't…. I mean, how could you be in your right…mind? How could anyone who does… what you did. What they're saying you did, the…" He stopped short of saying it. He couldn't bring himself to speak of the butchering. "How could that be considered right mind?" They sat like that for a while longer. Three people bound by blood and trauma, with so much unspoken pain between them. The guard indicated that visiting hours were over.

Joy stood, her face set. "Don't say anything stupid in court. People are already calling you a monster." She gave Katherine a quick, strained hug. Then she turned and moved off. Shane followed, a little slower. He couldn't hug her yet. He looked back once and was gone.

After they left, Katherine was escorted back to her cell. She lay back on the mattress and stared at the ceiling. Concrete walls, the scratch of the wool blanket against her skin. Monster. It was a word she'd heard before. At school. At the pub. In her own mind. She thought of her mother, and the tales she would tell the girls over cigarettes and tea at the kitchen table. The talk often centered on sex and men and betrayal. All of it mixed up, adult chatter spooned too early into a child's mind. She remembered her father's anger, the way it could turn rooms alarmingly still. She remembered other things, too, things she had never said out loud. Waking in the dark with the door half open. Someone sitting too close. A hand that didn't belong. Sometimes she told herself it wasn't real. Other times she believed it was the only real thing, and that's why she turned out the way she did. She thought of the trial. Of the photos they would show, the videos, the testimony, and the drawn faces of the jury. She imagined them looking at her, trying to decide what she was. A battered woman? A cold-blooded killer? A damaged child? A mad person?

She had never been able to stop her rages. Maybe that was the truth of it. Would she ever be able to stop herself? Would she ever find peace? She didn't know. And then…a thought struck her. It was one she had never had before and one she never would have expected to have. She wondered suddenly what it would feel like to be forgiven. Not by the court, not by the Prices or the judging world—but by herself.

43

REGINA V. KATHERINE MARY KNIGHT

Justice Barry O'Keefe entered the courtroom shortly before 10 AM. He settled behind the bench without preamble, giving a short nod to the barristers before him. The dock sat empty. Katherine Knight was not present. She had been excused from this procedural sitting.

"Good morning, Mr. Macadam. Mr. Thraves," he said. Mark Macadam stood first. "Your Honor, the Crown requests that a formal judicial warning be given to potential jurors tomorrow morning. Due to the nature of the evidence and the severity of the allegations, we believe such a warning is not only appropriate but necessary."

Justice O'Keefe nodded slightly, his pen already moving across a lined pad.

Macadam continued. "The material facts are, as Your Honor is aware, uniquely distressing. Graphic and violent. In the Crown's view, it is essential that prospective jurors are afforded the opportunity to withdraw if they feel, after hearing the warning, they cannot engage with the evidence impartially."

O'Keefe glanced briefly toward the defense. "Mr. Thraves?"

Peter Thraves rose, buttoning his coat as he did so. "Your Honor, the defense concurs. We recognize the potential for emotional harm, particularly where jurors may have personal histories or sensitivities that intersect with the content of the case."

O'Keefe looked between them. "I agree, gentlemen. I will address the jury panel directly. I will advise them of their right to seek excusal should they believe, in good conscience, that they are unable to hear out the evidence." He paused, then looked down at the bench. "It should go without saying that what they will hear—if selected—may be deeply confronting. But the justice system requires, above all, clarity and fairness. That applies to the accused, and to those selected to hear the case."

Thraves nodded. "Yes, Your Honor."

"Is there agreement on language?" the judge asked. "I don't intend to sensationalize."

"Yes, Your Honor," Macadam replied. "We trust your discretion."

There was a beat of silence while Justice O'Keefe wrote something down. Then he closed and tapped the spine of his notebook once against the bench.

"I will finalize the wording and have it circulated before the end of the day. If there are any issues, you may raise them first thing tomorrow." Both barristers murmured assent. "Then we are adjourned until tomorrow," the judge said and brought down his gavel. The Crown and the defense both thanked the judge and didn't linger very long. They gathered their papers and left as Justice O'Keefe stepped down and disappeared through the door behind the bench. By 10:20 AM, the courtroom was empty again.

44

THE WARNING

Wednesday, October 17, 2001. Case Number 70094/00. Supreme Court of New South Wales.

The courtroom was full. The murmuring of small talk and movement and throats being cleared as the jury pool waited for the proceedings to begin. Justice Barry O'Keefe entered and took his place on the bench as the courtroom quieted and settled in his presence. After the formalities, Justice O'Keefe looked down over the crowd of potential jurors. One hundred and twenty names, pulled from the electoral roll. Most had never been inside a courtroom before.

The judge began. He sat upright, hands resting on the bench, his voice steady and without flourish. "Ladies and gentlemen," he began, addressing the assembled panel. "What you will hear during the course of this trial will not be typical or ordinary. This is not a typical or ordinary case." A few on the panel shifted slightly in their seats.

"The evidence, if you are selected to serve, will be extremely graphic," the judge continued. "Most of it will stay with you long after the case is over. Most of it may disturb you. I say that, not to frighten you, but to prepare you." He paused for a moment, searching for the right words.

"As such, it is important that you understand you are not expected to look at what you cannot endure. The law does not demand that. If, after hearing this warning, you feel that you cannot continue, you may come forward and be excused." He scanned the room, allowing the message to sink in. "There will be no shame in that," he added. "No judgment."

One woman at the back lowered her gaze to consider the judge's warning. A man in the front row cleared his throat as he listened intently. Everyone listened *intently*.

"The trial itself will be lengthy," the judge continued. "The prosecution will present its case first. That will include testimony, forensic reports, and a number of photographs and videos of the crime scene. Those images will depict the deceased and the crime scene in a state that, frankly, many people would find confronting.

"The defense will then respond in kind. The court will also hear from expert witnesses. Pathologists, crime scene specialists, psychiatrists, and police testimony. You will be asked to listen carefully. To evaluate the evidence with attention and seriousness. But more than that, you will be asked to look at things most people should never have to see." He let the silence gather around them again while he made a note on some papers in front of him.

"These are not images from television. These are not reconstructions. These are the real aftermaths of violence." The panel remained still and attentive, almost transfixed by what the judge was saying, as though they were trying to imagine for themselves the gruesome things of which he spoke.

"If you believe you are able to hear that evidence and remain fair, impartial, and grounded in the facts alone, then the court asks that you stay." He scanned the panel briefly. "If, however, you believe that serving on such a case would compromise your ability to remain fair-minded—or if the emotional toll would be simply too high—please make that known." He went on to remind them that Katherine Knight, pleading not guilty, was innocent until proven otherwise by a jury of her peers. That the charge was serious, but the burden remained with the prosecution. No assumption should be made. A jury must be impartial.

As the judge was speaking, a court clerk entered and walked quietly through the room, stepping forward for permission to approach the bench. Justice O'Keefe waved him over. The clerk handed the judge a piece of paper. Justice O'Keefe took it without speaking and read it once, then again. His expression changed only slightly. He set the note aside, straightened his posture, and looked out over the courtroom.

"I'm sorry, but this session will have to be adjourned," he said. The pool of prospective jurors looked around at each other, confused. "I understand this is unusual. But the circumstances that have arisen are unusual as well." There was no further elaboration. The note remained unread by anyone else. The judge's tone held no urgency, only finality. "You are hereby requested back here tomorrow morning at nine-thirty for a ten o'clock start." He looked down at the clerk, gave a nod, then raised the gavel. The sound of it marked a close to the proceedings. The jury candidates stood. A few exchanged looks, unsure if something had gone wrong. Counsel gathered their papers and moved off in quiet discussion.

45

THE PLEA

Thursday, October 18, 2001. Case Number 70094/00. Supreme Court of New South Wales.

At 9:30 AM all but five of the original jury pool returned to the courthouse. Guided by court staff, they moved quietly into the courtroom and took their seats in the public gallery. The usual shuffling followed—files exchanged, screens adjusted, the low rustle of voices held just under the threshold of formality. No announcement had yet been made regarding jury selection.

John Price's three children entered the courtroom with their mother, Colleen. They walked in a close group, holding each other up emotionally. At the back of the room, on the right-hand side facing the bench, they found their seats. From there, they were about ten meters from the dock, where Katherine Knight sat forward on the wooden bench, her back to them. Two uniformed officers sat behind her.

The courtroom was divided. Journalists covering the hearing sat to the judge's left, pens ready, notepads balanced on knees or desks. To the right, beyond the bar table, were members of the public, court staff, and police. At exactly 10 AM, Justice

Barry O'Keefe entered through the side door and approached the bench. As he moved into view, the courtroom stood. The judge nodded once to the bar table. Counsel for the Crown and the defense returned the nod. Court officers followed. The journalists stood as well, lowered their heads in a nod, and sat again when prompted. A formality for all but the public and prospective jurors. The judge's associate rose and read the arraignment.

"For that, Katherine Mary Knight, on or about the twenty-ninth of February, 2000, at Aberdeen in the state of New South Wales, did murder John Charles Thomas Price." The formal call for a plea followed. All eyes in the room turned to the dock. Katherine was asked to stand.

"How do you plead?" asked the judge.

"Guilty, Your Honor," Katherine said, sending a stilled hush through the courtroom. Colleen and her children looked at each other, wondering if they had heard correctly. No one was expecting it. Her defense had entered a plea of not guilty during the pre-trial hearing.

The judge addressed Katherine directly. "You understand, Miss Knight, do you, the effect of changing your plea to guilty?"

She looked at him, her face unchanged. "Beg your pardon?"

"You understand the effect of that plea," the judge repeated. "That is, that you are admitting to the charge of murder?"

"Yes, Your Honor."

"You have taken counsel's advice, have you?"

"Yes, Your Honor."

"And I understand that you have had the opportunity to consider the matter overnight?"

"Yes, Your Honor."

"And you are content to lodge that plea, is that correct?"

"Yes, Your Honor."

"Okay, you may take your seat."

Katherine sat down. Behind her, John Price's family remained still for a moment. Then something broke open. His daughter, seated closest to the aisle, put her hand to her face. Johnathon looked down at his knees and let out a breath, as if he had been holding it in all that time. Jackie started to weep with this gift of closure. Colleen reached for her bag, her hand searching without looking. She found a small pack of tissues and passed one to Jackie.

They had been preparing themselves for a trial. They had been told it would take weeks. The witness list had been read to them. Photographs, and videos, they were told, would be shown in open court and described aloud. They had rehearsed the sequence in their heads. They had each made decisions about when to look up and when not to.

But as they would later learn, the day before this turn of events, when the prospective jury pool had been assembled, Katherine had sent a message via her solicitor saying that she would change her plea. The judge had received the note while preparing the jurors, which prompted him to adjourn proceedings before they even got started. The Crown had not known in advance. Price's family had hoped for this, but none of them had believed it would actually happen.

Hearing it in court, the word had landed differently. It felt like a great weight had been lifted. The courtroom held still. The jurors, still seated in the gallery, glanced toward one another, uncertain of their purpose. The judge looked toward the Crown prosecutor and the defense. Both sides gave slight nods. A clerk stepped forward to remove papers from the bench. The judge made a brief note on the file before him, then turned again to address the courtroom.

"In light of the plea entered, there will be no requirement for a jury trial."

He turned to the jury box and addressed them plainly. "Ladies and gentlemen, your services are no longer required in this matter." Some looked toward the dock at Katherine. A few shifted in their seats. "I thank you for your attendance and for your willingness to serve," Justice O'Keefe said. "You are now discharged."

A court officer approached the jurors and asked them to follow. They rose and filed out, exiting quietly, their footsteps soft against the carpeted floor. Once they were gone, the courtroom settled again. Justice O'Keefe addressed the bar table. The trial, he said, would not proceed. The plea had been accepted. The case would now turn to sentencing. They now had to decide how much jail time was appropriate for the crime.

46

THE SENTENCING HEARING

Tuesday, October 23, 2001. Case Number 70094/00. Supreme Court of New South Wales.

At ten o'clock, the television above the reporters flickered to life, showing the crime scene. The screen hung high on the wall, angled downward, casting light over the heads below. Justice O'Keefe remained in his chair, the red fabric rising tall behind him. He did not look at the wall-mounted monitor. He watched instead on a small portable monitor placed on his bench.

Katherine had requested permission to leave the room while the video played. She didn't say why, but it was likely she did not want to watch the carnage she had created. She was led through a side door and down a short passage to a holding cell. The floor in the holding cell was sealed concrete, the bench poured from the same material. A stainless-steel toilet and hand basin were mounted on the back wall. The front of the cell was thick Perspex glass, offering no privacy. A brass padlock bolted the door. A camera in the corner watched her from above. There was no mattress, no blanket or pillow, no softness. Katherine simply sat. Then she lay back and stared upward at the yellow ceiling and waited.

Soon the video played. It began with the outside of the house—St Andrews Street. Then moved to the interior, to the crime scene. The bedroom was first. The video showed the green bedsheets stained with blood. The camera panned slowly across the mattress, then to the wall, where there existed more stains. Smeared handprints. Blood spray. The lens followed the trails of blood down the hall, then the edges of the skirting boards, panning up to more stains on the walls—some narrow, others fanned wide. Drops turned to pools. One long streak marked a collapse.

The camera slowed at the archway. John's legs were visible first—one foot crossed loosely over the other. It moved in closer to show more clearly that his skin had been removed. That he had been beheaded. And had many, many knife wounds.

The camera operator walked to the other side of the lounge. The lens picked up fragments—flecks of blood and flesh on the coffee table, a broken frame, and a scrawled note. Then it moved into the kitchen. The screen showed the suit of skin hanging from the archway. A body emptied and inverted, left to dry in the air between the two rooms.

Beyond that, the camera moved to the kitchen sink. Dirty utensils. A pile of vegetable peelings. An ant trail crawling along it all. The lens focused on the two dinner plates. Knife and fork and spoon settings. The shot widened to reveal a tray on the stovetop. Next to it, a pot. The lid was lifted. Inside, the boiled head of John Price. No reaction came from the gallery. None was permitted.

At the bench, the judge's face held steady. He kept his eyes on his portable screen until the video ended. A clerk pressed a button on the remote, and the screen went black. The sentencing hearing could now begin.

Katherine was returned to the dock. Her solicitor leaned in to say something to her, but she didn't respond, only kept her eyes forward. The court officer beside the judge's bench adjusted the microphone on the stand, then stepped back. The first witness was called.

Detective Bob Wells, who had led the initial investigation, approached the witness box. After taking the oath, he sat and answered procedural questions from the prosecution. Senior Constable Scott Matthews followed. He took the stand quietly, gave his oath, and leaned forward slightly. He recounted first arriving at the scene on St Andrews Street, and the events as they unfolded on the day.

"I probably wouldn't have gone in the house if I had known what it was," he admitted. The courtroom remained quiet. A woman from the office of the director of public prosecutions took notes beside the Crown prosecutor. Photographs were tendered during questioning. Justice O'Keefe reviewed them briefly, then set them aside. The detectives continued answering each question directly. When he finished, the prosecutor thanked him and returned to the bar table. The judge looked toward the defense.

"Any cross-examination?"

"No questions, Your Honor." The next to be called were character witnesses, beginning with Cheryl Sullivan, who had known Katherine for many years and had considered her a good friend. Cheryl was asked about Katherine's relationship with John. "She dearly loved him, very much, I'm afraid. She was so wrapped up in him. That's what she used to tell me." Her voice quivered slightly as she continued. "She was really nice to me and my children. We would joke around, go power walking, to the pictures, to town. She would babysit my children. I have never seen a bad side to her, actually, not at all, not once. I never did."

Next came Robin Smith, who had worked with Katherine at the abattoir. Asked to describe the prisoner's character, she spoke without hesitation. "You couldn't find a nicer person than her, and she loved her sewing and embroidery and all that. Fantastic at anything like that. She was. But once you crossed her, that was it. I don't know whether you'd call it scatterbrained, but, you know, she was always hotheaded, and that type of thing. She was a nice person as long as you were nice to her and she thought you didn't do anything to hurt her, but then she could turn on you like anything. That was just Kath."

Testimony from family members followed. Natasha Kellett spoke first. "She was a good mum, and there is no doubt about that. I couldn't have asked for a better mother. I used to get smacked hard—Mum grew up that way. So that was the way things were."

Shane Knight followed next. "She was a good mother, a real good mother."

Then Barry Roughan, Katherine's half-brother. "Katherine had a heart of gold. It was just the stupid things she done, you know. The way she'd carry on with Pricey. It was just stupid some of the things she done. As I said, she would go and do all this to hurt him and five minutes later, she's back with him. That was her life…. It was just the usual thing. They fought today, made up and kissed tomorrow, and then fought again the next day—that was their relationship. It was a bad relationship, and everyone in the town knew that."

Katherine did not look at the witnesses. She did not look toward the bench or the prosecutors. Her posture remained unchanged, her eyes remained fixed ahead. The hearing continued in this way for five days. She had a change of clothing for each day. A white two-piece suit one day, a floral dress the next, a black pantsuit the third. Some days she came to court with a high ponytail, a fountain of red hair erupting from the top, listening without reaction. She was what one would call a model prisoner.

Until the sixth day, which began with the playing of a home video Katherine had filmed months earlier at her daughter Natasha's house. Katherine sat in the dock, eyes trained on the screen, watching the footage as it opened on a school concert in which her youngest daughter, Sarah, was performing. It then showed scenes of her granddaughter bouncing playfully on her knee, then Sarah and Eric playing on the floor. Then a hallway family gathering, voices off camera. Near the end of the recording, Katherine turns the camera on herself.

"I hope to see all my children again," she said to the lens, giving the unspoken impression to all in the courtroom that this might have been a farewell video. At 2:05 PM, the Crown prosecutor, Mark Macadam, rose from the bar table and called his third witness, Detective Senior Constable Peter Muscio. A man in a dark suit approached the witness box. He took the oath, gave his name and rank, and confirmed his position as head of the forensics unit, then attached to the Maitland Crime Scene Section. Katherine continued to watch from the dock. Macadam stepped forward with his first question.

"Detective Muscio, could you describe to the court your role in the investigation on St Andrews Street?"

Muscio nodded. "Yes. I arrived at the scene that morning at approximately eight-thirty and remained there for the duration of the day and was still at Muswellbrook Police Station until four the following morning, finalizing exhibits and processing all the evidence." Muscio went on to give a careful account of his method: how the scene had been secured, how items were photographed, collected, and logged. On a trolley beside the witness box sat several sealed evidence containers. One by one, Muscio referred to them. "These are the three knives used in the murder and subsequent dissection of the victim," he said. "As well as the stainless-steel meat hook recovered from the scene." He lifted the first knife, a long-bladed instrument with a yellow handle. The handle was darkened by fingerprint powder. He held it with gloved hands and addressed the judge.

"Your Honor, this knife measures thirty-one and a half centimeters. It was recovered from the kitchen."

Justice O'Keefe reached for a pair of blue latex gloves, which he slipped on before taking the weapon. He turned it slowly in his hands.

"There is a broken piece," the judge said. "And I can see what appears to be a finely honed edge. There is blood—perhaps skin—and some hair adherent to the blade."

The Crown prosecutor spoke then. "Your Honor will see in some of the postmortem photographs there is one there of the skull, which has a little chunk of it cut out, so that may explain… the gap in the blade."

Muscio reached for the next exhibit. A smaller, yellow-handled knife. Like the first, its grip was stained black from fingerprint powder. He held it briefly to show the court, then set it down and lifted the third item: a black-handled paring knife with a worn, blunt edge.

"These were recovered from the kitchen," he said. "This one," he gestured to the yellow-handled blade, "was found on the sink.

The black-handled paring knife was located on the breakfast bar." He paused for a moment. "DNA analysis was performed on all three. The profiles obtained were consistent with those of the victim and the assailant."

Justice O'Keefe looked up. "All three were used by the prisoner?"

"Yes, Your Honor. That's what the results indicate."

Macadam rose again. "Detective, can you speak to the apparent function of each blade?"

Muscio gave a slight tilt of his head. "I can't be sure of the exact use of each knife. But there was no significant staining on the smaller one. It may have been used in the preparation of vegetables."

"And the other two?" Macadam asked.

"They were suitable for inflicting the major injuries sustained by the deceased."

Macadam stepped closer to the witness box. "The large knife," he said, "was located fairly close to the body?"

"Yes," Muscio replied. "It was recovered from the carpet nearby."

It was at this stage that Katherine's composure began to fracture. When the paring knife was held up, Katherine leaned forward. Her jaw moved slightly. One of her hands lifted, then lowered again. She jittered in her seat. As Muscio spoke about the injuries, her mouth tightened. She looked toward the Crown, then back to the knives; her shoulders began to rise and fall.

Muscio continued, naming the positions of the weapons, the blood traces, the DNA. Katherine looked down at her lap, then back up. Her fingers moved—tapping her knees, then clenching into a fist. The judge removed his gloves and set them aside. He didn't look at her. The courtroom held still, but Katherine shifted again. She turned her head toward the witness box, her eyes sharp now, her breathing audible. The officer behind her leaned forward slightly, watching the side of her face.

Peter Muscio was asked to give his opinion on the sequence of events the night John Price was killed. He kept his voice clear and steady as he described what he believed had taken place. "In my opinion," he said, "the deceased was attacked in the bedroom and then tried to flee down the hallway. Once he was killed, the accused dragged him onto the carpet in the lounge, where she skinned and decapitated him." He paused and looked at the Crown prosecutor. "The head was later carried into the kitchen…"

As he spoke, a low sound began to rise from the dock. Katherine sat with her eyes closed. Her teeth were clenched, the muscles in her jaw twitched. A faint keening noise began to issue from her throat. The sound didn't stop. It came in pulses. Her body rocked once, then again. Justice O'Keefe looked at her briefly but said nothing.

Muscio continued. "It was placed in an aluminum boiler and left to cook on the stovetop." The sound from the dock grew sharper. Her low moans started again. Katherine's head moved slightly from side to side. Her eyes remained shut. Her top teeth pressed into her bottom lip.

"At some stage later," Muscio continued, "the pelt had been hung from the top of the dining room doorway on a stain-less-steel hook." Katherine's hands gripped the edge of the bench in front of her. Her body had started a short, rhythmic rocking motion. She didn't open her eyes. No one in the gallery moved. The officers behind her sat alert. The lawyers turned to look at her. Still, Peter Muscio went on. "The blood trail leads from the lounge to the kitchen, passing through the central doorway," he said. "That path—those drops—suggest the door was open at the time. Clean trajectory. No spatter on the frame, no smear consistent with it being ajar." He turned toward the bar table.

"When we found the pelt the following morning," he continued, "it was hanging from the center of the archway between the two rooms. A stainless-steel butcher's hook had been driven into the upper timber." He cleared his throat and looked at the judge. "The pelt took up most of the doorway."

Katherine's shoulders curled forward and her eyes were closed tight. The sound that came out of her was somewhere between a moan and a stifled cough. One of the guards behind her pressed his knee gently to the back of her bench. Muscio glanced at her, then back at his notes.

"I removed it myself. It was quite heavy…." His voice caught for a moment on the word heavy, but he pushed through. "I wasn't looking forward to it," he said. "It had dried somewhat, stiff in parts, but it was intact." A few seats back, one of Price's daughters buried her face in her hands. Katherine leaned forward, teeth grinding visibly. Her top lip had curled over.

"Excuse me, Your Honor," came a voice from the bar table. It was Mr. Thraves, her defense attorney, rising halfway from his chair. "I do apologize for interrupting, but I have some concerns for the prisoner." Justice O'Keefe raised his eyes to look at Katherine, then to her attorney. "Go on, Mr. Thraves."

"She appears to be in a state of mounting distress, Your Honor. I'm not sure how much more she's capable of hearing at present."

"I'm sorry, Mr. Thraves, but the prisoner will have to stay here while the evidence relating to these matters is given," said Justice O'Keefe.

"I was going to ask, Your Honor, if Your Honor could adjourn for five minutes so that I can assess, in a layman's way, the state she is in," pressed Thraves. The judge turned his gaze back to the dock. Katherine was rocking again, her lips pressed into two thin lines, her hands gripping the timber in front of her. Her jaw opened and shut, the sound of her teeth faint but audible in the silent courtroom.

"All right," said O'Keefe. "I am prepared to grant a brief adjournment. Testimony will resume in five minutes while defense attends to the prisoner."

After the short adjournment, the courtroom resumed under the steady gaze of the Justice. He adjusted his glasses and looked down at the bench, where Mr. Thraves had risen once more.

"Your Honor," Thraves began, "before proceedings continue, I wish to place on record my ongoing concern for the prisoner. She appears to be experiencing significant psychological distress, perhaps dissociation, or at the very least, a non-receptiveness to the nature and content of the evidence being presented." He paused, then added, "We maintain that Miss Knight has suffered a form of amnesia regarding the night in question. What is being described may well be inaccessible to her at present, and to press on could cause further disintegration of her mental state."

Justice O'Keefe listened. Then he spoke, deliberate and firm. "I appreciate the concerns raised by defense counsel," he said. "However, it is central to the court's task to determine whether the prisoner does, in fact, suffer amnesia or whether she is capable of recollection. If she does not recall the events," he continued, "then the recounting itself may assist in that recollection—even if a genuine amnesia exists."

He looked over at the dock, where Katherine Knight sat visibly distressed. "The events being recounted," O'Keefe said, "are those in which she was intimately involved. She remains the only living witness to them. Further, I must consider the Crown's submission—one foreshadowed already—that there may be an element of performance, even play-acting, on the part of the prisoner. I have not formed any view on that matter. But I will assess it." He folded his hands on the bench. "For these reasons, I am of the opinion that it would not be in the interests of justice to defer this evidence any longer. Nor do I believe it appropriate to excuse the prisoner from being present as it is delivered."

"Very well, Your Honor." Mr. Thraves returned to his seat at the bar table.

Peter Muscio returned to the evidence at the witness box. He produced another clear evidence bag. Inside was a thick stainless-steel meat hook. He held it carefully, one hand supporting the weight beneath.

"This," Muscio said, "is the implement from which the skin was suspended. It was driven into the timber above the doorway between the lounge and dining areas. DNA testing on slivers of meat removed from the cooked portions—what the scene photos show as plated meals—revealed tissue consistent with the right gluteal region of the deceased." He cleared his throat. "From the victim's right buttock."

There was an audible shift in the room. A stifled intake of breath from someone in the gallery. A scraping of a shoe.

And then Katherine began moaning again. Low at first, like a deep exhale pressed through the throat. Then came the rocking—sharp, repetitive movements, forward and back. She suddenly flung her arms over her head, shielding her face, as her eyes rolled back into their sockets. A correctional officer leaned slightly toward her in anticipation of her falling. The noise she made had grown into a keening hum, her breath catching between each wave. From the gallery, Price's son, Johnathon, stared at her with contempt. On the other side of the courtroom, Katherine's brother Shane watched with concern as his sister grew more distressed. He looked across at the officers, then back at Katherine.

The prosecutor resumed. "Detective Muscio, is there anything about the scene that could tell you one way or another whether the stabbing, killing, decapitation, and subsequent mutilation of Mr. Price appeared to be part of a consistent series of acts, or whether…" Mr. Macadam paused. In the dock, Katherine Knight had begun to murmur loudly once more. Her words were unintelligible, but the sound was a steadily growing guttural complaint. She rocked forward and back with increasing force. Her breathing was audible, fast, and erratic.

Justice O'Keefe looked toward the bar table. "Continue, Mr. Macadam." The prosecutor resumed. "Or whether it was…" But he stopped again, his eyes drawn to the prisoner's movements. "Your Honor, perhaps the prisoner is showing signs of…"

Katherine suddenly shrieked. The sound split the courtroom, startling everyone. She threw herself sideways and collapsed onto the floor of the dock. Her body bucked violently. She kicked at the base of the dock wall, legs flailing, fists hammering the air. The guttural sounds had turned to piercing wails.

Her brother Shane stood up from the gallery, fed up with what he was witnessing, and shouted toward the bench. "Do something for her!"

Three court officers rushed forward. They reached her quickly, kneeling to try to contain her limbs and prevent injury. She continued to writhe, her breath coming in gasps, yelling words no one could fully make out. One observer thought she might have been screaming the word blood—but couldn't be certain.

A call was made. Paramedics arrived within minutes, entering through the side entrance with the necessary equipment. They moved swiftly to her aid, crouching beside her, checking her pulse and her breathing. It was 2:50 PM. Justice O'Keefe watched the outburst with restrained skepticism.

"Given the nature of the prisoner's conduct, the court will have to adjourn for the day."

Detective Muscio was told he would be required to return the following day to continue his evidence. He stepped down from the witness box and exited through the side, passing close by the dock as officers and paramedics worked around Katherine.

After ten minutes, the paramedics left the courthouse. Katherine was brought a cup of tea, made milky and sweet the way she liked, which she drank slowly while seated under guard. She spent that night in a holding cell at Newcastle Court. A doctor attended to her and prescribed a mild sedative.

By the following morning, she appeared composed and docile—just as she had been before the outburst. She folded her hands in her lap and looked toward the bench with a neutral expression. One observer in the gallery, who had witnessed the chaos of the day before, remarked quietly to another: "She's bright as a button today."

The transformation was striking. Whatever had overcome her the previous afternoon had passed—or been tucked away, out of reach, for now. The courtroom settled. Justice O'Keefe entered, and the sentencing proceedings resumed without further incident.

47

THE JUDGMENT

November 8, 2001. Case Number 70094/00. Supreme Court of New South Wales.

Johnathon, Rosemary, Jackie, and Colleen arrived at court early, quiet and stiff with expectation. Each of them hoped—without saying so aloud—that Justice O'Keefe's sentence might somehow account for what had been taken from them. Not just John's life, but the shape of their own, what they had become in the aftermath, and for the version of reality in which they would now live. They carried the deep and raw sorrow that often follows a violent loss—disbelief, rage, and a gnawing ache that would not ease for a long time. Grief after homicide is complicated: survivors can feel trapped in time, replaying memories and questioning every moment, wondering what they could have done, or should have done, seeking answers that would never come. And so they sat— bound by their yawning grief and fatigue, hoping the sentence might, in some small way, fill the hollow left by John's absence and make the unbearable feel bearable, even just a little bit.

Across the forecourt, Katherine's brother Shane Knight and their father, Kenneth, made their way toward the courthouse entrance, a small cluster of reporters and onlookers trying to get a reaction as they passed through the metal detector. Neither man acknowledged the noise. They moved with a kind of inwardness that set them apart, a posture of endurance—that's all they could offer for now, just endurance. In the courtroom they took their place in the public gallery, seated on the far side of the center aisle from the Prices.

They were still trying to understand what Katherine had done. Still replaying the horror that had been revealed, questioning themselves for somehow reconciling it all with the fact that they had shown up to court most days to support her. It was a strange disconnect—unspoken but bone-deep. She was and would always be family. No amount of revulsion or shame could undo that. No sentence handed down in the courtroom would change the Katherine they knew and loved, the one who was generous and loving, the one who was a good mother and a good sister and a good daughter. Kenneth stared ahead as they waited. Shane glanced once across the aisle. There was no eye contact with the Prices. The distance was forever fixed.

At ten o'clock, Justice O'Keefe entered the courtroom through the side door, and the courtroom fell silent. He moved to the bench and took his place in the deep purple chair at the center, his red robe flowing behind him. He gave a single nod, revealing the top of his powdered wig.

Justice O'Keefe rested his papers in front of him. "Members of the court," he began, his voice calm and authoritative. "I have had considerable time to reflect on this case and its implications under the Crimes Act 1900."

He scanned a sheet of paper, then continued. "This murder plainly meets the criteria for the category of cases requiring the most serious penalty. The law allows me two options: to impose a life sentence—meaning incarceration until her natural death—or to exercise my discretion and impose a fixed term, which might permit her release in many years."

A hush spread through the courtroom. Katherine sat motionless in the dock. Her black patterned dress and matching jacket looked remarkably neat, not the dress you'd expect on a violent killer. Family members of the victim strained forward in the gallery.

Justice O'Keefe opened his judgment and began reading. With every turn of the page, the events of that night were recalled. Detail after detail—sketching the timeline, revisiting the forensics evidence, reiterating witness testimony. Muscio's evidence returned: the trail of blood, the meat hook, the knives, the DNA findings. The desecration of the body.

John Price's children sat together in the courtroom as Justice O'Keefe detailed the wounds inflicted on their father. The judge referred to the thirty-seven stab wounds and the severity of the injuries sustained as John tried to escape. The courtroom was heavy with silence, broken only by the quiet sobs of John's daughters.

Each time Justice O'Keefe recounted the knife's path through his flesh, John Price's family's tears grew louder. Their faces strained from the horror, their heads shaking with grief and shock. Rosemary finally rose from her seat and stepped out of the courtroom, overwhelmed. Outside, she gathered herself, drawing in a few calming breaths before returning. She sat back down, determined to hear the judge's sentencing.

Meanwhile, Katherine's expression remained neutral. Her eyes were fixed on a point ahead. Justice O'Keefe continued, describing the witnesses' accounts—Cheryl Sullivan, Robin Smith, Natasha, Shane, Barry Roughan—their recollection of Katherine's temperament, the volatile relationship with the victim, the swinging extremes of affection and anger. And the Crown's case that these facts framed a murder committed in full knowledge and intent. He paused.

"In my view," he said, "the nature of the act, and the deliberate mutilation that followed, demands classification as an offence of the highest severity."

From the public gallery, another sound caught the judge's attention: one of the Price children sobbing quietly. He nodded, paused, then returned to the text.

Justice O'Keefe addressed Katherine Knight's claim that she had attempted suicide. He referred to the toxicology reports, which showed that the levels of drugs in her blood were within therapeutic limits.

"There is no evidence to support a serious attempt," the judge said firmly.

He also dismissed her claim of amnesia, citing that the acts committed that night required a steady hand, great skill, and focused intent—qualities inconsistent with memory loss. He described her claimed amnesia as emotionally convenient and strategically beneficial in the legal process—in other words, a narrative shaped to gain sympathy or avoid full accountability. Turning to Katherine's relationships with men, Justice O'Keefe rejected any notion of her as an innocent victim. He said the evidence presented in court demonstrated that she was often the aggressor, not the victim.

"On balance," he said, "I accept the sworn written testimonies of her ex-husband and former partners over her own account." He made it clear that he regarded the testimonies of those who knew her intimately as more credible, painting a picture of a woman whose pattern of behavior was marked by aggression and volatility. Regarding the murder itself, Justice O'Keefe declared it was premeditated. "Miss Knight carefully planned both the timing and the method of the killing. It appears she sought to manipulate perceptions of her mental state, possibly to evade full responsibility for her actions." He paused briefly, then continued. "Her actions were deliberate and calculated, carried out with a precision that leaves little room for the suggestion of madness."

He then quoted from the psychiatric evidence provided by Dr. Martin: "'It is very important to realize that the pleasure in getting rid of him and getting away with it by making out she was mad, that, in a sense, is payback. But it is the manner in which she gets rid of him that reveals the absolute depravity of her conduct. That, however, does not in itself indicate madness. Such an interest might appear as madness to a layperson, but not to a psychiatrist.'" Justice O'Keefe concluded, "While this behavior may appear as madness to some, clinically it is understood as a calculated act of cruelty."

Outside the courthouse, a commotion was brewing. John Price's younger brother, Bob, had arrived at the court and had been seen breaking a beer glass and placing two jagged pieces, each about ten centimeters long, into his coat pocket. Although he passed through the metal detector, police stopped him before he could enter the courtroom and forced him out. His shouting and angry protests echoed through the corridors and the walls of the courtroom, a raw and vocal expression of grief and anger. His presence was a reminder of the pain rippling through the family, the impact of the crime far beyond the courtroom walls.

Despite the disturbance, Justice O'Keefe maintained his composure, his voice steady and unyielding as he neared the conclusion of his judgment. The courtroom sat in tense silence, the weight of the moment pressing down on everyone present. The judge's words carried the finality of the law, confronting the terrible facts and the human cost.

Mr. Thraves, Katherine's attorney, presented four matters in mitigation. He began with her guilty plea, emphasizing the acknowledgment of responsibility it represented. He then highlighted her diagnosis of borderline personality disorder, as given by both the defense's and Crown's forensic psychiatrists. He noted her lack of prior criminal record and previous psychiatric observations and finally urged the court to consider mercy in imposing a finite sentence. Katherine, he said, was a woman shaped by difficult circumstances.

Justice O'Keefe considered each point carefully. Addressing Katherine's diagnosis, he said, "Her borderline personality disorder is not inconsistent with either premeditation or a natural cunning which may cause a prisoner to put the best spin on the situation confronting her." He acknowledged her lack of a criminal record but was clear about its limited weight. "When I consider the catalogue of violence she has perpetrated against her previous partners, and particularly against John Price, her prior record holds little significance."

Turning to the question of mercy, the judge outlined the court's standard firmly. "Mercy," he said, "is reserved for prisoners who confess their crimes and express genuine remorse and contrition, and for those whom the court believes will not reoffend. The prisoner...does not qualify for mercy on any of these grounds. She engaged in cruel, vicious behavior toward Mr. Price. She showed him no mercy. She has not expressed any contrition or remorse. If released, I believe she poses a serious threat to the security of society."

He continued, "I am satisfied beyond any doubt that such a murder was premeditated. I am further satisfied that not only did she plan the murder, but that she took pleasure in the horrific acts that followed—acts which formed a ritual of death and defilement." The judge's voice remained steady as he pressed on. "The acts committed after Mr. Price's death demonstrate cognition, calculation, calm, and skill. I am convinced beyond a reasonable doubt that her actions were driven by resentments rooted in her rejection by Mr. Price. She was furious at his refusal to marry her, his impending expulsion of her from his home, and his unwillingness to share his assets—particularly the home he wished to preserve for his children.

"I also have no doubt," he continued, "that her claim of amnesia forms part of a deliberate strategy. It is an attempt to simulate madness, to evade the consequences of her actions, and to avoid detailed police questioning and punishment.

"As I have said, the prisoner showed no mercy whatsoever to Mr. Price. The last minutes of his life must have been moments of absolute terror for him, while for her, they were moments of utter enjoyment." Justice O'Keefe paused briefly before delivering a final, unflinching verdict on her attitude.

"At no time has the prisoner expressed any regret or remorse for what she has done. Not even through the surrogacy of counsel. Her consistent attitude is one of contempt, disregard, or cold indifference. This is consistent with the pattern of violence she has inflicted on her various partners, a pattern characterized by the belief that they deserved such treatment." The courtroom remained silent as the anticipation of judgment settled over everyone. The judge's words had painted a stark picture: this was not a crime of passion, nor one borne of uncontrollable madness. It was one borne of calculated cruelty and deep-seated resentment.

Mr. Thraves sat back while Katherine remained motionless, her eyes looking ahead at nothing and no one in particular.

Justice O'Keefe's summation left no room for doubt. He had weighed the evidence, the arguments, and the psychiatric assessments. The nature of the crime, the deliberate and ritualistic violence, the absence of remorse—all pointed to the necessity of a sentence reflecting the gravity of the offence and the risk Katherine posed.

"The court's duty," he said, "is to impose a sentence that protects society and delivers justice for the victim and his family. Mercy, in this case, is not warranted."

As the proceedings moved toward conclusion, those in the courtroom understood the gravity of what had transpired—and the permanence of the judge's decision.

He had been speaking for more than an hour by then. His voice, calm and resolute, had carried through the courtroom with an unwavering judicial cadence, each phrase chipping away at the last fragments of doubt. Now, as he drew toward the end, the sobbing of John Price's daughters—sharp and ragged earlier—had settled into exhausted silence. Their eyes were swollen, their hands clenched in each other's.

Katherine took a slow breath. The judge's words circled her. He looked at his judgment for a moment, weighing the facts and the law, and the fate of one woman, the hopes of a family, and the precedent of a nation. Then he lifted his gaze from the dense pages of his sentencing remarks.

"The only appropriate penalty for the prisoner is life imprisonment, and that parole should never be considered for her. The prisoner should never be released."

There was a pause. A stillness passed through the room. Then the judge looked directly at the dock.

"Katherine Mary Knight," he said, "please stand." She did so slowly, her shoulders square, her eyes fixed straight on the judge. The courtroom had gone utterly quiet. The press, the public, the grieving family—they all waited.

"You have pleaded guilty to and been convicted of the murder of John Charles Thomas Price at Aberdeen in the state of New South Wales on or about twenty-nine February 2000. In respect of that crime, I sentence you to imprisonment for life."

He closed the file in front of him. There was a beat—then a sudden burst of applause from the public gallery.

John's children stood as they clapped, unbothered by decorum. Their faces were flushed with emotion—part triumph, part disbelief that the moment had finally come. For a moment, the court was no longer a chamber of deliberation, but something closer to release. A long, grief-strained exhale.

Katherine didn't look at them. Her body remained upright and controlled, her mouth tight. Then she leaned sideways and spoke in a low voice into her solicitor's ear. Mr. Thraves nodded. What she said would never be known. But whatever it was, the sentence was final. Life meant life. Katherine Knight had become the first woman in Australian history to receive such a punishment.

For John Price's family, the sentence offered something close to justice—not complete healing, but closure, a sense that the person who had taken everything from them was now being stripped of everything. Two corrective services officers appeared at Katherine's side. She allowed herself to be guided without resistance. As they led her from the dock, she turned once, just enough to find her father in the gallery. Their eyes met, and he began to cry. She gave a small, almost imperceptible nod. Then she was gone, ushered through a door that led to the holding cells beneath the courthouse.

THE FUNERAL

They had come from all over the Hunter Valley to pay their respects. Friends and coworkers. Blokes from the pub and the mines. Distant relatives, neighbors, people from soccer clubs and school committees. The funeral was held at St Alban's Anglican Church in Muswellbrook. The casket was draped in native gum and bottlebrush. A photo rested on an easel near the altar: John Price grinning, beer in hand, sunburnt cheeks and crow's feet from years in the sun.

Keith[19], one of John's best mates since high school, had flown in from Darwin. He was the first to speak. He stood at the lectern, unfolding a sheet of paper.

"It's quiet here today," he said, looking at the three hundred or so congregants filling the pews. "Too quiet, for someone like Pricey." He let out a sad little chuckle. "How do you put thirty years of mateship into a few words?"

He cleared his throat and after a moment of considered thought, he began.

"John Charles Thomas Price was one of the good ones. The kind of guy who'd help you build a fence, then stay for a beer

---

[19] *Fictionalized composite character based on documented statements*

and drink your fridge dry." He let out another mournful chuckle, met with a smattering of the same from the pews.

"He was the guy who'd fix your ute, lend you money, give you the shirt off his back if you needed one. He loved the best things in life. Not in some grandiose way, but in the small stuff: a pint at the pub with his mates, dancing until the band clocked off, laughing loud enough to turn heads. He never judged, never gossiped, never left anybody out." Keith paused, squinting through the pale sunlight filtering through the windows. "But he was a dad first and foremost. Loved his kids to bits. Everything he did was for them. They were his reason." He looked toward the front row, where Price's children sat, shoulder to shoulder.

"You were his everything, you lot. He was proud as hell of you." Heads nodded through the pews, along with quiet sniffles.

"And Pricey wasn't afraid to take the piss outta himself." Keith basked for a moment in the warmth of a cherished memory.

"I'll tell you one story that sums John up pretty good. A few of us were up in Bonshaw a couple years ago, fishing. The trip turned to chaos—floods came through, the roads were buggered, Marty's car nearly got washed away. And old Ted's hand got a nasty insect bite. A lot to be miserable about. But Pricey? Nothing bothered him. Our mate Laurie said to him, he said, 'Hey Pricey, we're locked in by flood.'"

"Fine," Pricey said.

"Hey Pricey, Ted's got a poisoned hand."

"Fine."

"Pricey, Marty's car's gonna get washed away."

"Fine."

"Laurie said, 'It looks like we're here to stay.'"

"Fine," said Pricey.

"Then Laurie said, 'Hey Pricey, it looks like there's not enough grog to shout.'

'What!?' Pricey yelled. 'Quick, let's get out!'"

Laughter cracked through the church, brief and full-bodied. Keith grinned, wiping away a tear. "That was him. No dramas until the beer ran out." Keith laughed again softly, looking down at the sheet of paper in his hand. Finally, he folded it and looked at the congregation, the hundreds of people who loved John and came to pay their respects.

"So here we are," he said, his voice cracking as he held back his tears. "We came to cry for John—the bloke we danced with, the bloke we drank with, the bloke we leaned on. We came to mourn a father whose kids will grow older without their pop here. And also, we came to grieve, not only for what has been lost—a top bloke, a truly top bloke—but for the horror that has been revealed to us through his senseless death, a horror so complete it defies belief." He stood for a moment longer, remembering his friend. And then he stepped down without another word, his cheeks moist with tears as he returned to his seat.

ADDENDUM

In 2006, Katherine Knight lodged an appeal against her sentence of life imprisonment without parole. She argued that the killing of her de facto partner, John Price, did not fall into the "worst category" of murder and therefore did not warrant the maximum penalty available under New South Wales law. Her legal team claimed the sentence was "manifestly excessive" and that the post-mortem mutilation of Price's body should not have influenced the severity of the sentence.

The case was heard before the New South Wales Court of Criminal Appeal. Knight's lawyers also submitted that she had not been granted an adequate sentencing discount for her guilty plea, and that her psychiatric condition should have been given greater weight.

On September 6, 2006, the court delivered its decision. Justice Peter McClellan, writing for the panel, dismissed the appeal. In his judgment, he described the crime as "appalling" and "almost beyond contemplation in a civilized society." He affirmed that the sentence imposed in 2001 was appropriate and proportionate to the gravity of the offence.

Knight's rejection by the state's highest criminal court effectively extinguished any prospect of release. The ruling cemented her position as one of the most notorious figures in Australian criminal history and confirmed that her incarceration would see her die in prison.

BIBLIOGRAPHY

Books

- Lalor, Peter. Blood Stain: The True Story of Katherine Knight, the Mother & Abattoir Worker Who Became Australia's Worst Female Killer. Sydney: Allen & Unwin, 2002.
- Lee, Sandra. Beyond Bad: The Life and Crimes of Katherine Knight, Australia's Hannibal. Sydney: Bantam Australia, 2002.

Documentaries/Video

- Crimes That Shook Australia: "Katherine Mary Knight." Season 1, Episode 6. Crime + Investigation/ITVX, 2014.
- Crimes That Shook Australia: – "LIFE Sentence" (clip). Crime + Investigation, YouTube, 2019.
- Katherine Knight: Cannibal, Psychopath, Mother and Wife Crime Documentary. YouTube, Uploaded 2017.
- 7 Red Flags of Female Psychopaths Most People Miss. Lise Leblanc. YouTube, May 17, 2025

Podcasts

- Casefile True Crime Podcast. "Case 12: Katherine Knight." Casefile, 2016.

News and Journalism

- ABC News. "Court Rejects Appeal in Body Cooking Case." March 2006.
- ABC News. "Remembering Katherine Mary Knight…20 Years On." March 2020.
- 7NEWS. "Katherine Knight Butchers Husband John Price…" 2021.
- People. "Inside the Shocking Crimes of Katherine Knight…" February 2025.

Legal and Scholarly

- Crofts, Penny. "Monstrous Wickedness and the Judgment of Knight." University of Technology Sydney Law & Justice Journal, 2010.
- Knight v R [2006] NSWCCA 292. New South Wales Caselaw.
- Regina v Knight [2001] NSWSC 1011 revised 29/01/2002 File Number 70094/00 Judgment of: O'Keefe J

ACKNOWLEDGMENTS

My deepest thanks to Debra Englander, Caitlin Burdette and Allie Woodlee at Post Hill Press. Your support, guidance, professionalism, and belief in this project have made all the difference.

To my agent, Jennifer Cohen—thank you for the years of encouragement, steady advice, and for walking beside me through every stage of this journey. I would not have reached this point without your persistence and faith.

To Cassandra Hampson and Lisa Thomas at Morii Media, thank you for stepping in when I needed it most and for bringing clarity, structure, and energy at exactly the right moment.

To the Glebe gang—your enthusiasm, humor, and unwavering support sustained me through the long drafting months. I'm grateful for every conversation, every push, and every spark of encouragement.

My heartfelt thanks to Greta Augustin, Sydney Augustin, Christine von Steiger, Edward Galla, Eric Longo, Craig Pearce, Dijana Delay, Bertrand Delay, and Luka Delay. Your love, friendship, and encouragement have been constant anchors.

And finally, to Tom, Marley, Stevie, Janet, and the whole Donald family: thank you for the patience, belief, and generosity that made this book possible. Your support is the foundation beneath every page. I am, and always will be, profoundly grateful.

ABOUT THE AUTHOR

Rojé Augustin is a native New Yorker currently living in Sydney with her Aussie husband and two daughters. She is also an Australian citizen. Rojé works as a writer, producer, and journalist. She has studied in Paris and London and is a graduate of Columbia University's Bachelor of Arts Degree with honors from the literature and writing program.